"... a compound of many things ... of drugs and dildos and Impressionist paintings and guns and World War II secret codes ... A compound, yes, a put-on with a manipulative bravura which will remind you of others—say Fowles or Pynchon or indeed, Southern ... should startle, tease, and entertain you simultaneously."

— *Kirkus Reviews*

"... everything is random—character isn't stable, people can't be said to exist in any fixed, describable way. The reader may expect rational cause and effect sequences ... but that's his problem. As Hill says ... 'This is definitely an intellectual contest.'"

— *Newsday*

"A dazzling patchwork, coyly asserting that 'in the realm of the mind, anything is possible.'"

— *Library Journal*

"It isn't a masterpiece. I haven't time. I'm calling it a little something for everyone—it's for when you're in bed with a cold or a partner and you need something entertaining and outrageous ... also pornographic."

— Carol Hill
LET'S FALL IN LOVE

# LET'S FALL IN LOVE

## CAROL HILL

BALLANTINE BOOKS

NEW YORK

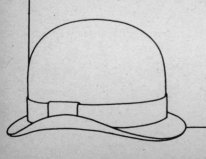

*Acknowledgments*

Grateful acknowledgment is extended by the author for permission to reprint the following:

Browne Vintners Company and J. Walter Thompson Company: For the C. G. Mumm & Co. Cordon Rouge Champagne advertisement, "Victor Hugo was writing, Renoir was painting, and Mumm was the word."

Jacques Desoye (Edition Lanchère): For four photographs from post cards, Paris 1900–38 Première communion, Paris 1900–19 Les transports parisiens, Paris 1900–58 Rue du Chevalier de la Barre, and Paris 1900–33 Promenade dans le bois de Boulogne.

Funk & Wagnalls Publishing Co., Inc.: For excerpts from *Modern Criminal Investigation,* by Harry Soderman and John O'Connell, edited by Charles O'Hara. Copyright © 1962 by Funk & Wagnalls Publishing Co., Inc.

Grove Press, Inc.: For excerpts from pages 65–66 and for "The Magic Ring" from *The Folklore of Sex,* by Albert Ellis, Ph.D. Copyright © 1960 by Grune & Stratton, Inc. For excerpts from pages 462, 463, 470, and 471 from *My Secret Life,* by Anonymous. Copyright © 1966 by Grove Press, Inc.

Rapho Guillumette Pictures, Paul Guillumette, Inc.: For the photograph "The Beach at Villerville, 1908" by Jacques Lartigue.

Indiana University Press: For 7 lines of "Comical History of Don Pedro, Knight" from *Gypsy Ballads*, by Garcia Lorca, translated by Rolfe Humphries.

McGraw-Hill Book Company: For pages 46 and 112 from *Victorian Inventions*, by Leonard De Vries. Copyright © 1971 by Leonard De Vries.

The Museum of Modern Art: For the photograph "The Menaced Assassin," an oil-on-canvas painting (59¼" × 77") by Rene Magritte. Collection. The Museum of Modern Art, Kay Sage Tanguy Fund.

*Newsweek:* For "The Watergate Five: Chapter II" and "Arab vs. Arab" from "The Periscope," July 10, 1972. Copyright © Newsweek, Inc., 1972.

*The New York Times:* For "Auction Brings $13 Million" by Sanka Knox of 5/5/73, "British Paper Reports Bormann Alive" of 11/25/72, "Israelis and Commandos Clash Just Inside Lebanon" of 11/25/72, "Arabs in Perugia Meet Hostility" by Paul Hofmann of 9/11/72, "Detained Peking Official Asks to Return to China from Paris" of 5/7/71, "A Phone Snarl, a Murder, an Exiled Yemen Premier" of 9/7/71, "Official of Al Fatah Shot Dead in Rome" of 10/18/72, and "Arms Network Sought in Rome" by Paul Hofmann of 6/17/72. Copyright © 1973/72/71 by The New York Times Company.

G. P. Putnam's Sons: For excerpts from *Memoirs of a Woman of Pleasure*, by John Cleland. Copyright © 1963 by G. P. Putnam's Sons.

Yale University Press: For an excerpt from the Foreword by Norman Holmes Pearson of *The Double Cross System in the War of 1939 to 1945*, by J. C. Masterman. Copyright © 1972 by Yale University.

To anyone who has ever been in bed
with a cold, or a partner

All that happens is symbol,
and as it perfectly represents
itself, it points to the rest.

*Goethe*

---

I love you
I love you
I love you
I love you
. . . one never know,
do one?

*Fats Waller*

# BODY ONE

## THE MAN FROM MAGRITTE

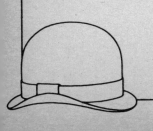

One can only see what one observes, and one observes only things which are already in the mind.

*Alphonse Bertillon (1853–1914), Founder,*
*Bureau of Criminal Identification,*
*Paris Police Department*

"Everything," said Avian Braine, "has a beginning, a middle, and an end. Unfortunately, they do not always appear in that order."

# 1

## Zurich 1:22 p.m.

Cold.

He stood in the dense cold of the mountain snow waiting to see her. His hands in his pockets he stood, the wind cutting his face, his small derby laced with ice, his black wool overcoat glazed with frost, he stood frozen into a landscape, stood still as stone when she darted suddenly from the bathhouse, the steam rushing the door a cloud at her heels, shining she ran pink and warm and beautiful into the snow, her buttocks rippling in the sun she ran tumbling into the soft white snow, her apricot buttocks a soft goldness flashing beneath the sun, her blonde hair flying, laughing, her breasts tumbling, her flanks moving like a tiger smooth and soft, plunging, crying joyously. She turned suddenly then and raced toward him, his heart thundering as she reached him and thrust her firm nipples against his chest, those firm pink orbs igniting his buttons, melting the snow from them as she squealed and shivered against him and then tilting her head upward nibbled his ear and cried "Papa! Papa!" She leapt then, as suddenly as she had come, running to the sauna, pausing, her full breast against the frame of the door, balanced for a moment she stood on tiptoe and waved.

Then she slammed the door; and only the vapor escaped. He sighed. It was not in keeping for a man of his station, a man of his education, to be seized by erotic longings for his daughter. And yet, the smoothness of her thighs obsessed him, as did the calling of her name, Madeleine.

## Leeds: 4:01 p.m.

"Madeleine. That hardly sounds Swiss, does it?" said Avian Braine, as the train hurtled down the track from Glasgow into London. Farthingdale red-faced and plump at work studying the shipping schedules.

"Swiss?" said Farthingdale, looking up. "Madeleine? Heavens no. I suspect it's French, originally. It's what you call those dreadful little cookies Proust was always going on about."

"Hmmm," said Avian Braine, opening a small tin of candied violets and nibbling one, "Switzerland has a new beauty queen, with skin, it says here," he pointed to the front page of the London *Daily Express,* "the color of apricots. She's quite fetching, I daresay, and at least in this photo, she has a most remarkable rump. Her name is Madeleine." Avian sucked thoughtfully on one of the violets.

"Apricots? Skin the color of apricots?" said Farthingdale, his glasses sliding to the end of his red nose, his pudgy finger placing them back. "Why apricots? I thought beauty queens were supposed to resemble peaches."

"Peaches," said Avian Braine, slowly as though instructing a child, "are red and yellow. This girl is golden," he leaned forward, drawing the word out, "a g..o..l..d..e..n girl with a golden ass," said Avian.

"A golden ass," said Farthingdale chuckling, "in the best tradition of Roman comedy."

"What are you talking about?" said Avian.

"Apuleius, of course," said Farthingdale. "He wrote *The Golden Ass.*"

"The golden ass sounds like an East End stripper to me," said Avian, "but ah!" he snapped the paper, and the violets dribbled all over his lap, "she has a golden papa as well, Miss Apricot, who does all of his banking on the Bahnhofstrasse. A professor."

"A professor of what?"

"Victoriana. A social historian with a special interest in inventions, according to the paper."

"A social historian who banks on the Bahnhofstrasse?" said Farthingdale. "Highly unlikely."

"Oh, the money is because of his business," said Avian, getting out another tin of violets and brushing the spilled ones from his lap.

"What sort of thing?" said Farthingdale.

"Apricots, of course," replied Avian.

"I say," said Farthingdale, his eye on the time of ships arriving in Genoa, "perhaps we'll nab him in Genoa."

"Him, or her? Who's to say?" said Avian, puffing on his pipe and gazing across the fields. The train continued its cutting track across misty streams and blooming heather.

It had been months since anyone had spoken of the murders.

## 2

## Rome: 4:17 p.m.

It was 4:17 and Plato had not arrived.

"Damn that pimp," said Anna throwing open the sash. Below her the black and white tiles of the palazzo gleamed in the last rays of the Mediterranean sun. No sign of Plato, no sign of his dark presence in his neat pressed white slacks, his bare chest, dark and hairy, "all that classic machismo shit, upfront and outfront," she would curse him for, no sign of the strange combines of ethnic jewelry he wore around his neck, his beringed hands, his classic dark impassive face, and bracelets of hair, no sign of Plato yet.

"Fuck Italy," Anna cried, slamming the window shut. "First the Fascists and now a pimp who can't tell time."

## The Riviera: 6 p.m.

We were on the beach at Toulon.

"Do you see that girl?" Santiago said, pointing down the long strip of sand.

I said that I did.

The beach was deserted except for the girl, Santiago and me.

"I'm going to rape her," Santiago said. "Do you care to watch?"

I said that I did. Santiago stood up. "Now? You're going to do it now?" I said.

"Yes."

"Is now a good time?" I said, looking down the beach. "She's leaving."

"She's waiting," Santiago said as he strode toward her, his muscles so renewed by the promise of attack they flickered now in waves beneath his skin, weaving through his long body, Santiago tall and purposeful and very beautiful I thought; Santiago, the carrier of the myth.

As we approached her the sky turned yellow, deepening, and the green from the sea seemed to rise and penetrate it, whirling circles of color across the sky.

"It's going to storm," I said.

The girl was lying on some small flat stones surrounding her like a grey mesh, her belly small and flat and glistening with sand, sparkling as the sun moved slowly over her, back and forth in a soft undulation behind the clouds.

"Good evening," Santiago said, standing at the edge of her blanket. The girl opened her eyes, flooded with a grey green light. Wide and sparsely lashed, heavily lidded; a Renaissance eye.

"I have been watching you," Santiago said.

"I know," the woman said, and she stood suddenly then, her hair brown and blonde and falling soft behind her shoulders, the body muscular, yet full, she bent suddenly folding her blanket, the thin film of bikini stretched across the roundness of her buttocks.

We stood on either side of her, watching, waiting for her to finish. The sky had darkened. There was barely any light, only the yellow green haze of the storm. She shivered in the wind from the ocean. The cold raised small pebbles on her flesh.

"I'm going to rape you," Santiago said.

The woman turned to him slowly, a shadow in her eyes, her face immobile, one corner of the blanket clutched tightly in one hand.

"That is impossible," she said softly, released the blanket and prepared to fold it.

"Lie down," Santiago replied. He touched her lightly on the arm.

She pulled away, suddenly, and said hoarsely, "Don't force me." Then she looked away. She stood there, motionless, the wind lifting her hair behind her. She was determined not to submit, I saw that immediately, and yet I knew, as Santiago knew, as we both knew from the movement of her lips as she sat down on the blanket, she would comply.

We waited for the terms to emerge.

The woman reached into a wicker basket and pulled out a pack of cigarettes. Gauloises, and blue; predictable I thought. She lit one, puffed once, twice, then threw it into the sea, turned quickly to Santiago, smiled, shrugged and said, "Are you very rich?"

We were startled by her remark.

"Rich enough," Santiago said uncertainly, his poise toppled for a moment.

"Good," she said, smiling again, and lay back on the blanket. The remark was curious, but no more so than the casualness with which she lay back on the blanket, her face sad, her hair mixed with salt and sand falling across the light brown skin. She was quite beautiful, lying back, as she casually removed the top of her suit, manipulating one nipple with her hand, and smiled, then, spreading her legs and saying, "But remember," excited I could see now that she had somehow taken Santiago on her own terms, and she was smiling as she began a slow rolling movement, "remember, I must be in Milan by eight."

"Take her pants off," Santiago said to me as he stood there naked, facing the sea. His back was to us. I knelt on the edge of the blanket. She lay there, those great grey green eyes studying me as I slipped the small black silk from her, down her thighs; she raised her legs then, ankles together, bringing her knees back to her chest, to make it easy for me, and then, in a minute, her feet shot out over my shoulders. Pushing herself up with her arms, she wound her legs about my neck and, hanging upside down, she pushed the elastic band of my bathing suit aside, maneuvered her head inside and fed on me.

It was, I thought, a perfectly shocking thing to do. In a moment Santiago's hand and then him behind me. I thrust my hands behind to grab him, but his head shot past my waist, moving my arms aside as his head bent forward, seeking the girl's breast. I saw his tongue dart for it, and then his teeth. I was smashed between them.

"Oh," I heard her cry, and raised my head then and tore at her until her mouth incredible against me I cried as I came and tossed her aside, collapsing as Santiago came in me. It was over. But for the girl. In a rage now she rose and leapt for Santiago, pressing herself into his face, moaning as she beat him with her fists, and when it was clear she could bear it no more, he rose, suddenly and long and standing over her, flipped her, her head dragging the ground; grasping her by the thighs, he held her upside down and dove into her, plunging in and out, while the veins in her neck grew thick and violent. She tried to turn to claw at him, he was not enough for her, could not abate her, and in his fury, pounding her, came again, and threw her aside. She lay there on the sand, her fists clenching until Santiago, rising, slapped her furiously and pulled her to him, kissing her, caressing her, she succumbing to him, folding into him, until, pinning her arms back, he urinated, the cascade heavy and vast until she shrieked and fell to her side silent.

---

"Did it strike you as prurient?" Santiago asked as we drove along the highway, the night air fragrant with the smell of honeysuckle and the sea. I said that I didn't know.

"It wasn't," he said, driving swiftly now, the wind tossing his hair in waves over his head; it was longish now, almost to his collar.

"It got in her face," I said.

"So what? You're not going to be stupid, are you, and be metaphoric?" Santiago was laughing. "The only thing depraved about it was its metaphoric possibilities, remember that." He turned a corner sharply then, and it threw me against his side.

"Santiago," I said, "I love you."

Later I remember, as we attempted to formulate

some kind of meaning in regard to the Act, we consulted several dictionaries. Santiago said it was a waste of time because the American Heritage Dictionary said prurient meant inciting to lewd thought, and the Oxford Dictionary said it meant an itch.

DOCUMENT #1

On the morning of April 18, 1875, Charles Eddington Cartwright, a London gunsmith, was startled awake by a sudden premonition. He had dreamed that thirty-six of his guns had been used in a series of unsolved murders ranging from the lakes of Scotland to a small island off the coast of China. The years of the murders were 1970-1974.

Charles Eddington Cartwright was not a mystic; he had in fact, a reputation among the townspeople as a fierce advocate of the sciences, with a strong bias against religion in any of its forms, and was known to become engaged in heated argument whenever anyone tried to defend the supernatural. A one-time student of philosophy, he had returned to his life as a gunsmith after the death of his father nearly twenty years before. He sat up now, the sheets drenched in perspiration as he quickly reviewed the events in his dream. Then, springing from his bed, he moved to the small washstand, not stopping even to heat his water. He splashed the water onto his face and hands, threw his nightcap aside, and crossed quickly to the fireplace. Hurriedly he lit the grate, threw a log on the fire, and then, pausing only to put on another robe and pull his blanket across his lap, for it was cold for such a late day in April, he carefully recorded in the family diary the details of the dream.

His hand trembled as he finished. So strange, so forceful was the impact of the dream that he did not even pause to reflect why almost a hundred years in the future should be the time of the murders using his weapons.

It was enough to consider that his guns, those he had made and collected over the years, thirty-six of those guns, including one entire pistol of the finest handwrought silver, had been involved in murder. For it was a gunsmith's pleasure, and the collector's art, to put together such things for the beauty of themselves.

Dressing hurriedly he paused only to nod briefly to the cook, who stood astonished at the bottom of the stair, seeing him running out at this hour without breakfast and forgetting his topcoat.

Charles Eddington Cartwright walked swiftly toward his shop. For twenty years he had been exactly on time—never a moment late, never a moment early, but arriving precisely at 7:30 a.m.— and had never missed a day, with the exception of the time during his apprenticeship to his father in the winter of 1845 when he had worn himself to exhaustion in preparation for the Great Exhibition of Small Arms in London.

Rounding the corner, he saw the face on the clock above the bank read 5:42. It was absurd he told himself, not yet slowing his pace, to be rushing to his shop almost two hours early because of a dream. He wanted to smile to himself, to chide his fear, but he could not, for approaching the store he felt a strange sense still, a cold curious presence that startled him all the more because Charles Cartwright was a rational man, had always considered himself above those boundings of the mind that turned back upon themselves in fear, and yet at this moment he felt so impelled by something in the dream that he could not slow his pace as he ran, breathless now, toward the store. Then, reaching the front door, he stopped. The door was open, and swung slowly on its hinges, banging against the interior wall, as if someone had just left. The lanterns in the store were lit. Walking directly to the back room, the pressure in his chest acute, Charles Eddington Cartwright hesitated only a moment before he unlocked the door to the gun collection. Of his private collection of over three hundred of the finest guns in the world, thirty-six guns were missing.

## London: 10:15 a.m.

"Life," said Avian Braine, "is a most peculiar affair."

The body, when it was found, was determined to be two weeks old, a rather extraordinary length of time for a corpse to be lying unnoticed in the midst of London.

"You would have thought the smell," said Avian, wrinkling his nose in distaste.

"Embalmed," Farthingdale replied, never once taking his eyes off Waterloo Bridge.

"What?"

"It was treated," Farthingdale said. "Embalmed."

"You never bothered to tell me that," Avian said.

"So sorry," Farthingdale replied, "I thought you'd figure it out yourself."

"We're supposed to be partners."

"Well, that's all right. Partners don't tell each other everything all the time, now do they?"

"But we're supposed to be working on a case, if I may remind you."

"I don't need reminding. If there's anyone who needs reminding, it's you."

"Not about professional details."

"That's true, of course, actually," Farthingdale said looking at him, "you're rather good professionally; it's a pity that same astuteness of mind simply crumbles in regard to your private affairs."

"Your kindness overwhelms me. You know perfectly well these lapses, those memory lapses, that temporary amnesia is beyond my control."

"Things beyond one's control are not always causes for sympathy," Farthingdale replied. "Now let's get something to eat."

Avian looked at him oddly. Twenty years partners, and yet he wondered if they really liked each other at all sometimes. He rather thought they didn't. They were often like this, not particularly nice to each other, not particularly hostile. A fairly easy alliance from which they each, on occasion, profited and in other times were spared from loneliness.

"Well," said Avian, "it certainly is odd. An embalmed body in Trafalgar Square, dead approximately two weeks. Female. Age eighty-four. Occupation millionaire. Survivors none. Cause of death," Avian sighed, "overdose of LSD."

"Name," Farthingdale said as they arrived at the restaurant, "you forgot name. The name is Lady Sarah Covington. I myself don't believe that falderal about the LSD."

"Well, they found it."

"I know they found it, but they also found a bullet wound."

"Yes, well, clearly she was shot."

"The LSD, I suspect," Farthingdale said, "is some sort of gallows humor."

"Odd, isn't it," Avian said, ordering some smoked salmon, "that she was there two weeks and no one noticed?"

"Which means, of course, she wasn't there for two weeks."

"Quite," said Avian. "Perhaps she was in cold storage."

"Perhaps she was," said Farthingdale dipping into a large serving of foie gras, and then, savoring a large teaspoonful in his mouth, and ignoring the bread, said, "and perhaps she wasn't."

"You know how many this makes," said Avian.

"Yes, if it's part of the others, it makes three. The third murder," Farthingdale said, "but the first body."

"Yes," Avian said, "perhaps he's making it easier for us. Although he's always leaving us something. The body, the weapon or the clue."

"Yes, notes from a murderer," Farthingdale said. "It's most extraordinary."

"Is it a woman do you think?"

"It's hard to say," said Farthingdale, and ordered another ale.

Santiago stroked my thigh as we drove into the drive. We had rented this house for the summer. It was a small white house surrounded by flowers.

"Did the woman excite you?" I asked as we strolled up the small walk to the house.

"No."

"But you were erect, early."

"I was thinking about the film."

"Even then," I asked, "before we had begun?"

"Even then," he said sighing as he locked the door behind him.

"I think you might be lying," I said.

Santiago yawned and took off his shirt. "That is always a possibility we must bear in mind," he said, and got into bed.

---

The next morning an envelope arrived from Milan. It was a bill for 5,810,000 lire, and bore only the signature "Anna." Santiago is on the phone now, talking to Victor.

"And why did you not tell me or her, surely you must have known . . . I am not usually interested in courtesans, but an expensive courtesan like that . . . five million eight hundred and ten thousand lire, Victor, really she must be crazy. No whore gets that kind of money. Who is her pimp?" Santiago laughed. "I'll see you Thursday, Victor. Bring this Anna." He hung up the phone. "Can you imagine," he said, "what I thought was merely playful little late afternoon rape turns out to be the grand sweepstakes?"

"What are you talking about?" I said.

"That woman on the beach turns out to be the costliest courtesan in Europe—nothing less than a ten-thousand-dollar fuck."

"Ten thousand dollars," I said. "Heavens how does she get her prices?"

("It's a self-fulfilling prophecy," Anna said. "There are certain men you tell them it's ten thousand dollars, and they have to have it because it is ten thousand dollars and because it is ten thousand dollars it is of course ten thousand dollars' worth."

"Does anyone come back for seconds," I said.

"The semi-rich," said Anna.

"What of the very rich?"

"For multimillionaires," she said, turning on her lovely back, "I'm willing to work out a tax-deductible yearly contract. For a million dollars they can have me whenever they want me, but never," she said smiling, "on Sundays.")

"She claims it is not possible to rape a prostitute and that I owe her five million lire. A bill!" Santiago outraged swore as he paced about the room.

"Does she know who you are?" I asked. "Did she, on the beach?"

"Victor says no," Santiago replied, reaching for some strawberries, "but I wonder."

"When do we meet her?"

"Thursday, at Fiorio's. Victor says her pimp's name is Plato."

Avian Braine and Farthingdale were hiding in the bushes. Avian said, "I think this is eucalyptus. I'm allergic. I'm going to sneeze."

"Don't be absurd," Farthingdale whispered. "We're not in Martinique. Eucalyptus doesn't grow in England."

"Oh," said Avian, and he sneezed.

Just then, the man appeared. They watched as he carefully rolled his umbrella, buttoned it, adjusted his small black derby hat, and smoothed his grey suede gloves. In a moment two more men, dressed exactly alike, came out of the house, and then the three derbies, with the men under them, proceeded down the walk.

"Come on," Farthingdale said, "now's our chance," and bounded from the bushes to the porch of Lady Covington's estate.

When they entered they noted the vast accumulation of sculpture and paintings in the foyer. They paused before one of them.

"Magritte—terrible taste," said Avian.

"He *has* been overexposed," said Farthingdale, moving across the room. "Did you know she was something of a bibliophile? An old manuscript nut of some sort —absolutely dotty on the subject. Perhaps we ought to have a look at the library."

"Of course I know that," said Avian. "I always know more than you know. I also know that she translated several rare things from both Latin and Chinese. An expert in ancient languages. Also codification. Greek, for example. Both Linear A and Linear B were known to her. What doesn't fit is that she was a major shareholder in the American rock groups."

"Which one?"

"The Seventy-second Street Vagina."

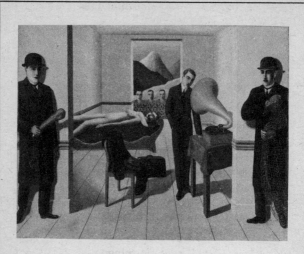

*The Menaced Assassin*
MAGRITTE

"Upon my word," Farthingdale said, wrinkling up his nose in disapproval, "vagina yet. And an old Tory at that."

"Well," they both said, as they stood in the door of the library, "somebody's beat us to it." Along the entire wall were pockets and spaces where books and manuscripts had been removed.

The desk was untouched, however, including a small silver frame with a photograph of a young girl in a bathing suit, waving.

"Upon my word," said Farthingdale, look at the photograph, "look at this."

"At what?" said Avian, engrossed in dusting the shelves for fingerprints. "I haven't eyes in the back of my head."

"This photograph," said Farthingdale. "Why, I do believe it's your Miss Apricot."

"Miss who?"

"Apricot, the apricot girl with the father on the Bahnhofstrasse. Isn't that she?" Farthingdale handed the photograph to Avian.

"Why, I do believe you're right," he said.

"What an odd coincidence," said Farthingdale.

"There is no such thing," said Avian.

"As what, coincidence?" said Farthingdale. "Look, you're not going to give me more of your falderal about ESP I hope."

"No," said Avian, "there is such a thing as coincidence, but there is no such thing as an odd coincidence. An odd coincidence, I am tempted to think, is a plant. Did you have those gentlemen in the bowlers followed?"

"Of course I did," said Farthingdale. "I just got a call on the radio, however."

"What happened?"

"They lost them."

"Where?"

"They said they left their clothes on the beach."

"What beach?"

"At Holyhead."

"Their clothes, all the bowlers and umbrellas were neatly piled in little squares, they went into the sea wearing striped wool bathing suits, circa nineteen twenty—very entertaining, and never came out."

"You mean they drowned?"

"No," said Farthingdale, "they just never came out."

"It gets stranger and stranger," said Avian.

Farthingdale looked at him and nodded. This meant that they both agreed that things did.

DOCUMENT #2

At five o'clock on the evening of February 2, 1922, the train from Dijon pulled into the Gare de Lyon and a conductor handed a package to an unidentified woman. She hurried by taxi across the Pont d'Austerlitz and up the Left Bank of the Seine past Notre Dame and Place St. Michel to 9, Rue de l'Université.

There she examined the parcel, which contained two manuscripts. At exactly 6:17 the woman, nude, descended the staircase. She got into her clothes at the bottom, and stepped out into the street, and handed one package to a waiting messenger. Then she hailed a taxi, and hurried back up Rue de l'Université and Rue Jacob past the street market at Carrefour Buci and up to 12, Rue de l'Odéon. There in a bookstore, the group was waiting. They examined the parcel and then moved to a restaurant, Ferrari. They each ordered a glass of Fendant. The parcel was brought out and examined again.

After a careful examination, each of the four men, wearing black coats and derbies, took out pens and made notations. Then the manuscript was wrapped up again, tied, and the party moved on.

In the meantime, the messenger had arrived at his destination and handed over the other manuscript.

"Did you know," Avian said, "that the manuscripts she collected were pornographic?"

"Of course I know," said Farthingdale. "How did you find out?"

"I made a few calls," Avian said.

Farthingdale shrugged. "Did you hear about the false wall?"

"Yes."

"That means you spoke to Harcourt."

"Of course I spoke to Harcourt."

"However did you find him?"

"When one is desperate, one can always find him."

"And of course he knew."

"Of course he knew," Avian said in an irritated tone.

"How does he know these things I wonder," Farthingdale said.

Avian shrugged. "Harcourt just knows things."

They proceeded to the third floor of the house, where they found a locked cabinet. They opened it; inside was a manuscript page and a cerulean blue velvet case. Inside the case was a nineteenth-century gold-plated revolver. A small white card attached. It read: THE MURDER WEAPON.

"Well," Farthingdale said, "the murderer clearly doesn't think we're very bright." He turned the pistol over. "It's a lovely pistol—Adams revolver, it was an English-made gun, the Adams—sort of England's answer to the Colt revolver. A collector's item. No doubt about it."

Avian was looking over the manuscript. "It reads a bit like Frank Harris, although it seems even more enthusiastic."

MY SECRET LIFE

got in a fortnight plumper, altho I took so much
semen out of him; but he was young and strong.—
What pleasure for him!—the only annoyance to me
was that his prick, when he got randy and it stood,
had a strong smell.—The smell of most cunts I like.

After I had sucked him that night, I never repeated
it but once.—Altho we had lost all modesty, I did
not like Sarah to see all, until late in the evening
when whiskey and baudiness told on me. Whatever
we did together, I never lost sight of my principal
object, which was to frig him, and see either his tool
or his face when he was spending.—When Sarah
came in, at first we used to sit round the fire drinking and smoking, all as naked as the weather permitted. Sometimes he told his adventures with ser-
vants in the houses where he had worked, she about
what men had done. The conversation always was
erotic.—Until the spirit moved me to action, I usually
sat by him in an easy chair, with his tool in my
hand. Sometimes he laid hold of mine. "Look at you
two feeling each other's pricks." Sarah would say,
with a toss of her head.—"Shew me your split, and
see if it will give his cock a rise."—She would show
it gaping, and his cock would rise. Perhaps he'd
kneel in front of her, fingering her cunt, or licking
it, whilst she cocked her leg up to facilitate his work.
At times both *his* and *my* fingers were up her cunt
at the same time, and fifty other baudy tricks we did.

I had now made Sarah suck my prick, but I dis-
liked still to tell here that I had had *his* prick in
my mouth; yet one evening did so. Behold us soon all
three on the bed, *she* with *his* prick in *her* mouth,
and *he* with *my* prick in *his* mouth. I feeling about
*her* cunt and *his* balls, as well as the difficult attitude
permitted. Another night we followed it up, by his
laying on the bed and she kneeling over him with his

## MY SECRET LIFE

prick in her mouth, her backside over his feet, and I at her backside fucking her—I alone could plainly see this in the looking glass, and a most delicious sight it was.

My most satisfactory amusement, I think, was frigging him whilst I fucked her. I used to lay him down so that his prick was well within reach of my hand and in view whilst I did so. At times Sarah laid her head on his chest or his belly, as a pillow, he laying across the bed, and then his prick was just by my shoulder. Then putting my hand up I frigged him. At other times, laying partially on his side with his legs up against the wall at the bed head or near her head, his prick was equally close to me.

Once his tool looked so beautiful that it seduced me entirely—I had again vowed to myself that having had his prick in my mouth and felt it swell within it from flabbiness to a poker, under my lingual pressures, I would never do it again.—But now lying with my prick up Sarah, my left hand under her smooth backside, my right round his prick; my pleasure coming on I could not resist it, and engulfed his stiff cunt-rammer in my mouth. My backside was then oscillating, his hand could just reach my arse and he was feeling my balls. I felt he was near his crisis, withdrew his prick, and at that instant out shot his sperm, just between Sarah's naked breast and mine.

Instantly, for such was the lascivious effect, Sarah and I mingled our mucilages in her cunt. I never had his prick in my mouth afterwards.

He got fond of Sarah and constantly besought me to let him have her. Then after I had frigged him, we would all three sit round the fire. "Shew us your cunt, Sarah"—She'd open her legs so that the article was visible. I watched his prick, which perhaps....

### MY SECRET LIFE

spittle. His prick was still stiff. There was the small round hole—the balls beneath—the white thighs.—I closed on him half mad, holding him round one thigh. I pointed my prick—my brain whirled—I wished not to do what I was doing, but some ungovernable impulse drove me on. Sarah's words rang in my ears. I heard them as if then spoken. My rod with one or two lunges buried itself up him, and passing both hands round his belly I held him to me, grasping both his prick and balls tightly. He gave a loud moan. "Ohoo I shall faint," he cried. "Ho, pull it out."

It's in—don't move or I won't pay you, or something of that sort—I said, holding myself tight up to him. "Ohooo, leave go, you're hurting my balls so"— I suppose I *was* handling them roughly—but his bum kept close to my belly.

I recollect nothing more distinctly. A fierce, bloody minded baudiness possessed me, a determination to do it—to ascertain if it was a pleasure—I would have wrung his prick off sooner than have withdrawn for him, and yet felt a disgust at myself. Drawing once slightly back, I saw my prick half out of his tube, then forcing it back, it spent up him. I shouted out loudly and baudily (Sarah told me), but I was unconscious of that. She was in her sitting room.

I came to myself—how long afterwards I cannot say.—All seemed a dream, but I was bending over him—pulling his backside still towards me.—My prick still stiff and up him. "Does it hurt now." "Not so much."

His prick was quite large but not quite stiff. A strong grip with my hand stiffened it, I frigged hard, the spunk was ready and boiling, for he had been up to spending point half a dozen times. My prick, still encased, was beginning to stiffen more.—He cried—

## MY SECRET LIFE

"I am coming, I am coming"—his bum jogged and trembled—his arsehole tightened—my prick slipped out—and he sank on the bed spending over the counterpane—I stood frigging him still.

He spent a perfect pool of sperm on the bed. The maddening thought of what I had done made me wish to do it again. I forgot all my sensations—I have no idea of them now—I knew I had spent, that's all. "Let me do it again." "That I won't for any money," said he turning round.

Then I frigged myself and frigged him at the same time furiously. Fast as hands could move did mine glide up and down the pricks. Pushing him down with his arse on the sperm on the counterpane, I finished him as he lay, and I spent over his prick, balls, and belly. In ten minutes our double spend was over.

Immediately I had an ineffable disgust at him and myself—a terrible fear—a loathing—I could scarcely be in the room with him—could have kicked him. He said, "You've made me bleed." At that I nearly vomited—"I must make haste," said I looking at my watch, "I forgot it was so late.—I must go." All my desire was to get away as quickly as possible. I left after paying him, and making him swear, and swearing myself, that no living person should know of the act.

Yet a few days after I wrote the narrative of this blind, mad, erotic act; an act utterly unpremeditated, and the perpetration of which as I now think of it seems most extraordinary. One in which I had no pleasure—have no recollection of physical pleasure—and which only dwells in my mind with disgust, tho it is against my philosophy even to think I had done wrong.

Tomorrow we were to meet Victor at Fiorio's. I asked Santiago how I might recognize him.

"He always wears a red shirt," Santiago said.

"And carries the proverbial writer's notebook?" I asked.

"Ummm." Santiago drove skillfully along the Amalfi Drive, the sun warm and the air sweet with the smell of spring flowers, the blending of flowers and the salt from the sea something I always remember. Victor was an American Negro, who called himself that, who introduced himself at parties by saying, "Hi, I'm an American Negro. My name is Victor."

"It is as though he thought being a Negro were an occupation," Caldwell once remarked. Caldwell, whose complexion is black, does not describe himself as an American Negro. He and Victor are clearly two of the most notorious blacks in Rome. Victor, for his impudence; Caldwell for Lola. Santiago, who had the displeasure of meeting Caldwell only once, said, "Nobody knows where he was born. No piece of earth wants to claim him." Caldwell, all of Rome knew, was brilliant, and handsome in an insidious way. There was some talk of his being a Soviet agent. All of Rome knew that someone in the top literary and social circles was a Soviet agent. But no one knew who or how or why or even how they knew this. Caldwell was reputed to be cruel with women and as if to emphasize the exotic air that surrounded him, he wore capes which were said to be made from some ancient threads rewoven from Persian tapestries. They were quite beautiful. When he took the cape off he always wore a mirrored vest with nothing under it, and leather pants. He shaved his head, carried ornate and elaborate cigarette holders, and seemed fond of making a spectacle of himself.

Everyone thought him fabulously rich, but this was difficult to know, for if he were a man of property he kept it well hidden. One saw his clothes, but never his circumstances. He had no telephone and no address. People anxious to see him would have to go to Lola, who occasionally still modeled for Valentino. She saw Caldwell every night but she would shrug when asked. "I don't know where he lives. He always stays at my place."

"Has he money?" I asked her once, and she looked at me astonished. "Oh yes," she said, and I did not know whether this meant that it was foolish for me to suppose otherwise about Caldwell, or that it reflected poorly on Lola who was careful about sleeping only with gentlemen who were eager to establish tax losses.

Lola had long red hair and skin a startling ivory, a soft gold white skin. She was thirty-seven, and her eyes were a deep and some said vicious green. As even women who hated her admitted, she had a magnificent back. When I first met her she was wearing a dress cut high around her neck, with black sequins, and long sleeves, and on her back was cut out this enormous question mark. The dot under the question mark exposed the beginning of her buttock, and I have never seen a back quite like that, so firm and fleshy you had to run your hands all over it, which everyone immediately did.

Occasionally Lola would dally with a person of political power. It was rumored that her politics were quite radical, despite her penchant for money, and people talked the way they do, saying that Lola had slept with Kissinger during some Caribbean jaunt, a rumor she made no effort to put down, and clearly enjoyed. Women love to sleep with men in power, of course, and knowing Lola who has a simplistic, albeit symbolic mind, it would perfectly fit her needs. She made no secret of the fact that when she could arrange it, she preferred an evening with four or five men, being sexually tireless, and we all agreed if she slept with Kissinger it would have compensated her enormously, for it would be the equivalent of fucking the entire State Department, something that would accord her tremendous satisfaction.

On Thursday we drove to Rome. Anna was to meet us with Victor at the Casino Veladier. She was waiting for us when we arrived. I barely recognized her. She was more than beautiful, more than dazzling, she had an elegance that is born not only of clothes and money, which it was clear she had, but of some inner aristocracy of the spirit which, combined with her physical qualities, made her altogether a woman of most extraordinary qualities. She was wearing a new Valentino, one that I privately thought was one of the best in his collection, and a magnificent pair of soft brown sueded boots. There were seven or eight silver bracelets on her arm, which I learned later she always wore, and she had thrown a sable coat, cut in something of a trench coat style about her shoulders. As I sat down near her I thought too that now the body had a different odor, an aroma, the flesh gleamed with a light I did not appreciate on the beach, under the soft glow of the candles in the restaurant, her flesh was almost translucent, and yet round and firm. And the face, the face was most changed of all. This I recognized was the professional face. The face of an elegant, but nevertheless hot, bitch.

Santiago is arguing with her, very gently, and laughing about the bill.

"It was rape," Santiago said, "I told you that. I owe you nothing."

"It was not rape," Anna said in a magnificently modulated contralto. "I supplied you with services for which I am demanding a fee. You stole my services. That is illegal. You owe me Santiago."

"It so happens that this poses an interesting legal predicament." Santiago grinned. He was handsome today I thought, looking as he often did like a combination of Ricardo Montalban, some Italian diplomat (for even though he was Argentinian he had a finely molded aquiline nose that made one swear he was the son of Caesar) and one of those square jawed faces that do toothpaste commercials. He had a perfect chin and even teeth. The shirt I thought was a bit tight however. It pulled across his chest. But then it was a magnificent chest, to say nothing of his ass. I love you Santiago I thought. There were several women in the restaurant who noticed him.

I looked at Anna. Did he excite her I wondered. I wondered if he was close enough to her so that she could feel that peculiar heat he radiated which he attributed to his metabolism, but which I of course attributed to magic. When sitting next to him, that heat began to penetrate. It was like sitting next to a sun lamp, I told him, or a hot brick, something that amused him no end.

"The legal question is, madame, the nature of your services. You have just admitted that I stole. To have stolen from you, madame, due to the nature of what it was I stole, was to have committed rape. I owe you nothing." It was then I became aware that Santiago's face was changing. I noticed then that Anna's head was leaning close to his, but her hands were under the table. Santiago had drawn the tablecloth up as far as his waist.

"My services are pleasure," Anna said smiling. "You obtained yourself of my services, you owe me for them."

Santiago's eyes were closing. "Is the pleasure for yourself or your client?"

"My client of course. Don't be a fool."

"Just checking," Santiago said. "Ahhhhh." But his voice dropped, his face changed, one hand of Anna's emerged on top of the table. Her eyes glowed. "You owe me five million, eight hundred and ten thousand lire, now, or I leave," she said.

Santiago's throat worked quickly. "You bitch, I owe you nothing. You gave no pleasure. I did it only for the film. Your skills," he leaned back, "had nothing to do with it." He clenched the tablecloth then with his fist.

"What film?" Anna asked, her face trembling.

Santiago leaned across the table, his face tense and she to my surprise complied and he fell across the table, relaxed and breathing heavily. No one said anything for some time. Anna lit a cigarette and then, Santiago sat up and adjusted his clothes.

"Come." Santiago took her hand and stood up.

I was annoyed. I did not like the way things were going. Santiago seemed interested in her in more than a sexual way. She was dangerous from one point of view, although I confess my attraction for her also. I have always found there is something quite magical about physical beauty, some bewitching trick which however brief and temporary, solved for me and surmounted certain basic paradoxes. I felt this magic being near her, but I was prepared too, to hate her.

We drove along the shore, the wind billowing Anna's hair up from the nape of her neck. She stretched her arm out on the red leather seat and I could see how beautiful the lines were, the line from her neck along her shoulder down along her arm. She was graceful Anna was and Santiago, driving easily now, occasionally would smile and glance her way. He was full of pleasure in her presence. And she, like some milking cat, would just lean her head back, loving the warmth of the sun, loving what he was taking from her, giving it to him with a certain sweet satisfaction, a sense of feline control that made her I thought even more marvelous. I began to experience the strange sensation, somewhere during the drive, that they had met and loved before and that their seeming strangeness, their sense of discovery, was only for my benefit.

This was absurd, of course, and so I soon forgot it.

It was late by the time we got to Turin, so we stopped for supper in a little restaurant by the sea. It overlooked the azure blue Mediterranean, from a fairly high cliff and one part, a small area, was separated from the other diners. This was a small white gazebo filled with yellow roses. Anna walked deliberately toward it, and once inside immediately asked the waiter to shut the gate. It was suddenly then, with the shutting of the gate, very dense, very private, and quite wicked. There was a slight wind. I could hear my heart. I could hear Santiago's heart, as we looked at Anna, soft amidst the roses, the green thorns and hedges, and wilting wisteria forming private lattices around us. Small greystone slabs led to the little gate which opened again as the waiter appeared. Anna ignored him completely, staring only at Santiago, and began to unbutton her dress. The waiter hesitated, then retired, to the little world of diners closed out beyond us, only the laughter, the occasional clatter of glasses reaching us here in the corner, the air so fragrant, the strange intensity like a gathering storm, and I saw that Anna had opened her blouse and her breasts rolled out, full and soft, and perfect, the nipples dark scarlet going firm in the cool breeze, and then I watched as Anna unpinned her hair which fell almost to her shoulders, full wavy almost muscular hair and then her long smooth arms coming forward pulling Santiago's mouth to her mouth to her breast and then beneath her skirt, and I watched. I watched excited, and carefully as Santiago's head dropped beneath her skirt, watched at Anna gasping, falling backward her skirt over her head, watched then as Santiago's cock, stiff with blood, seemed to burst from his body like an independent force and enter her. Saw Anna's face, saw the silk curve of her hips above the table, her fists clenching her teeth then small and white digging tiny tears in Santiago's shoulder as Santiago's hips thrust with a vengeance he never had for me, as if he would plow through her very back and then the two of them in a steady rhythmic rolling as her head fell from the bench and Santiago pressed her shoulders down, riding her higher her head dragging the ground, her hair spread amid the roses, the sharp small bone of her ankles seemingly tied behind his back and then Santiago pressing, pressing her head turning side to side he looked as if he was choking her then and then a sudden still falling, something I saw and did not see and then he was shivering, clutching himself against her chest, while there along his back a small thin red line, a seven-inch scratch along his back thin and rather deep, seeping like a knife cut. Anna finally saying, her voice back far in her throat, "Let me up."

When they had gotten dressed, the waiter came, I wondered if he'd watched us. His timing seemed too perfect. We had a bouillabaisse, which was very good, but Santiago took one swallow of the wine and spit it out. "You should never drink French wines in Italy," he said. "They always put the bottles where they sour. I swear it."

---

In the film, there was no question but that we were being watched.

"Who is that?" Santiago said rising suddenly from his chair. "I never saw him, did you?"

"I didn't know," Anna said smiling, "we had company."

"A man in a bowler hat on the beach? Don't be absurd. The negative must have been run over another shot, he's been dubbed in."

"Not a chance." I said. "Look at it."

We looked. Clearly he was there. Hands folded in front. Umbrella in the sand, stationed like an officer at his post, watching.

"Well," Anna said, brushing her skirt off as she

stood up, "perhaps he's only a vapor that emerges on contact with silver nitrate."

No one laughed. We said good night and I drove Anna home.

When Santiago entered the bank the next morning to make some routine deposits, an officer called him aside and asked to speak to him. He was surprised; as far as he knew his account was in scrupulous order.

Signor Castelli led him to a magnificent mahogany-paneled office and offered him a seat.

"I had thought, signor," Santiago said, somewhat annoyed, "that my small account was in perfect order, and certainly not something to call to the attention of the vice-president."

Signor Castelli smiled. "I will come right to the point. A certain signorina has informed me that you may wish to make a loan of five million lire in order to pay her a debt."

Santiago started . . . a courtesan informing a bank officer. He waited and said nothing.

"We can make it available to you at very very low interest."

"This is outrageous," Santiago stood up, "absolutely outrageous and I intend to report you to the authorities, signor. Clearly that certain signorina has simply charmed you or bribed you or God only knows what."

Signor Castelli interrupted him. "It was simply a

financial offer; I apologize, signor, if it does not meet your needs."

"About my private life!" Santiago pounded the table, "Who the hell do you think you are to discuss my relationship with a certain signorina?"

"Signor, I think you do not know and you should that this is a private bank, signor, and one of the most respected in Italy."

"You, Signor Castelli, are a corrupted flunky and I intend to write a personal letter to the chairman of the board. I will have your head, signor, for cavorting in what is doubtless dubious company."

"I think you should know, signor," Signor Castelli continued, with total aplomb, "that the chairman of the board is the signorina in question."

Santiago stood still several seconds, not quite able to hear it. "What?" he said.

"The signorina in question is the chairman of the board."

Signor Castelli opened the door. "Anytime you wish to reconsider, signor, just let me know."

Santiago nodded slightly as he walked out of the door and toward the elevator.

Anna was waiting for him in a silver limousine when he left the bank.

"Well," she said, as he walked over to her car, "have you reconsidered?"

"Do you own all of Italy, is that what I am to find out next, Countess?"

"How did you know my title?" She looked surprised.

"Oh God," his hand hit the handle of the window, and Anna laughing, nodded to Bacco to drive off. Then Anna leaned at the window and said, "I'm going yachting this afternoon, meet me at the Bay at three if you want to come."

Santiago did not even turn back. She was clearly going to make an ass out of him, one way or the other.

It was half past midnight on a February evening in what seems to be many years ago now, that I heard a knock at my door and opened it to find a parcel with a note attached. The note explained that the manuscript in the parcel would be of more than casual interest to me, that I was to translate it as rapidly as possible, and to publish it soon thereafter. There was no indication of an author, and I had no idea how the manuscript arrived at the house. We live in a country estate several miles outside of the nearest small town, and the house is surrounded by a guard, a high-voltage gate and several dogs. The guards heard nothing; the dogs made no noise.

I took the manuscript inside and to my horror saw that the entire thing was constructed in three languages: English, French and Italian. Any sentence contained all three of these languages. It promised to be an enormous task, and I did not know if I had any appetite for it. I was curious, however, and sat down immediately to work on it. When I had deciphered—perhaps a better word than translated—thirty pages, I was quite fascinated, as well as profoundly disturbed, and remained at my desk until five a.m. when I quite fell asleep over the manuscript. The next morning when I awoke, I picked up those portions I had deciphered, and read them, and it was then that I realized how the manuscript, and the events related in it, bore an uncanny resemblance to certain memories in my own life. I could not at first be certain, and because my feeling was so ambivalent, it was not necessarily a pleasant discovery. I decided not to work on it further and put it away.

During the next few years I came to work on it daily, and to such an extent that the thing very nearly became my own. It was my choice about which meaning the original language bore, and I could not any longer distinguish between what was in the original manuscript and what was my own invention. For I confess that as I translated, the words seemed almost to seep into my very existence until the fantasy produced on the page, if indeed I any longer believed it was a fantasy, became a memory of actual experiences in my own life. And who is to contest the propriety of such an action? Is this not the author's real wish? For how many of us, when caught up in a work of fiction, have not wished to rush into the pages and halt the conversation of the characters with our own news of the day?

In a scrupulous move, finally, I decided it would be necessary to reread the original manuscript, only to discover of course that it no longer existed. There existed only this final copy, for which I take credit as editor and translator, and for which the original author must of course remain a mystery.

"Hers, do you think?" said Farthingdale when he had finished reading it.

"I don't know," said Avian, "it has a distinctly Victorian flourish. It may have been something she'd bought, you know, some old manuscript."

"But why isn't it identified?"

"I don't know. We can check the handwriting. It may be hers."

"What manuscript does it refer to?"

"I don't know," said Avian, looking puzzled. He photographed the document, then put the camera in his pocket.

When they left the house it was just after five, and dusk and shadows filled the yard which was surrounded by enormous trees. As they walked down the stone walk, Farthingdale had the distinct feeling he was being watched. He put his hand on Avian's arm and they stopped. There was no sound. Once they were in the car, Farthingdale said, "Did you feel it, that someone was in that yard?"

Avian nodded. They got into the car, and Farthingdale drove very slowly, glancing into the rear-view mirror as they pulled away. When they were no more than fifteen yards from the gate, he saw a figure in a hat, darting from the drive. He stopped the car and Avian was ahead of him running down the drive. But the gate was closed; there was no trace of anyone.

Back in the car Farthingdale said, "By the way, an odd thing turned up while you were gone," and reaching into his pocket he handed a slip of paper to Avian.

"It's in Latin," said Avian, surprised.

"Quite. Can you translate it?"

"Yes," Avian said. "It says, 'The Jew will bring you any dream you wish.'"

"What's it from?"

"I haven't the faintest."

"Your favorite author, Juvenal; odd you don't recognize it."

"Yes," said Avian, brooding.

"It turned up in, of all places, a Chinese fortune cookie found near the body. Some old queer, eighty-four years old, was shuffling through the park and got it near the bench, although he said at the time there was no body on it."

"What time?"

"Three o'clock."

"The body was found at three-fifteen."

"Quite."

"What an odd thing to come up . . . was it on the ground or the bench, and did he pick it up, why would he pick it up? If it was a plant, a risky one, a fortune cookie. Good God . . . a dog could have gotten it, anything."

"Oh, he didn't find it, a woman with red hair and a black cape handed it to him."

"Well, what the devil," Avian said starting, "what did she look like?"

"We don't know . . ." As usual, Farthingdale was being very reluctant about giving Avian information.

"Well come on, man, was she masked or what?"

"The cape covered everything, head to toe, he couldn't even see her eyes."

"But you just said, she had red hair . . ."

"Pubic hair," said Farthingdale. "She exposed herself to him in the park and handed him a cookie. Poor fellow never'd seen one so close up and he about died."

"But he took the cookie?"

"Well, she'd sort of paralyzed him."

"How extraordinary," Avian said. "I've never heard of a woman exposing herself."

"To an eighty-four-year-old queer at that," said Farthingdale. "You can't help but think she knew all about him and decided he ought to have a glimpse before he died."

They pulled up to their offices and Farthingdale started to get out when he noticed Avian was coming toward his side of the car. "Are you taking it?"

"Yes," Avian said, "I thought I'd go see Harcourt; he's the only one who knows the erotic literature well enough."

"Oh, perhaps I'll go with you then," Farthingdale said. "That foie gras at the little restaurant around the corner was very good indeed."

"It's closed," Avian said.

"How do you know that?"

"That American writer I met yesterday mentioned it."

"Oh, pity," said Farthingdale. "Well, I did so want foie gras."

"What about Henley's?"

"Oh, I'm not going there anymore. Albert Wesker told me, he's just got back from Lyons and knows the farmer who supplies Dominic, who supplies Henley's, and they don't stuff their geese nearly enough."

"The entire thing disgusts me," Avian said. "How can you relish a force-fed animal?"

"Oh bother," Farthingdale said, "you moralists are all so boring. You forget that appetite comes before anything else." He got reluctantly out of the car then, wondering where he would have dinner, and brooding that he would have to have it alone.

Avian slid into the seat behind the wheel. "Where are you having dinner?"

"I don't know," Farthingdale said. "If I can't have foie gras, I must have escargots."

"Did he say what it looked like?"

"What?"

"The quim."

"Yes," Farthingdale said, "but what do you expect from an old queer. You know what Bertillon said."

"What did he say?"

"Bertillon said . . ."

"Not Bertillon, the queer."

"Oh, he said it looked like a jack-o'-lantern, only it had teeth and when he ran away it started to laugh, and when he turned round he saw the teeth shining in the dark."

"So much for the vagina dentata." Avian said sighing. "You don't usually get it so direct I suppose."

"No, I suppose not." Seeing that Farthingdale was about to leave, Avian caught him by the sleeve and said, "What did Bertillon say, by the way?"

"Bertillon said," Farthingdale replied, "one can only see what one observes, and one observes only things which are already in the mind." He tipped his hat then, Avian nodded, and they said good night.

## ANONYMOUS FOLK TALES

Sexual stories are abundant in the anonymous folk tales of all peoples, from Siberia to the Dauphiné, from the Bretagne to Norway, as well as from the Near East, Asia, and the Pacific Ocean. There is so much of this material that it was necessary to exclude the Oriental and to focus on folk tales of Europe. However, many of these tales, especially the Russian, have undoubtedly come originally from the East.

For our selection we have relied primarily on the vast documentation known as *Kryptadia*, carefully prepared by collectors of folklore from various countries and published in Paris between 1897 and 1905. (This collection is multilingual; all of the stories here were translated by us either from French or German.)

Among the most interesting of these stories are those from Russia, some of which we took from *Kryptadia*, others from a rare French collection entitled *Contes Secrets Russes* (*Rousskiia zavetniia skazki*), published clandestinely by the Bibliothèque des Curieux (Paris, 1921).

## THE MAGIC RING

In a village there lived three brothers. As they were no longer on good terms, they decided to divide up their inheritance. However, the property was not apportioned evenly: chance favored the two elder brothers and left almost nothing to the youngest. All three were bachelors. One day when they were together in the street, they agreed

that it was time they married. "That is all very well for
you," said the third brother, "you are rich and you will
find rich wives, but what am I to do? I am poor and in the
way of riches I have only this cock of mine that comes
down to my knees."

Now, a merchant's daughter was passing by just then;
she overheard the three brothers' conversation and said to
herself: "Ah! if only I could marry that young man! He
has a cock that reaches down to his knees!"

The elder brothers married and the youngest son did not.
However, the merchant's daughter went home obsessed
with the idea of marrying him. Several shopkeepers asked
for her hand, but she spurned them all. "The only husband I want," she said, "is so-and-so."

Her parents lectured her. "What are you thinking of,
you silly fool? Be reasonable. How can you marry a penni-
less peasant?"

"Don't worry about that," she answered, "you won't be
the ones who will have to live with him."

Then she got together with a professional matchmaker
and sent her to tell the fellow to come and ask for her
hand. The matchmaker went to the peasant's house and
said to him: "Listen to me, dear boy! What are you moping
about like this for? Go and ask the daughter of such-and-
such a merchant to marry you; she's been in love with you
for a long time and would be glad to marry you."

Hearing this, the mouzhik put on a new smock and a
new cap and went straight to the girl's father. As soon as
she saw him coming, the daughter knew him as the man
with the cock down to his knees. She was so insistent that
her parents finally agreed to let her marry the young man.

On their wedding night, the bride discovered that her
husband's cock wasn't even as long as a finger. "Ah, you
rascal," she cried, "you boasted of having a cock down to
your knees, what did you do with it?"

"Ah, dear wife, you know that before our marriage I was
very poor; when I had to pay for the wedding feast, I had

no money and nothing to borrow on, so I had to pawn my cock."

"And how much did you get for it?"

"Oh, not much: fifty rubles."

"All right. Tomorrow I'll ask my mother for fifty rubles and you can redeem your cock; you've absolutely got to get it, or never darken my doorway again!"

The next day, the young bride hurried to her mother's house: "Please, mother, give me fifty rubles, I need them very badly!"

"Why do you need them, pray?"

"Well, mother, this is why: my husband had a cock that came down to his knees, but on the eve of his wedding the poor man had nothing else to put up for security, so he pawned it for fifty rubles. Now my husband has a cock that isn't even as long as a finger. He simply must redeem his old one!"

The mother realized that this was a matter of dire necessity, and she gave her daughter the fifty rubles. The young woman immediately took them to her husband and said: "There! Now hurry up and go redeem your old cock: I don't want anyone else getting the benefit of it!"

The young man took the money and left with a heavy heart. "Now what is to become of me," he thought to himself; "how can I get such a cock for my wife? I shall go on walking as long as the earth will carry me."

He had been walking for some time when he met an old woman: "Good day to you, little mother!"

"Good day to you, young man! Where are you walking to?"

"Oh, little mother, if you knew how wretched I am! I don't know where to go!"

"Tell me your troubles, dear boy, perhaps I can help you."

"I would be embarrassed to tell you!"

"Don't be afraid, speak right out!"

"Well, little mother, here is how it is: I boasted that I

68    *The Folklore of Sex*

had a cock that came down to my knees; a merchant's daughter overheard me and married me; but on our wedding night she discovered that my cock isn't as long as a finger. So she got angry: 'What did you do with your long cock?' she asked me. I told her I had pawned it for fifty rubles. So she gave me the money and told me to redeem it or never to darken her doorway again. I don't know what is to become of me!"

"Give me the money," said the old woman, "and I will help you out of your trouble." The peasant immediately counted out fifty rubles to her and in return received a ring. "Here," she said, "take this ring and slip it over your fingernail, but no farther." The fellow did so and instantly his cock grew to a cubit in length. "Well," the old woman said, "is it long enough now?"

"But little mother, it still doesn't come down to my knees."

"All you have to do is slide the ring down your finger, dear boy."

He slid the ring down to the middle of his finger and he suddenly had a cock seven versts long. "Hey, little mother, what am I going to do now? A cock this long is a real calamity!"

"Slide the ring back up to your nail and your cock will only be a cubit long. Now I expect you'll be satisfied with that! When you use the ring, be careful not to slide it below the nail."

The young man thanked the old woman and started home again, happy at the thought that he was not returning empty-handed to his wife. When he had walked a long while, he felt the need to eat a morsel and, stepping off the road, he sat down by a stream, took some little biscuits out of his sack, dipped them in the water and began to eat them. After that, he lay back and admired the effect of the ring: he slipped it over his fingernail and his cock stood a cubit high; he slid it down to the middle of his finger and his cock rose to a height of seven versts; he took the ring off and his member returned to its former, modest proportions.

When the peasant had amused himself in this way for quite a while, he felt sleepy but he forgot to put the ring in his pocket before he fell asleep and left it lying on his chest. A gentleman and his wife happened to be driving by in a carriage. Catching sight of a peasant sleeping near the road with a ring shining on his chest, the gentleman stopped the carriage and said to his footman: "Go fetch that mouzhik's ring and bring it here." The servant immediately carried out his master's order, and the carriage got under way again. However, the gentleman was fascinated by the beauty of the ring. "Look, darling, see how pretty this ring is," he said to his wife; "let's see if it will fit me." And he slipped the ring down to the middle of his finger: instantly, his cock shot out, knocked the coachman off his seat, passed over the horses' heads and stretched out seven versts in front of the carriage.

Seeing this, the panic-stricken gentlewoman shouted to the footman: "Go back to that peasant and bring him here!" The footman ran back to the mouzhik, woke him up and said: "Go to my master and hurry up about it!" Meanwhile, the peasant was looking for his ring: "The devil take you! Did you filch my ring?"

"Don't bother looking for it," replied the footman, "go to my master, he's the one who's got it; that ring of yours, my friend, has got us into a fine kettle of fish."

The peasant ran to the carriage in a twinkling of an eye. "Forgive me," began the gentleman in a plaintive tone of voice, "help me out of this predicament!"

"What will you give me, sir?"

"Here, take these hundred rubles."

"Give me two hundred and I'll help you." The barine gave the mouzhik two hundred rubles and the mouzhik slipped the ring off his finger. Instantly, the gentleman's cock returned to its former size. The carriage went on its way and the peasant went home.

70 *The Folklore of Sex*

His wife saw him coming from the window and rushed out to meet him. "Well!" she asked him, "did you redeem it?"

"Yes."

"Come on, show it to me!"

"Come into the house, I can't show it to you in the street." When they were inside, the wife kept repeating: "Show it to me! Show it to me!" He slid the ring over his fingernail and his cock grew to a cubit in length; he took it out of his trousers and said: "Look, wife!"

She started to kiss him: "Don't you think it's better, little husband, to keep such a treasure at home instead of leaving it with strangers? Let us hurry and eat dinner, then we shall go to bed and try it out!"

She immediately spread the table with dishes and bottles. The couple dined, then went to bed. Once the wife had tested the vigor of her husband's member, she spent the next three days peeking under her petticoats, for it constantly seemed to her that she could still feel it between her legs!

One day, she went to see her mother, while the mouzhik lay down for a nap under an apple tree in the garden. "Well," the merchant's wife said to her daughter, "did you redeem that cock?"

"Yes," answered the young wife, and she went into great detail on the subject.

As she listened, the merchant's wife became obsessed with the idea of slipping away during her daughter's visit, going to her son-in-law's house and testing that stupendous engine for herself. She managed to steal out and secretly hurried to the peasant's house. She saw him asleep in the garden. The ring was over his fingernail and his cock rose to the height of a cubit. "I'm going to perch myself on his cock," said the mother-in-law to herself as she took in the scene. No sooner said than done. Unfortunately for her, the ring on the sleeper's fingernail slid down to the middle of his finger, and all at once the merchant's wife shot up to a height of seven versts as the cock suddenly stretched. Meanwhile, the wife had noticed her mother's absence and, guessing what was behind it, she hurried home. There was nobody in the house; she went out into the garden, and what did she see? Her husband was sleeping with his cock in the air, and way up on top, so high you could hardly see her, was the merchant's wife, spinning in the breeze like a weather vane. What was to be done? How was she going to rescue her mother from such a dangerous predicament? A crowd gathered and an argument arose as to the best solution to the problem, with everyone giving his opinion. "There is only one thing to do," said some; "we must get an axe and chop down the cock."

"No," replied others, "you musn't do that, it would mean the death of two people. If we chopped off the cock, the woman would fall to the ground and break every bone in her body. The best thing is for all of us to pray; perhaps God will work a miracle and save the old woman." In the midst of all this, the sleeper awoke, realized that the ring was in the middle of his finger and that his cock, which rose perpendicularly to a height of seven versts, was pinning him so firmly to the ground that he couldn't even turn over on his side. Very gently, he withdrew the ring; his cock shrank slowly, and when it was only a cubit high, the peasant realized that his mother-in-law was on the end of it. "What are you doing there, mother?" he asked her.

"Forgive me, dear son-in-law, I won't do it again."

"Another murder," Santiago said, reading the papers that morning. "Things are getting very uncomfortable in Rome."

"Particularly for the terrorists," I said.

"The terrorists are always uncomfortable, it's the businessmen who are in trouble," Santiago said.

Lucia interrupted at that moment. They were having troubles of their own. Lucia is Santiago's wife. When I first met him, two years ago, he told me he was vacationing with his wife in Italy for the winter. He then decided to stay on, the way people do in Rome. I had never been able to find out exactly how he lived. He made "deals" for people, he said; he was an art dealer who made expensive purchases for private clients, or so he told me. Later, this appeared to be true, although one is never of course quite sure . . . It was during August in Naples when I had first stopped near his table that I overheard him arguing heatedly about the murders. Like most amateurs he thought it was a drug ring. I myself because of certain sources, and certainly because of the guns, knew there was no question but that they were political murders. This was clear, however, only to me, the murderer, and pos-

DOCUMENT #4

*THE NEW YORK TIMES, WEDNESDAY, OCTOBER 18, 1972*

## Official of Al Fatah Shot Dead in Rome

ROME, Oct. 17—A Libyan Embassy employe, a Jordanian who is believed to have been a member of Al Fatah, the Palestinian guerrilla organization, was shot dead last night outside his suburban apartment.

The 38-year-old victim, Abdel Weil Zuaiter of Nablus, Jordan, was described today by Fatah's

# Jordanian, Fatah Aide, Is Slain in Rome

Continued From Page 1, Col. 8

press agency in Beirut as its representative for Italy. It said he was a martyr and hero of the Palestinian cause, "assassinated" by Israeli secret-service operatives.

A Jordanian Embassy official said Mr. Zuaiter was a nephew of Akram Zuaiter, Jordan's Ambassador in Beirut, but declined to confirm reports that he was also a second cousin of Yasir Arafat, leader of Fatah.

The police said the murder had been carefully planned. Neighbors told the police they saw two men fire and then escape in a waiting car.

The car was found a few blocks from the scene. The police said it was rented Sunday by a man who showed a Canadian driver's license, on which he was named as Anthony Hutton, 47, of Toronto.

The police disclosed that Mr. Zuaiter, who officially was a translator for the Libyan Embassy, had been ideologically involved in activities on behalf of Palestinian refugees and guerrillas. Two of his brothers were killed four years ago during an Israeli incursion into Lebanon, it was said.

According to the police, Mr. Zuaiter had been a contributor to Palestina, a pro-Palestinian periodical issued here until a year ago, and organized and led meetings of Italian leftist pro-Arab and rightist anti-Jewish movements. Recently, he collected funds to build a hospital in a Palestinian guerrilla camp.

In September, 1970, he was reported in Amman and was a frequent traveler to Libya.

Mr. Zuaiter was questioned in connection with the attempt by two Jordanians to blow up an Israeli airliner on Aug. 17, the police said.

A statement by the Ambassadors to Italy and the Vatican of the 18 member countries of the Arab League said that the "horrible crime recalls the actions of the Zionist bands that have written notorious pages in the history of terrorism and violence, in Palestine and elsewhere."

## 'Zionist' Terrorists Accused

Special to The New York Times

BEIRUT, Lebanon, Oct. 17— Al Fatah, the major Palestinian commando organization, accused pro-Israeli terrorists today of killing the Fatah representative in Rome.

"This is part of the Zionist terrorist campaign being carried out in all parts of the world by the enemy," a Fatah statement said.

The dead man, Abdel Weil Zuaiter, was born in Nablus, now part of the West Bank of the Jordan River, which was occupied by Israel in 1967. He was "another martyr whose blood will be avenged," the statement said.

sibly one or two other interested and highly motivated parties. Eventually having overheard more of his conversation I stopped at his table and introduced myself. Why? Because he was very handsome, very vital, very tan, very manly, very dark, very charming, very gay, very brooding, very intense, very savage, and, observing these qualities as I strolled by the pier that particular August afternoon, I thought that I would like, therefore, to fuck him.

This eventually came to pass.

As I got to know Santiago it became clear to me that his sexual practices were not conventional in any regard. He went so far as to have his wife trained like a dancer so that she could accommodate his need for diverse and difficult positions. My impression on the whole is that she has no other life than pleasing him, something which breeds eventual havoc, or at least such has been my observation. This particular afternoon at their house there seems to be some special disruption. She does not guess as to why I spend so much time with Santiago, and thinks simply we share intellectual and artistic interests.

We are having cocktails around the pool. The Mediterranean sun is very white today. I see Santiago splashing about in the blue water of the pool. He is very beautiful. I do not think I will ever tire of looking at his form. He is wearing black trunks today and they are tight and wet now, clinging to the outline of his penis and his balls. I love to watch the curves as he stands by the side of the pool, the water dripping off his legs, running down the hairs curling against his skin pulling the soft material down further, one ball rising slowly then falling, like a soft, full lung.

"Lucia," he says now, drying his head with a towel, "if you're going to have this affair, I want you to consider it carefully." Lucia turns her chair away from us and pouts. "Really, Lucia, you had better listen to me, you know I always tell you what is best. It would be best if you did not have it, but if you are determined to have it listen to me. Choose very carefully. Be sure it is someone you would find it impossible to live with, whom you could not marry. For you I think it would be best to have a polite, aggressive, cordial bastard."

"A bastard!" Lucia turns around. She is a lovely woman I think, especially when hurt. Her face, incredulous holds nothing but love for Santiago. "So," she said, "you wish me to be hurt."

"But of course." Santiago stopped, pulling the white towel from his tanned, lean cheek. "You want to suffer don't you want to feel humiliated abused, risk everything that matters to yourself in order to satisfy your body . . . that's the point, isn't it?" Santiago stirred his drink. "Or perhaps," he smiled, "I have misunderstood."

Lucia crossed her arms and tapped her fingers nervously against her elbows. "Don't bet silly," Lucia said. "What would I want to be abused for. I want a man," her chin tilted, piquant towards the sky, "who will love me." She put her hand back nervously through her copper-colored hair.

Santiago of course laughed. "But Lucia, I love you."

"But you are never here." Lucia's eyes blazed. "You go out, you travel around the world, you sleep with other women."

"So what," Santiago said, his mouth again now in a straight line, getting angry. "I love you. Don't you see, Lucia, you need a man who will love you, no matter what you do. Unconditional love, Lucia, that is your requirement. I am the only man who can give it to you."

"But you mistreat me!" Lucia said, pleading. She stood up now, lighting a cigarette and paced about the pool.

"I do?" Santiago seemed surprised. He turned and asked me to bring him a beer. I got up and went into the house. Andrew was playing on the floor with his blocks. A lovely child, soft and delicate, his hair was blond. He grinned and waved at me. "Blah, blah," he said. "Yes," I said, "pretty block, lovely block." I got the beer from the refrigerator and when I passed the living room again, Andrew began to cry loudly. I stopped and picked him up and carried him with me out to the pool. The sun was white hot now, the clouds had dispersed and it was two o'clock in the afternoon. I set the beers down on the table and saw that Santiago and Lucia at the far side of the pool were arguing heatedly.

"I have never mistreated you!" Santiago said, furious. "How can you say that. I give you everything you want."

"I want," Lucia wailed, "companionship, to sit by the fire," she was getting hysterical now, "I want to be normal to live like other people I want."

"Shut up!" Santiago slapped her. Startled Lucia stepped back, tears falling from her face. I do not think he had ever struck her before.

"I hate you!" she spat at him. "I hate you, Santiago!" He grabbed her wrist as she tried to slap him and she lifted her knee and caught him in the groin. Santiago bent over and Lucia dived into the pool. The pool was long and Lucia was swimming underwater. I saw her arms and legs folding in and out her red hair curling above her as she swept along the bottom of the pool Santiago was after her in a minute, swift dark and moving quickly he caught up to her and still under water grabbed her and pushed her against the side of the pool Lucia struggled and he clapped his hand over her mouth as she struggled trapped against the wall of the pool. Her legs kicked out and I wondered how much longer she could stay under there when I saw Santiago tearing her bathing suit, he tore it from her in shreds as she struggled desperately under the water and then I saw in a minute he was into her, pounding her up against the wall. Lucia's head moving from side to side desperate for air her eyes wild I thought he would drown her but then in a minute he let her surface, still inside her as she struggled against the wall her eyes bulging her head above the water then Santiago's head above, gasping for air, Lucia coughing gasping a hoarse whisper. Santiago ducking her head under, letting her up for a moment, then he twisted her arm behind her back and pushed her head down under the water as she struggled then and he pushed her head between her knees and jacknifed her and entered her from behind. I thought Lucia might be drowning. I stood up, not knowing what to do and brought Andrew inside. I sat him on the floor and went out again on the veranda. Lucia, sputtering coughing and gasping in her torn suit, a huge gash ripped in it just below her belly, was leaning against Santiago now on the side of the pool, he was dragging her, "No No No more," Lucia cried, he dragged her along the concrete, her knees bruising and pulled her up to the diving board. She was weak and faint coughing still. He pulled the last of the suit from her and Lucia, fair-skinned Lucia stood pale and naked, trembling in the bright noonday sun, the red hairs of her pudenda curling down, despairing, with water. "NO!" she screamed as he took her then, her arm behind her back, Lucia crying as she did as he bid. "Do it," he whispered fiercely against her neck, "I will I WILL STOP!" Lucia screamed and I watched then as he bid Lucia grasp the diving board with her hands, and moving to the end, stand on her hands, her hands holding to the edges of the board.

"Now," Santiago said and Lucia then not a dancer for nothing, straight in the air bent slowly back for him in a beautiful arc, legs out straight, then spread, until her legs, were at a sharp right angle to her body and just below his waist now her feet spread open and Santiago walking from the end of the board ran and plunged into her.

Lucia moaned, as Santiago screamed at her to dive. "Dive, Lucia." His penis plunged into her, she still gripped the sides of the diving board. His arms held her legs firmly gripped beneath his armpit.

"JUMP WITH ME LUCIA!" Santiago sounded the warning, and then jumping from the board, Lucia pushing off with her hands they went as one into the air, Santiago still pinned into her, legs still straight they went up into the air, white and glittering against the sun and then they fell, Lucia diving with her arms over her head, her legs out straight Santiago astride her his head high in the air, Santiago cried then just before her head was buried beneath the water, and I saw the look on his face as his head disappeared and the blue water covered his open mouth.

DOCUMENT #5

---

*THE NEW YORK TIMES, TUESDAY, SEPTEMBER 7, 1971*

# A Phone Snarl, a Murder, An Exiled Yemen Premier

Special to The New York Times

BEIRUT, Lebanon, Sept. 6—Maj. Gen. Hassan al-Amri, three time Premier of Yemen, has been sent into exile by a crossed telephone line.

General Amri, who arrived here unexpectedly last week, has locked himself into his hotel suite, refusing to talk to reporters or even to deny the charges made against him, but the story of his downfall has trickled out.

It all started on Aug. 25, according to newspaper accounts, when General Amri—commander in chief of the Yemeni Army for more than five years and Premier for the third time in nine years since about two weeks earlier—made a telephone call to the chief of guards at the army's general headquarters.

Or so he thought. In fact, due to an electronic mixup, he reached instead Mohsen al-Harazi, the owner of a photographic shop in downtown Sana, the nation's capital.

General Amri, the newspapers reported, thought he was speaking to his military subordinate. Mr. Harazi thought the caller, who said he was the Premier, was a friend being funny. General Amri was not amused. Neither was Mr. Harazi, and mutual confusion led to mutual insult.

The Premier, according to the

Continued on Page 4, Column 4

United Press International

**Maj. Gen. Hassan al-Amri**

# Phone Snarl, a Murder, an Exiled Yemen Premier

Continued From Page 1, Col. 3

accounts, went to military headquarters and ordered Mr. Harazi brought before him. The shopkeeper pleaded for mercy.

But General Amri had Mr. Harazi beaten by the guards, according to the newspaper accounts, and then he himself beat the shopkeeper with an iron bar. He ordered the guards to shoot Mr. Harazi. When they refused, the newspapers reported, the Premier took one of the guards' pistol and shot the shopkeeper in the head.

General Amri, 55 years old, had maintained himself in a variety of powerful positions in the Government and the military since Yemen, in the southwestern corner of the Arabian Peninsula, became a republic in 1962 with the ouster of Imam Mohammed al-Badr.

Regarded as the heir apparent to Abdullah al-Salal, who led the 1962 coup d'état, General Amri became even more powerful after Field Marshal Salal's ouster in 1967. His popularity with the military grew when he headed the successful counteroffensive against the royalist forces that broke the siege of Sana in 1968, leading to the end of the civil war.

After the death of Mr. Harazi Abdul Rahman al-Iryani, President of the Republican Council, forced General Amri to resign from all his posts or stand trial for murder. General Amri was then bundled aboard the first flight to Beirut with the understanding that his family would join him later.

His resignation—as Premier, commander in chief and member of the Republican Council — was unanimously accepted by the Yemeni Consultative Council, the country's 159-man legislature, which met in emergency session Saturday, according to Yemeni sources here.

But several council members insisted that General Amri be tried for murder. "The killing of people like animals cannot be tolerated," said one.

Judge Mohammed al-Siyaghi, a prominent jurist, said: "The murder has brought Amri down from the top to the gutter; for people to feel safe, Amri must be presented to trial."

The victim's family refused to bury him for several days until the President promised to take action against General Amri.

## 10

"Did you see this absolutely asinine incredibly stupid telephone affair in Yemen?"

"Yemen?" the little priest said. "More trouble in Yemen. The Al Fatah."

"This was not Fatah, this was that idiot General Amri who murdered a man all over a wrong number. It's like a bad movie." Anna crumbled the croissant and looked gloomily over at Bacco across the table. "I don't know what to do," she said.

Just then the pussycat came in and Anna picked her up and stroking her said, "Pussy, can't you tell me what to do?"

Bacco said, "What time is the delivery due?"

Anna shrugged, "Sometime this week," and put the cat down. "I'll have to wait."

Bacco watched her face as she sat, drinking her tea, and looking out to sea. He saw how troubled she was, and knew immediately it was more than professional complications. Actually he knew Anna never worried about being caught. It was her birthday coming up that caused it. He sighed, got up and went into the kitchen. He mixed up the flour and the yeast and took great pleasure in the kneading. He was genuinely concerned about her. The fat man in the white suit had done it. Things were fine until then; she had always *wondered*, but she didn't worry about it.

"Damn fool," Bacco said out loud suddenly, smacking the doughy mass against the board, "bringing her the letter." A letter written to her as a child, and somehow gotten by the man in the white suit. Until then he had been an abstraction, but the letter had obsessed her—with the desire to know something, who he was, or if he was alive, or dead or something. But the fat man had only delivered the letter—he said he had no idea who her father was. He had simply been asked to deliver the letter. A trick or not, it had worked its havoc. That was years ago, Bacco thought, and each year, at birthday time, like magic, the obsession began to overtake her. He wished she would forget it. Some things were impossible that was all, he's told her that. But he knew Anna well. She would find him. That was that.

## London: 8:48

"But my dear fellow," Harcourt said, puffing as he moved his huge form into a more comfortable chair. "I *have* told you everything I know." Avian gazed at him, but not uncomfortably. There was something so finally mysterious about Harcourt that one accepted it. He did not accept, however, his statements about Lady Covington. But in case Harcourt did not co-operate, and it was characteristic of him not to co-operate, he had made the necessary arrangements.

"Pity about the old girl," Harcourt said, taking out his pipe cleaner and working his white pipe. "I knew her rather well; that is to say, as well as anyone could know her. Most peculiar."

"What's that?" Avian said. He knew Harcourt would get chatty and pretend to give him information, yet say finally nothing. He sighed and decided to wait it out.

"Her interest in American rock music, most particularly since . . ." Harcourt dribbled off then, hunting for something with which to pack down his pipe.

"Since?" Avian said, leaning forward.

"Well, the old girl far as I could tell was stone deaf." Harcourt searched the floor now, eagerly for the pipe cleaner he had dropped.

"How do you know that?" Avian said. "I mean what makes you so sure?"

"Well," Harcourt said harrumphing, "when I was there once, in the garden, and some of these young people were there too, you know all long-haired and blue-jeaned, and they were having a marvelous party," Harcourt's eyes grew misty, "quite marvelous, but when I said to her, 'You know that young man,' there was one particularly I noticed, 'is a marvelous saxophonist,' she shrugged and listened a moment, and at that moment, you see, the saxophone solo had finished, and this clarinetist was playing, and at that moment she said, 'Oh yes, he's fine.' So I knew you see the old girl couldn't tell."

"Perhaps she was referring to the saxophonist in any event," Avian said, getting bored with the approach of amateurs like Harcourt.

"Well no, because she actually paused, to listen to the clarinetist, and she said, 'Yes, he's really fine. The notes are so pure.' It would have been all right, if she'd left it at that, but like all unpracticed liars," Harcourt said, "she went on. She said, 'He's very close to Johnny Hodges in his tempo, don't you think?' Well, Hodges played the saxophone, dammit man. He wasn't a clarinetist."

"Hmm," said Avian, wondering if a gaffe like that could have been deliberate.

"Tell me," Avian said, "what do you know about her sex life?"

"Her sex life," Harcourt's brows shot up, "good God, man, she was eighty-four years old."

"Nonetheless, you always seem to know everything about everyone's sex life. Did she have any peculiarities?"

Harcourt squinted at Avian. "I wouldn't know. I've told you everything I remember about her."

"You seem to have a rather poor memory," Avian said.

"I wouldn't be quick to make allegations about poor memory if I were you," Harcourt said, raising his huge form from the chair and stirring the fire. "Despite your reputation," Harcourt said, "you never know when you might begin to slip, things can suddenly simply *vanish,* you know. Hubris is a dangerous thing."

Harcourt stood there in his white suit silhouetted against the fire, his eyes suddenly bright and menacing.

Avian shifted his weight in the chair. It was a remark that was all, he assured himself. Mere coincidence. He'd known Harcourt fifteen years and he'd never suggested such a thing before. Avian stood up.

"It would be embarrassing for you I think," Avian said, "if your car, transporting your paintings, were to reach Rome only to be searched and found containing several pounds of heroin. Most embarrassing."

"This is blackmail," Harcourt replied.

"But it's just among friends," Avian said smiling.

"I know you don't bluff, but I don't see that you would have gone to the trouble of lacing my car with heroin and if you have done that I must know why the information is so important to you."

"You can't know any of that. Your car will be at the Italian border in about six hours. Call me if you change your mind before then."

Avian picked up his hat, did not shake hands, and turned away. As his hand reached the doorknob Harcourt said, "Dildoes. She collected dildoes. She got them from a man in Amsterdam. His name is Silverstein. He's a Jew."

Avian's hand grabbed the door. "Cheerio," he said, tipping his hat, and left.

---

I noted that Santiago read all of the international papers—Peking, *Le Monde,* the London *Times,* the New York *Times*, *La Nación* and *Al Ahram*. This morning studying the papers he seemed very disturbed.

"What's the matter?" I asked, reaching for more strawberries. It is one of those things I can't help noticing that after a night of loving strawberries are a most compatible thing to breakfast on. "There was an owner of a photography shop killed in Yemen. Aaman I know, that's one, and two, Lady Sarah has died."

"Who is she?" Lucia asked jealously.

"The woman in London."

"Oh, the poor old one, poor thing, the translator. Did she get to finish the work for you?" Lucia said.

"No," Santiago said. "She didn't die of old age. She died of murder."

"Oh dear," I said, deciding to put some lemon juice and sugar on the berries this morning, instead of cream, "it's getting to be so commonplace. Why just the other week that embassy agent or whatever."

Santiago stood up suddenly. "We're going to have visitors I think." He walked out the door. When I heard the car start I raced out and caught him just as he was pulling out of the drive. I hopped in.

"She was murdered on November tenth," Santiago said. "Three days before that I had sent her a check for a half million pounds."

"Why so much?" I said.

"I was making a purchase." Santiago was nervous. The wind was whipping his hair in his face, something he usually seemed to enjoy, and he kept pushing it away a perfectly hopeless gesture. He gunned the motor as we took an uphill turn that I always found particularly risky and then he began to drive very fast.

"Well, what about the Yemen thing, did you have anything to do with it?"

"Nothing that can be traced," Santiago said.

We were going well over a hundred miles an hour and Santiago was discussing the murder as thoughtfully as if we were having afternoon tea. His entire body, however, was taut as a wire.

"Were you working for Silverstein?" I said finally. Santiago nodded.

"You think he planned it, planned to frame you?"

"It's going to be difficult," Santiago said.

I knew I was partly responsible for implicating Santiago. I had glimpsed Silverstein on several occasions over the years, always it seemed from the rear. He was forever leaving places in a hurry, but I had had no opportunity to speak to him until one night, some months ago. It was a grey October evening in Amsterdam. Santiago had explained to me that Silverstein was an antiquities dealer of dubious leanings, but that nevertheless, although it was rumored to be dangerous, it was extremely profitable to deal with him. That recently he had expressed an interest in getting some African masks out of Uganda, and Santiago had thought he might help him. Then with General Amri being so difficult, and the Ugandan murders of Americans, they had let it cool. Silverstein seemed particularly anxious to get the masks, however, I remembered, and since Santiago had suggested he might have a connection, I went to his shop one evening in Amsterdam, for my own purposes.

Of course I did not like him. He was ominous looking—rather like a penguin in a long black coat. He carried expensive canes, which I had once commented to Santiago I was sure contained hidden swords, but Santiago had laughed and said I had a foolish imagination. In any event, I decided to pursue the matter with Silverstein and so it happened that particular evening that I made my way to his shop. He was entertaining a visitor, a rotund English gentleman, a rather Sidney Greenstreet looking character in a white suit, and a blue tie with peacock feathers on it. He wore several expensive scarab rings and squinted at me from a wicker chair which could barely contain him. On his shoulder was a myna bird which ominously uttered only the names of special organizations: Gestapo, Mafioso, Fascista, all of which amused Mr. Harcourt enormously. That was his name. He smoked a cigar.

I told Silverstein what I wanted and he replied with characteristic brevity, "Impossible."

"I can get it," Mr. Harcourt offered suddenly from the chair. Even Silverstein seemed surprised.

"Are you a rare book dealer?" I asked.

"Among other things."

"What other things?"

"Things that are hard to find."

"Such as," I asked, pressing him further.

"Books that are hard to find, jewels that are hard to find, fortunes that are hard to find, and uh," Mr. Harcourt cleared his throat, "people that are hard to find."

"That's quite a scope of specialization," I replied somewhat tartly, partly annoyed at my obvious fascination with him.

"Diversification is the secret of good profits," Harcourt replied smiling. He was menacing, and I did not like his British manners. He was sailing in the morning for Casablanca and told me he would notify me when he found what I was looking for.

Santiago was very annoyed when I told him. He said then he thought that Harcourt was an agent, and that in any event he did not trust any of Silverstein's connections.

"Silverstein seemed smaller than when I first saw him years ago," I said to Santiago.

"Saw him?" Santiago said sneeringly. "No one has ever *seen* Silverstein. Harcourt, of course. But Silverstein? Never."

# 11

Silverstein stood on a street corner in Amsterdam. He wore a faded black coat, a homburg, and tapped an onyx cane with a head in the shape of a serpent, carved of silver and ivory. It was five o'clock and Plato had not arrived.

THE NEW YORK TIMES, TUESDAY, SEPTEMBER 7, 1971

# Detained Peking Official Asks To Return to China From Paris

PARIS, May 6 (Reuters)—A Chinese official, taken semiconscious to a hospital by the French police after an airport row with Peking diplomats here last week, has asked to leave for China as soon as possible, the police said tonight.

The 31-year-old official, Dr. Chung Chi-jung, left the Hotel-Dieu, a hospital, today and went to the Chinese Embassy, the police said.

He has told two French officials that he would like to return to China, but no date has been set for his departure, the police added.

Informed sources said he would leave by Monday at the latest. Chinese Embassy sources were not available for comment.

Dr. Chung, a technical adviser, was reported to have originally sought political asylum at the French Embassy in Algiers before a group of Chinese officials tried to get him aboard a Shanghai-bound airliner at Orly Airport here while he was under sedation.

The French police detained him after a struggle with the Chinese diplomats and took him to the hospital.

After the incident, the French Ministry of Interior said that Dr. Chung would be allowed to stay in France if he wished.

His return to the Chinese Embassy today apparently ended a potentially embarrassing affair for the French Government, which had been accused by Peking of "kidnapping" a Chinese citizen.

At 5:12 Silverstein returned to his shop. There he heard on the wireless the news of the China agent.

## Amsterdam: 7:17

"One of those manuscript pages has been identified," Avian said as they sat down to dinner. "Although it was part of a nineteenth-century erotic memoir it also appeared in a major intelligence document used during World War Two."

"What was that?"

"The Rosedale Manuscript."

"Never heard of it," Farthingdale said, mumbling something about finding sand in his salad.

"Well, you wouldn't, of course. I wouldn't if I hadn't worked in British intelligence. It's never been declassified, although ironically, in order to keep the cover intact, there has always been a copy in the rare manuscript collection of the British Museum."

"How amusing," Farthingdale said. "What code did it conceal?"

"Well, I don't know the code of course. I do know the cover names were for two remarkable agents during World War Two."

"Oh, those marvelous cover names. I remember hearing of the agents, working for the Germans and us, called Mutt and Jeff, I do believe."

"Yes," Avian said, looking preoccupied.

"And then," Farthingdale said carefully, "there was the one called Snow."

Avian said nothing.

"Whatever happened to him?"

"Snow?" Avian said quickly. "The name isn't familiar to me, there were so many, but I do recall Mutt and Jeff. The most imaginative names of all though, were two particular agents who were referred to as Quim and Bun. There are some remaining photographs of Quim, who worked for years undetected." He slid the photographs across the table.

"She had a remarkable ability to change her appearance as you can see . . . she was very valuable in providing us with information about Nazis but she disappeared shortly before the end of the war."

"A remarkable looking woman, she appears different in each photo . . . what eventually happened to her?"

"We don't know for certain, we believe she was drowned in a Scottish lake. There was some talk of a child but no one seems sure. The body was badly decomposed when it was found, and it was difficult to make any definite identification."

"You're certain, are you," Farthingdale said, reaching for the sherry, "that there is a double agent connection in these murders?"

"I'm not certain," Avian said. "It could be there to put us off, but I've got a very strong hunch. There's more here than politics. I have an even stronger hunch that Mr. Silverstein holds the key."

DOCUMENT #7

**The Rosedale Manuscript: Classification and Analysis. War Office. Department 008.**
The following list is a summary of double agent activity of those agents listed in the Rosedale Manuscript. In this list **w/t** stands for wireless telegraphy; **s/w** for communication in secret ink or by microphotography; **p/c** for personal contact in neutral enemy countries.

| Agent | Method of Communication | Assignment | Began Assignment | Assignment Ended | Reasons | Observations |
|---|---|---|---|---|---|---|
| 1. Dick Tracy | s/w | Arms and Armament | May '40 | June '43 | Germans considered that other Quim connections made it unnecessary to continue with Dick Tracy | Dick Tracy might have done more if he had been less distracted by Gravel Gertie |
| 2. Caesar | w/t | To create fifth column in England | May '41 | Dec. '44 | Refused to continue to work. Believed to have been heavily influenced by Cleopatra | His personal conduct and the consequent impossibility of controlling him spoiled a promising case |
| 3. Cleopatra | s/w | R.A.F. information, especially delivery of aircraft | July '40 | Mar. '43 | Fear of disclosures in trials of French acquaintances of Caesar | An unpaid agent working for ideological reasons |
| 4. Bun | — | Reports to Vichy Government | June '41 | Dec. '41 | Attracted too much attention | Purpose was really to discover if Vichy was trying to penetrate organizations here |
| 5. Arnold | p/c | General | Jan. '33 | Aug. '45 | | — |
| 6. Quim | p/c | Observation of troop movements. Daily weather reports; military and general information | Apr. '33 | Jan. '44 | Misfortune. | Her messages were responsible for capture of the spy Jello |
| 7. Winston | s/w and w/t | Details of aircraft factory. Air raid damage | May '44 | May '45 | Inability to control sexual behavior | — |

| Agent | Method of Communication | Assignment | Began Assignment | Assignment Ended | Reasons | Observations |
|---|---|---|---|---|---|---|
| 8. Batman | s/w (no method of reception) | Suppliers and manufacturers, attitude of miners and railway employees and coastal information | Dec. '41 | Jan. '42 | Hanky-pank with Robin | — |
| 9. Selms | s/w | Organization of German High Command | July '41 | Mar. '43 | Could not reach agent. Line always busy | — |
| 10. Rabbit | s/w and w/t | Aircraft and scientific apparatus, and methods used in antisubmarine warfare | July '41 | May '44 | Unknown | — |
| 11. Snow | w/t and p/c | General | Sept. '33 | Mar. '44 | See text | — |
| 12. Bicycle | w/t | General travel | Sept. '40 | Mar. '43 | No further use | — |
| 13. Lizzie | Spanish diplomatic bag | Morale, food situation, etc. | Aug. '39 | Mar. '42 | Agent kept losing bag | — |
| 14. Poseidon | w/t | General information (see text) | Sept. '40 | June '44 | Kept having nightmares about being washed up on beach at Coney Island | Operated for more than four years |
| 15. Topless | s/w and w/t | Military information and news about projected invasion | May '41 | Jan. '45 | Tendency to catch colds readily. Excessive sick leave | See text |

## 12

Anna's house was on a high slope overlooking the Mediterranean. On three sides, it was surrounded by hills and on the fourth a sharp series of cliffs, white and carved that dropped down to a small beach before the sea. Towards the rear of the house the cliff jutted out on a small narrow promontory, covered with moss and fern that angled out very sharply and narrowly for almost a quarter of a mile from the mainland. As a protection for boats, Anna had lights put into the cliff of the wall, so that in the fog it could be avoided. What no one seemed to know was that Anna lived that high on the cliff overlooking the Mediterranean for the extraordinary privacy this promontory offered. There were days when she would practice diving from it. It was a 150-foot drop, and she would dive this, going down very deep, and trying to increase the amount of time she could hold her breath. The longest she had managed was 3.4 minutes. She sighed that morning, arching her back over the rings, and testing the exercise equipment, her lung capacity would never be very much greater than that. It was the only part of her body, she thought, that was not extraordinary, extraordinary in its capacity for development. She was careful so that men never knew in bed the full strength of her legs, and her arms could lift enormous weights for her size, and she could have tried lifting more, but she did not for she thought it would require distending the muscles in her neck in a noticeable way. She sighed then, turning over the bar, and hanging by one leg, swung out over the ocean, turning in the glittering noon sun, her body full of heat, from the sun, from the cliff, from the water, she was aware then of the reflected heat coming from below and around her, and the stark heat from the sun above. Then a breeze would come and ruffle across her like a million turkey feathers. She was naked. She loved the feel of the sun on her body, naked like this, she loved, as she swung another ankle into a ring, and hung upside down for a moment, the sun pouring over her genitals, would tilt like that, hoping not to burn, until the heat made her feel immense, and swollen as if Apollo himself had come down and emblazoned her with his scimitar.

There were days when she would awake feeling stone cold, dead, wanting to die, unable to go on, only to feel someone open the shutter, and the sun would crash in on her, enveloping her, until miraculously it seemed the heat and light would creep into her very bones, and she would begin to live.

She lay now feeling its heat between her legs, and when she could bear it no more she swung up, amazed always at the strength in her back and abdomen, and began the long careful series of exercises on the bars. Her athleticism was kept to a public minimum. She skied well, people knew, and had a flair for racquet sports, but no one knew she was capable of extraordinary physical feats, like 150-foot dives off a cliff, or could swim underwater holding her breath for close to four minutes. And with a tank on her back, she was very skilled indeed. She remembered that she had even surprised Bacco, who taught her after all, how to use the tank, with her strength. That day when the three of them had taken a boat towards Malta, and she had spent almost twelve hours under the water. She loved it there, amidst the dark and shadows, the green lights flashing, the fish, the sweet swelling presence of the fish, gliding, and turning, she loved their mass and their stupidity, and traveling, she had latched onto a porpoise once, and the creature had played with her and let her ride it almost a quarter of a mile. She swam then, more than three miles back to the boat, and Bacco was beside himself by the time she arrived. She saw his small fat form in the sun hat pacing the deck in a frenzy, his red nose bulging and his small black eyes bloodshot with worry and fatigue. She saw the relief as she surfaced and pulled herself over the side.

"You're very foolish," he said angrily to her, helping her out of her gear that day, "and totally irresponsible. I had no way of knowing what happened to you. Even for you, my dear, a three-mile swim in a rough sea is not a good idea."

She knew it as she lay exhausted in the boat chair, she knew how fitting was Bacco's panic, knew that someday she would die in the water, because always she had to test her strength to the ultimate when she was in it, knew that always in some part of her she was intoxicated with drowning, that she often had the narcosis of the deep, the sensation that she didn't want to come up, ever, even when she knew she had almost no air left. "You will get the feeling," she remembered years ago, centuries ago it seemed when Bacco was instructing her to deep-dive, "and you won't want to come up. It will feel very pleasurable. That you know is the end. If you don't come up when you get that feeling, you will never come up." Anna loved to get that, that giddy, sensual, gliding sensation, her head saying, "Stay down, don't go up, just stay a little more" —it felt like the happiness one must have had as a child if one had had happiness as a child—the air running out of her tubes, knowing if she didn't go up she would die, and she would fight it finally and go up. She thought, however, someday she wouldn't.

She turned over now on the chair, as Bacco offered her some wine. "Do you get that, Bacco, jumping out of planes?"

"Get what?" Bacco said, studying the marine maps.

"That feeling, that you don't want to pull the rip-cord? I get that, like the narcosis, I don't want to come up and I don't want to pull the cord and stop floating—it feels so slow," she said smiling, thinking of the jumps, "you feel as if you've got forever to fall."

"No, I am not infatuated with dying, I told you, I

pull the rip cord while I still have one foot in the airplane."

"You're not as bad as that," Anna said turning over.

"No, perhaps not as bad as that at all; I wait until I count three, then I pull it."

Anna laughed, she remembered her dragging him out to the airport, she was amazed she ever got him to jump at all.

She turned to ask him a question and saw he was intent on the maps.

"You think the submarine will surface here?"

"I think so," Bacco said, "but who knows. I have the terrible feeling that they are smarter than we are."

"They're not smarter than me," Anna said.

"They fooled Lola," Bacco replied.

"Yes . . . hmmmm, I forgot that. So they did. And Lola is smarter than me, bless her little red-haired cunt."

"You seem to think," Bacco said mildly, never surprised at Anna's vulgarity, at least where Lola was concerned, "that the brains are in the genitalia."

"No, I don't think Brains, as in some capital B abstract universal law are in the capital G Genitals as in some abstract universal law, but in this particular case it's true—Lola's mind is in her cunt, that's where she does all her thinking."

Anna rolled over and then turning to him said, "Bacco sweetie, peel me a grape."

In a few minutes there was a clamor on the staircase and Lola appeared in the doorway. She said to Anna, "Who do you think you are? Mae West?"

"That's what I love about you, carrot top," Anna said, rolling over in her direction, "you're always just as predictable as the color of your pubic hair."

"Fuck you," Lola said and turned down the stairs. She heard Bacco say he was going down to check on lunch because Lola was such a terrible cook.

Several minutes later Anna felt someone standing

near her. She opened her eyes and found herself staring straight into Lola's bush of pubic hair. "You shouldn't make Lola angry," she heard Lola say in that savage voice she used with Anna, and she put her hands under Anna's head. That did it, as soon as her hands were under Anna's head Anna felt herself lose control, felt the mystique begin to rise, and with it the curious and in a strange way disgusting excitement that Lola could provoke in her found herself staring at Lola as she raised the mass of pubic hair like a curtain exposing the plump folds underneath, "Come on now," she heard as though it were far away the voice of Lola's cooing, as she felt her head pulled relentlessly inexorably forward, fascinated transfixed by the fat pink rolls coming towards her, Anna like a child whimpering softly, "No, Lola, don't make me," yet excited, trembling, feeling the excitement as Lola's hands brought her head forward that last few inches, as Lola murmured, "Come and give me, come, be a good girl," and Anna was lost lost in the slow sweet sucking of the furrows and folds beneath the auburn hair.

# 13

## Malta

"Reverence, Bunny?" she said. "Reverence?" in her creaking voice. "I revere nothing," she said haughtily making for the humidor, "and certainly not God. Do you want a cigar?"

"If you don't revere God," Harcourt said, "what do you do instead?"

"Really, Bunny, what do you mean what do I do instead. Even for a priest, reverence is not a full-time occupation."

"I mean, what do you do about God?"

"God? I acknowledge him," she said settling herself down in a chair, in front of her Ming Dynasty case. "I acknowledge everything. I just can't believe in it. Not even you." She smiled then and drifted past him, her dragon flowered peignoir floating behind her like yellow fog on little cat feet.

"You shouldn't read poetry, Bunny," she declared at breakfast. "It ruins the mind. It prompts imagery, mimicry and boggled thinking."

"Boggled?" Harcourt said. He looked at her in amazement. All his life she had made him feel precisely that— boggled. And now she attacked poetry as the cause. How like her he thought, and waited for her further chastisement. But she said no more and drifted out to the terrace—for ninety-two she moved with surprising grace—her robe flowing behind her like when in the silks my Julia goes the undulation of her clothes or something like that. Americans he could recall, but Englishmen, particularly the minor poets, he could remember with no accuracy.

It was hot, the bougainvillea bloomed. He secretly wondered how long they would have to remain on Malta.

# 14

## Amsterdam

Several days had passed. Avian Braine had had no luck tracing Silverstein the Jew. For it appeared that that was how he advertised himself: Silverstein the Jew: Moneylender, Pawnbroker, Collector.

"It's an odd combination, isn't it," Farthingdale said, squinting into the window of the old Amsterdam shop.

"What?" said Avian.

"Guns, moneylending and collecting."

"Seems wise to me, putting to use some junk you hold for lending the money when the poor bastard doesn't pay you back."

"But I mean, collecting is a much more gentlemanly pursuit than moneylending."

"Not to mention erotica."

"The sign doesn't say a thing."

"I don't see any dildoes," Farthingdale said again, peering intently, "perhaps the guns doubled."

"Very clever and most uncomfortable."

"Did you hear of the girl who—"

"Yes, the gun went off and she thrilled herself to death."

"Bleeding," Farthingdale said. "Gory, isn't it?"

"You like gory things," Avian said distastefully.

"I don't know," Farthingdale rose to his own defense, peering intently through the dirty window of the shop. "I do have a dirtier mind than you, it's true, but then I have more everything than you."

"Except investigatory talent."

"Perhaps even that, everything except your looks," Farthingdale said, staring at him, "which aren't that good, and your phenomenal memory."

Avian smiled. "That you haven't got. No one has."

whorl" or "inside whorl." If there are only two ridges between them, the pattern is known as a "meeting whorl."

### E. IDENTIFICATION AND RECONSTRUCTION OF DEAD BODIES

When an unknown body is found, the following items should be noted:

1. Place where the body is found.
2. Time when found.
3. Cause of death.[14]
4. Time when death occurred.[14]
5. Supposed age.
6. Supposed profession.
7. Description of body (see page 44).
8. Description of clothing (with special attention to laundry and dry cleaning marks).
9. Jewelry and other objects.

Hands and nails may give important information as to the profession of the person. Cobblers, blacksmiths, musicians, seamstresses, etc., have characteristic callosities on the hands. The appearance of the nails may give information. We should note their shape, length and cut, and whether or not they are torn, bitten, manicured or well kept. Bleeding under the nails caused by blows or clamping persists for a long time and extends forward to the tip of the nail. Fingernails will grow about one-twenty-fifth of an inch in a week, and the toenails about one-fourth as fast. A characteristic appearance of the nails will be seen in laundrymen on the thumb and index finger of the left hand; in cobblers on the left thumb; in engravers and jewelers on the right thumb, and in lacemakers on the right index finger. Dyers,

[14] These questions should be answered by the medical examiner or coroner.

photographers and pharmacists usually have brittle nails.

All unknown dead should be photographed in the same manner as a criminal is, *i.e.*, front view and profile.

For photographic purposes it becomes necessary to have the face of the dead appear natural and with as lifelike an expression as possible, because of the difficulty encountered by most persons in recognizing a dead relative or friend from a postmortem photograph. The eyes are in most cases shut, or if open, they are sunken and covered with a gray film. There is no contrast between the color of the skin and the lips, and finally the rigid, unnatural appearance of the face gives the impression of something unreal. In order to make the face more lifelike, one should improve on the appearance of the eyes and the lips. Numerous methods have been proposed for this purpose. Generally, a mixture of equal parts of glycerin and water is inserted in the eyesockets with the aid of a syringe with a fine tip. The eyelids are then raised. The lips are covered with a mixture of carmine in alcohol, which is applied with a small brush. If the body has been submerged in water for a long time and the skin is already partly gone, one can give the face a more natural appearance by powdering it with talcum, which is gently massaged over the flesh and the remaining skin. Rubber gloves should be used for this purpose.

If putrefaction is so far advanced that large portions of skin and flesh have disappeared, one may be able to reconstruct the face even in seemingly impossible cases. The putrefaction ceases when corrosive sublimate solution is used as an external wash. Plastelina, clay, or cotton fixed with collodion and covered with the proper shade of wax, replaces the lost flesh. As the eyesockets are generally empty, glass eyes are inserted. The missing hair is replaced by a wig and the face is made to assume its natural color with make-up.

Dead bodies, or parts of them, that have become mummified as a result of being buried in dry places, may be returned to their natural shape by putting them in a 3 per cent potassium hydroxide solution. They should be allowed to stay in the solution until they have resumed their natural contour. They should be soaked for a short time in water and then preserved in a weak solution of alcohol or formalin.

Attention should be drawn to the possibility of making lifelike casts of the faces of dead bodies through the moulage process (see page 435). In certain Continental police laboratories, as, for instance, in Vienna, casts are made of the heads of practically all unknown dead bodies. The casts are painted in natural color and placed in a gallery for future identification. A cast is superior to a photograph for identification purposes, and should if possible be made in cases where a major crime is suspected. Continental police records show that such casts have aided in solving certain crimes. The assistance of a sculptor is employed when reconstructions or repairs are needed. The results obtained through casts sometimes are quite remarkable.

In cases where teeth have been treated by a dentist, there is a possibility of identification if the dentist can be located. Fillings, crowns, bridges and other items of dental work are mainly individual, and may sometimes be traced to a certain dentist through his records and teeth charts.

The teeth are the hardest and most lasting of tissues. Heat and chemicals have little influence on them.

When a skull is found, the possibilities of identification are indeed small if the teeth are missing. However, a method invented by the German anatomist, Wilhelm His, may be of aid in such cases.[15] When the supposed skull of the famous composer Johann Sebastian Bach was found, Professor His modeled a head, in clay, over the skull of Bach, in order to bring out the similarity with contemporary portraits. To determine the average

[15] For more comprehensive information, see Wilder and Wentworth, *Personal Identification*, Boston, 1918.

thickness of the layers of flesh on the face, measurements were made on dead bodies in a normal state of nourishment. The measurements were made by introducing a needle deep into various parts of the face. The thickness of the fleshy portion was thus obtained. With the aid of the average measurements determined, a table was computed which was utilized by the sculptor. The same method has been advantageously used for the reconstruction of other faces.

The method, tho, has its weak points. By modeling the ears, no clue to their original shape can be obtained. If the individual who is to be reconstructed was unusually stout or unusually thin, the similarity would not be very striking. It is also quite difficult to reproduce the lips and the contour of the mouth, both of which give the face its characteristic countenance. The reproduction of the nose appears difficult, but the results are good, because of the distinctive length of the nasal bone.

The La Rosa murder, which occurred in New York in 1916, is a good example of resourceful reconstruction.

On September 12, 1916, a skeleton of a human being was found in a house on Hegeman Avenue at Powell Street, Brooklyn. It appeared to belong to a man about 25 years of age, and 5 feet 6 inches tall. He had a small amount of brown hair on the scalp, and the lower jaw contained two gold teeth. The body was dressed in trousers and coat of blue fabric, with a black belt surrounding the waist. The only article found in his pockets was a briar pipe. The wisdom teeth had not yet grown. Some dark brown hair was also found on the neck. The autopsy showed that the skull had been fractured in four places. Since the investigations as to the identity of the man proved fruitless, it was decided to attempt a reconstruction of the face.

A sculptor remodeled the face with plastelina. Dark brown hair was obtained from a barber, and two brown glass eyes were bought, on the assumption that the man was Italian. Rolled newspapers covered with plastelina formed the neck. The eyes were put in place, the eyebrows were made of brown hairs, and a quantity of hair was put on the top of the head and down along the neck. This reconstructed piece of work was photographed.

A few days later, a new skeleton was found in the same vicinity, together with a check payable to a certain Rosario P. The Bureau of Missing Persons reported that a man of that name had been missing. The skeleton was identified by a sister, together with the clothing and the contents of the pockets. When friends of P. were questioned, they were also shown the reconstructed head of the first skeleton, and one of them quickly cried: "This is Domenico La Rosa," whereupon he tried to open the lips of the head saying: "Domenico had two gold teeth besides being inclined to baldness." Another witness testified that he had known La Rosa for many years and that the reconstruction was similar, altho La Rosa's face had been stouter. When this omission was corrected with plastelina, the witness declared that the reconstruction was now absolutely similar to La Rosa's facial appearance.

Naturally, a skull, with teeth, is the most valuable part of a skeleton for identification purposes, but most of the bones will give some information.

The height of the person, relative size, relative age, and very often the sex, may be determined from the bones. Diseases of the bones, their shape and fractures may also give information.

For the determination of sex, the skull, the hip bones and the sacrum are most important. Each may, in most cases, reveal the sex; but if all three are missing, the determination is uncertain. In such cases the size and proportions of the other bones may, however, be of help.

The age of a skeleton, during the first eight to ten years of life, can be determined within approximately one year; and under one year of age examination of the skull may determine the age within approximately one month. The older the individual, the less precise must be the determination of age. During growth, and until 25 years of age, various changes in the bones and teeth are still going on. This fact may give good clues to the age of the person. In the adult stage no such changes take place. In the aged, slight and very approximate changes may be noticed.

In order to determine the height of the person from various portions of the skeleton, there are numerous tables and calculations worked out by anthropologists. The length of the thigh bone, for instance, multiplied by 3.7 (in women 3.6) is equal to the height of the body; the length of the whole skeleton plus 1 to 1½ inches is equal to the height of the person, etc.

Determination of the race can only be made from the skull, and even here the conclusions are far from certain if the racial characteristics are not distinct. Examinations of this kind should be made only by experienced anthropologists.

DOCUMENT #9

**The Rosedale Manuscript: Classification and Analysis. War Office. Department SNOW 008.**

Several days later SNOW acquired some new instructions in the form of microphotographs hidden beneath postage stamps in several letters he had received. In one of these microphotographs instructions were given to SNOW to contact ARNOLD. ARNOLD is an Armenian raised in Germany who speaks perfect English and German. ARNOLD was recruited by the Germans in 1940 by use of a threat of reprisals against a third brother in Germany. At that time ARNOLD was living in London. The idea of putting SNOW in touch with ARNOLD was that ARNOLD was then working with QUIM who was an expert photographer and might be able to develop the microphotographs.

Two days prior to his visit to QUIM's studio, SNOW was informed by the Germans that he would for the future be paid by a woman in London, whose name was Anna Kleibourg. At this time, it was not thought that SNOW knew this was an alias for QUIM.

"Except him."

"He's dead," Avian said quickly.

"You think."

"He was dead," Avian said finally, "I saw him myself."

"Your perceptions are not always reliable," Farthingdale said, "they're like your memory. Full of curious inconsistencies. You have the best memory in the world, and the worst."

"The worst for personal things, not professional. Anyway, dead is dead," Avian said with some finality.

"We'll see," Farthingdale replied and they continued their walk towards the docks.

It was several days later when Anna announced to Bacco that she had begun writing her memoirs. "That should be interesting," the little priest replied, "as well as impossible. You're always saying you can't remember anything, you have the worst memory in the entire world, and here you are writing your memoirs." He paused in the doorway of her study, the trowel in his hands, and wearing mud boots.

"Where are you going?"

"Out to prune the figs."

"Oh. Anyway, what's having a bad memory got to do with it? Just because I write my memoirs doesn't mean they have to be true. Just now I'm talking about my days at the Courtley School for Girls in Philadelphia."

"Hmm," Bacco said, "considering the fact you've never set foot in Philadelphia that ought to be challenging."

"Of course I've never set foot in Philadelphia, now go away and stop bothering me. It's not important. I met a girl once who came from Philadelphia, and then I met her friend, he came from Philadelphia too, and they both said things and thought things in exactly the same way, so since everyone in Philadelphia is basically alike it shouldn't be hard, should it?"

"No," Bacco said, pulling down his sun hat, "no, I suppose not."

When he came in several hours later he saw Anna in her silk print kimono busily at work at a desk, and reams of paper flying from her hand into a pile on the floor.

"Is that the memoirs?" he said.

"No, I've changed it to a novel—pornographic. I'm halfway done. Memoirs are too boring."

"Halfway done. You must be working under the pressure of creative genius," he said, going to the closet and putting away his boots.

"It isn't a masterpiece, I haven't time, I'm calling it a little something for everyone—it's for when you're in bed with a cold and you need something entertaining and outrageous, also pornographic."

"Is pornography good for colds?" Bacco asked quietly.

"Of course. It's good for everything. I read somewhere that its effects are positively beneficial."

"You don't say. How are you taking care of everyone?"

"I have a wall chart, every ten pages you get a sex scene, I alternate, bisex, homosex, and heterosex and orgies."

"No masturbation?"

"No. Too much of a downer," Anna said. "This is a book to cheer people up."

"I don't think of it as a downer," Bacco said.

"You don't?" Anna seemed genuinely surprised. "Well, perhaps then if I can fit it in," and she scribbled on, paying no more attention to him.

"I suppose Lola has begun her memoirs or something of that sort?" Bacco asked tentatively.

Anna turned. "Lola? What's this got to do with Lola?"

"You're so competitive, eventually everything has to do with Lola. Has she been writing her memoirs?" he asked skeptically.

"No," Anna turned pouting towards the desk, "she has not. She's writing haiku."

"My my, the entire world is going literary." Bacco said, "Well, I'm taking the car and doing some shopping. I understand there is some very superior rutabaga on sale from a small farmer ten miles out of town, and I need a dash for this incredible Russian eggplant dish I have to make."

"All right," Anna said, "but be back by four, I want to go shopping."

"What do you need?"

"I need necklaces—you know, for the gold wool jersey, and also my red silk caftan. And don't fall asleep this time."

"Oh wonderful," Bacco said, "what an opportunity. I think perhaps you should think of some amber? Does that appeal?"

"I can't talk now," she said scribbling away and tossing another paper onto the stack. She waved at him with one hand and busily scribbled with the other as he closed the door, shaking his head in amazement at her perpetual insouciance.

---

The third day in Amsterdam, Avian flew to Rome. He left on the 8:35 KLM flight out of Amsterdam and arrived in Rome at 11:50 a.m. At 2:25 p.m. he left Rome and was in Amsterdam at 3:50 p.m. He did not tell Farthingdale of his visit.

When they met for dinner that evening, he said to Farthingdale, "Did you comb the shop?"

"Yes," Farthingdale drew a small paper from his pocket, "the name of Karl Werner, I could barely make it out."

"Karl Werner?" Avian frowned. "Shades of World War Two?"

"The very one."

"Where did you find it?"

"In the back of a false drawer . . . which makes me think of course." Farthingdale paused to relish the salmon mousse. It was superb. "That it might have been deliberate."

"In what sense?"

"Well, Silverstein would never leave it in a false drawer, not after the Covington murder, he's too smart, he's also too smart not to have combed everything he had."

"Planted again?"

"It may be. You must try this salmon, it's extraordinary, and the bread." Farthingdale's eyes rolled heavenward.

It annoyed Avian, his passion for food which amounted almost to a fetish.

"This is Werner's record, just to refresh your memory." Farthingdale pushed it across to Avian.

"Born Mannheim, nineten twenty-one. Father, a theater director, Mother, Helene, a Jewish actress. In nineteen thirty-four, Mother emigrated to Palestine, taking him. Attended an agricultural school at Ben Shemen and learned to ride horses very well. In nineteen thirty-seven joined the Haganah. At the outbreak of World War Two enlisted as a British volunteer, a double agent. Died, or so we thought, in 1941 when his Nazi cover was broken."

"He wasn't circumcised," Avian said, "because of the father?"

"No," Farthingdale said, "of course not. There is an unexplained portion of the story. Somehow someone in the Nazi high command entrusted a painting, or perhaps more to him, one known Memling for sure."

"And?"

"And he tried to make off with it."

"Why? Surely not the money?"

Farthingdale shrugged. "Perhaps he had another buyer."

"Where is the painting?"

"God only knows, and Karl Werner. Do you remember the incident at all?"

Avian shook his head, "No, I'm afraid it's from that period in which I remember very little," he sighed, "very little indeed."

"Who is looking for Werner at this moment?" Avian asked.

"Interpol. Israeli intelligence. Egyptian intelligence, the CIA, and the FBI."

"This isn't FBI territory."

"No, odd isn't it, but that's what I was given to understand. Werner is valuable I suspect because he knows who in the Israeli high command is a double agent. There is some speculation that a current Israeli general is a Jordanian agent—and that he is really protecting Martin Bormann who is part of the Jordanian command."

"Oh really, now I've heard everything. You honestly think Bormann could disguise himself as a Jordanian?"

"Possibly," Farthingdale said. "I have a marvelous fantasy that he will get shot at the border by his own men because they will mistake him for a Jew."

They finished dinner and Farthingdale ordered a cognac. They said nothing for a time, for when they were not discussing professional matters, they were genuinely uncomfortable with each other. Farthingdale on the other hand was the only human being to whom Avian had ever entrusted the information of his curious mental history. They had worked together for twenty years and he had never known if Farthingdale resented it, respected it, was sympathetic to it, or even believed it. He had suffered only one breakdown, ten years ago. But another was due soon. He knew. Approximately every ten years. He knew all the warning signs. The sudden increasing amnesia, inability to carry numbers in his head, sequences, anything that related to numbers. He hospitalized himself during such times. The doctors said it was the price he had to pay for such a brilliant associative ability. It was true, he knew, the way he held events and names and places in his mind; it was not an ordinary intelligence. He was more than a detective, his reputation was international, if quiet, he was a detector, and he had only one equal. And he was dead. He hoped. He prayed. Something in these last months had created in him a sudden fear of the other man. He did not believe in God but he prayed the other man was dead.

"Oh, there's one other thing," Farthingdale interrupted suddenly. "Silverstein has a submarine."

"A submarine?" Avian said blankly.

"Yes," Farthingdale leaned back and looked thoughtfully at his cognac, "but no one has ever found it."

"Well, how do they know?"

"He paid for it by check."

"You're joking."

"Alas, not," Fathingdale said, "it's some relic from World War Two. It was used to torpedo the Germans.

He bought it as a souvenir. It has his name painted on it."

"Upon my word," said Avian, "his name?"

"Well, more than that. The painter who painted it said it reads, 'Silverstein the Jew,' and it shines in the dark."

"The submarine?"

"No, the lettering."

They paused for a moment over this, and then both said at the same time, "Did you hear of the matter of Elmer Lee?" Avian said, "Tell me what you've heard."

Farthingdale continued, "Missing since last December. Disappeared from view on his way from Peking to Cairo by way of Rome. Many dealings with Lady Sarah. He was extraordinarily wealthy. A millionaire. Spent time in Rome with a noted courtesan who goes by the name of Anna."

"Anna what?"

"No one knows." Farthingdale shrugged. "Officially she's a bastard. Foster families. Never took a last name."

---

"Really, Bacco," Anna said as they went into Valentino's for Anna to buy some new clothes, "you should never have become a priest; you would have made an excellent dress designer. Why *did* you become a priest?" She turned to look at him as though it were the first time she had ever considered the question.

"What else could I become?" Bacco said, stopping to admire some beads. "These would look lovely on you," he held them up to Anna's neck, "no," he shook his head, "too yellow, you need more gold," he put the beads back and surveyed the case, his fat fingers tapping along the glass top, "anyone as repressed as I was had to become a priest. I really had no choice. It's all written, all designed, I fear." Bacco wheezed and asked a saleswoman to find Anna some beads with more gold in them.

"Weren't you called by God at all?" Anna asked in a tone of mock amazement.

"You can look at it that way too, I suppose," Bacco said, "a calling, fate, psychically determined, call it anything you like." He sat down suddenly in a chair. "Excuse me, my dear, I am tired," he said, and in a few minutes, like the dormouse, was fast asleep.

# 15

"There are several people in Rome," Farthingdale said the next morning, "whom Interpol suspects of art robberies."

"What has that to do with anything?" Avian asked, rather crossly.

"It doesn't have anything to do with anything, much," Farthingdale said, "except that Harcourt put you on to the famous Silverstein, whom we never found, and that Silverstein and Harcourt both deal in international artifacts as it were. That Covington was connected to Silverstein and also to someone in Rome—who had sent her a check for a million pounds and that Karl Werner's name shows up in a drawer."

"Yes, that check from Rome was for the dildoes, has anyone come up with the dildoes?"

"Someone at Scotland Yard found them, there were half a dozen involved, one is still missing, but that's what I'm getting at, one of these dildoes, if that is indeed what they are, are very intricately carved. No one seems to be able to decipher it, but some chap at the British Museum says he thinks the damn things are Chinese oracle bones, one of the earliest records ever of civilization in China."

"Terribly enlightening, I'm sure," Avian said.

"Well, it all fits somehow," Farthingdale said, "we just don't know how."

"What else did they give you?"

"The Yard has something going on some Rumanian who's been living in Rome for several years. His name is Plato. He has some sort of pimp-whore relationship with a very beautiful courtesan, who is called Anna."

"Anna again!"

"The very one. She has been seen with Santiago who buys from Silverstein. Anyway, she also hangs out with a redhead named Lola whom they *have* traced. Lola is some sort of Egyptian agent, they think, who is very heavily into international cartels, and money rates. She goes with some black called Caldwell, who is said to be the link with Soviet support of African independence movements, particularly Uganda."

"Good heavens," Avian said, pouring himself a glass of Perrier, "the place is positively seething with intrigue."

"Yes," Farthingdale said, "my feelings exactly. It's a little too seething to be true. So I think we ought to go to Rome and check this little group out."

"Well," said Avian, "actually I was going to go to South America."

Farthingdale's brow shot up. "Why didn't you tell me. Who are you on to?"

"An old friend," Avian smiled.

"South America?" Farthingdale puffed on his pipe. "One of your damn Nazi hunters has come up with a live one?"

"Very live. There's a lot of money in this old ex-Nazi, especially if you're searching for paintings they confiscated, old Impressionists and other things. They're worth millions and millions of dollars."

"You think your old boy knows where they are?"

Avian nodded. "I think."

"Why at this particular moment have you chosen to track down ex-Nazis who've hidden major paintings, and why did you pretend to know nothing about it when I mentioned Interpol's interest in all of this?"

"I was annoyed," Avian said, "that they were onto it. I want to find him myself."

"And before your Nazi headhunter, I should presume."

"Considerably before," Avian said. "I may have to guarantee to save him."

"Well, it's cold in Bolivia this time of year."

"Did you know?" Avian said. "Or are you guessing?"

"No, I knew. After all, I get around," Farthingdale replied.

Consequently Avian decided to go to Rome.

# 16

I asked Santiago if he knew how unhappy Anna was and all he replied, in that irritated tone he has, was that yes, she was moody. And yet we sat, Anna, Friar Bacco, Santiago and I, for three hours tonight in one of Rome's best clubs, with marvelous entertainment and Anna did nothing but stare at the tablecloth. When she did speak, it was only to Bacco. The attraction she felt for this warty fat little priest who always had the aroma of garlic about his breath eluded me. She depended on him for everything—he was her cook, chauffeur, dresser, and as far as I knew, her most trusted companion. At one point we had had an extremely awkward conversation. "I believe in moderation," Santiago had remarked in response to some provocation.

"That's why you're boring," Anna replied tartly. "I," Anna said, "I on the other hand do *everything* in excess. I eat excessively. I drink excessively. I fuck excessively, I cry excessively, I laugh excessively, I sing excessively, I take baths excessively—and it's me and my kind that shall save Western Civilization. It's you and your damn moderates that are sending us all to hell." With that Anna guzzled her brandy, something one should never do to brandy, Bacco remarked, and with a somewhat tilted salute, pushed her chair back and careened towards the dance floor. Victor, an elegant dancer, was waiting for her. He had sat at a separate table with another woman but he and Anna had been looking at each other all evening.

Whenever I inquired of Anna what was troubling her she told me to shut up, so I was relieved when we finally decided to leave and we got into Anna's marvelous white Rolls-Royce, with Bacco driving. He was short and had to use a pillow to see over the wheel, something which for various reasons I found enormously amusing, and Anna and I and Santiago sat in the back. Anna's long legs are showing beneath a dress, slit to the thigh, but a nonetheless sedate dress. The collar is like a bathrobe, rolled back, and there are long sleeves, and it is in brown wool, tied with a brownish rust belt. Around her neck she is wearing, and it somehow highlights the crest of her cleavage, a very long pair of single-strand and perfect, black pearls. She is still astonishingly beautiful, regardless of her mood. When we arrived at her house she leaned over to kiss me good night. Anna was full of affectionate custom like that and to my surprise I said, "You don't mean it. All night you treat me like an enemy, like we are all your enemies, as if you have nothing but enemies."

She looked at me then and shook her head. "I need

no enemies, I am my own adversary. Like everyone else, I have only one adversary." She gathered up her coat and prepared to leave.

"You can defeat it," I said, delaying her with my arm.

She shook her head. "How do you defeat," she said suddenly passionate as she turned to me those great green eyes piercing now, "a voice in yourself that says, kill kill kill kill yourself. He is very strong in me that voice."

"He, why he?" I said.

"Because that's who it is." Anna got out of the car and slammed the door.

Bacco drove us home, and when I asked him what was wrong, he said, "She will be with Plato tonight."

"Well," I said, "she certainly didn't seem to be looking forward to it."

"Lola and Plato," Bacco said, "they try to destroy her."

Santiago said, "No one can destroy her."

"Plato can," Bacco said, "he makes her a slave."

When Bacco drove back to the club the waiter told him he had a visitor.

---

Anna lay there, the dildoes circling her breasts, moistened and wet, the stir of the small electric vibrator rising over her nipples, making the full circle of her breasts then directly on the very tip of her nipple, Anna moaning then as she felt Lola start, licking her first, burrowing in her, her tongue darting in and out, and then the vibrator, the steady weight, and vibration into over and under each fold, then Lola pressing it on her clitoris, then pulling away, gently back, lightly teasing, feeling her head rise for it looking for it, feeling it again on her nipples then feeling Lola and the small machine working its way up her anus, scooping around turning her insides to jelly, waiting and moaning then, asking Lola to come back, come back and suck her while the vibrator was up her ass, and Lola would, suck and tongue, and bite, bite gently, and then hard, until Anna breathing heavily called out for him, now now, and Plato came in, and bending down, he would press the lips open, stretch her with his hands until she thought she would scream, and then move into her like a barge, brutally and huge and hard tearing her, paining her, Lola still tonguing her, and then she would cry out, and Plato would push Lola aside, push them all aside as he rode her like no man on God's earth had ever ridden her, rode her like a machine gun a hundred thrusts a second, his hair flying, his head spinning in a circle around his neck like a loop, he would ride her and then, when she was on the edge of coming he would pull out and shove it up her ass, while his hands moved over the front of her and she would come again and again and she was both overwhelmed by it and cheated by it, released by it and still needing him inside her, and then he would turn her again and suck her until she, exhausted, collapsed under him, but still he would tongue her fiercely until it hurt her, and then it would begin again, the long slow waves would begin rising through her until the pleasure was so painful she would not, she could not, endure it, could not endure the need for him deep inside her, the need, savage now, for his penetration, she could feel her insides contracting wanting him until she thought she would die if he did not enter her, and then he would still hold off those final seconds until she would feel him crash hugely into her as she grabbed him by the hips, pushing herself onto him, insanely insatiably holding him like an elasticized wrapper, stretching herself over his huge hulk and pumping and coming until that moan moved up from the center of her and she collapsed again, the sweat coating her skin, her breath nearly driven from her, collapsed against him, panting and breathless, her chest heaving as she whispered no more please no more, that was his moment then, when he would tilt her over one last time, she like a soft limp doll now, her insides thick and clinging and he rode her roughshod and relentless, plunging into her in circles, backing and circling, plunging right and left, pummeling her, her nails deep in his back, her teeth sunk in his side, rode her flushed and savage in the pleasure of his victory until her screaming split the air and the white rush oozed down her thighs.

# BODY TWO

# THE
# FORTUNE
# COOKIE
# CLUE

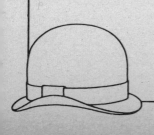

They were known only by their cover names and in them they lived and operated. But each life was shared. "It cannot be too strongly insisted," Masterman out of experience asserts, "that the most profitable cases were those in which the case officer had introduced himself most completely into the skin of an agent." Nuance became all. Even the methods of communication, between the agent and the enemy, whether by wireless, by secret writing or by personal contact in neutral countries, required empathy on the part of the case officer and the planners. The details of a man's wireless style, for example, the warning signals, the very rhythm of the key in sending messages must be mastered so that if the agent should die or for one reason or another be removed, a substitution could be made but not recognized. The dermal and the subdermal took on new and nerve-wracking significance.

*Masterman, xiii*

## Ostia

"Snow had a daughter," Farthingdale said, "does that surprise you?"

After a long time Avian said, "I don't remember." Then he turned away.

Avian Braine and Farthingdale had spent the night in a local hotel. They were breakfasting, like tourists, on the balcony. When the waiter had left, they noticed the fortune cookie. Only one. It was on Avian's tray. It read: "This disintegration is witnessed by a cool observer who is inside Bloch but is not precisely Bloch himself."

"What put that there?" Avian asked. Farthingdale noticed his hand was trembling.

"I can't imagine," said Farthingdale, looking at Avian. "And who is Bloch?"

"I never heard of him," said Avian, almost fiercely.

"Someone's fond of aphorisms, and fortune cookies," Farthingdale remarked.

"And observation," said Avian. "We're being very carefully watched."

"There's been another murder, this time in Rome," Farthingdale said.

"The same clues?"

"I don't know. The papers only reported that it was some Libyan official, some Al Fatah connection. Nevertheless, I thought I would go down and inquire. Care to come?"

"No," Avian said, looking tired, "I really think I ought to go to the beach, and think about all of this a bit."

"You ought to try this jam," Farthingdale said, "it's Amialle's White Barle Duc, I brought it with me," and Farthingdale held up a jar of tiny glassy white currants floating in a champagne-colored gel.

"Now just now," Avian said, "the beach is beckoning."

"I'm most curious about this murder," Farthingdale said, "I have an odd feeling that this place will turn out to be more interesting than its wine."

"Don't be a wine snob," Avian said.

"I'm not," Farthingdale said indignantly, "you just have to put up with a classification by grape here, and I'm not crazy about it."

Farthingdale excused himself, and Avian went in and got into his bathing suit. He took a blanket and a hat and to his surprise, tucked his revolver in under a towel. Something in this entire matter was causing him great mental fatigue. Some major obstacle seemed to be working on him; he had lost his ordinary facility for connection, and found that in an inexplicable way, he had become more interested in waiting for the next round of clues than even in preventing another murder.

This was totally unlike his ordinary behavior, and because it was so, it worried him. Some usually reliable mode of thought and feeling had been totally disrupted. He thought about this for some time as he made his way down to the sea. It all, he thought, began when he noticed the photograph of Miss Apricot in the papers. Then the Covington murder. In some strange and seemingly illogical way he felt that in the mind of the murderer, as well as his own, they were inexorably connected . . . He sat there for some time staring at the blue still ocean, the sun white-hot, staring at the horizon until a fine glaze began to seep over his body, a light coating of senses from another life, until he felt his body disappear, felt some strange presence replace it, felt himself rising out of his body, toward the sky, evaporating, until he could survey the entire beach from the point of view of a single, condensed drop of water. He hung there like a raindrop observing himself on the beach, and feeling himself on the beach, and yet suspended in the sky. The colors were green and yellow and they separated into each other, pure and gleaming, and then combined into the ocean, turning it blue. Suddenly he was lying on the blanket, and a woman, an astonishingly beautiful woman, approached him. She was accompanied by a man in a bowler hat who carried an umbrella. He did not seem at all uncomfortable in the heat. It was only then that Avian noticed that the beach was otherwise deserted. The woman was wearing a diaphanous white silk caftan, which swayed about her in the breeze, and one enormous jewel, a diamond-like pendant, hung about her neck. She said, coming toward him, in a magnificently modulated contralto, "We've come to see you." Then she stood up and took off the caftan and stood before Avian naked, except for the blazing light from the diamond on the chain. Suddenly he felt her hair, falling warm and thick about his ear and she said, her face against his, her hair engulfing him, "You will forget everything when you wake up." And he nodded obediently even as he noticed her eyes were almost violet and then switched again to turquoise. Then the man in a bowler hat sat down, and opened a small picnic basket full of pale brown truffles and sweet cold pears. Then he unwrapped a Brie cheese, spread it on a pear and offered it to Avian.

"No," Avian said, "I never take food from strangers."

"But you must," the man said, leaning close to Avian and offering it again, in an admonishing tone, "or you would be rude."

"Oh," said Avian, his voice soft, "but of course, then you must forgive me." He bit into the pear and cheese, and no sooner had he done so than he saw the woman standing before him, swaying and naked, he thought he heard a song, yet he did not hear it—for he was paralyzed now as she came toward him, the sea suddenly seeming to rise up right behind her, seeming to crest in a huge wave at her back while he sat there on the sand, and she, pushed by the enormous wave floated toward him, in a kind of silent crescendo, a sound one saw rather than heard, she came toward him, seeming huge and wet and soft and kissed him, kissed him so that the soft full wetness of her mouth overwhelmed him, felt his body liquid with desire, felt himself dissolving into the sweet full rosebud of her mouth, was about to swallow her by entering her mouth, to swallow and be swallowed, suddenly her mouth huge and he puny, like Pinocchio at the brink of the whale, about to feel the insides pressing around him, suddenly small inside the great soft wetness of her mouth undulating against him, the jaws sliding in, the teeth starting a steady descent until in the voluptuous rapture of his terror, he screamed.

Farthingdale said later it must have been an hallucination. "You didn't anticipate the sun."

"However," Avian said, "it felt drug-induced. I mean in the sense that it was so full of information."

"What kind of information?"

"I don't precisely know," he said.

It was some time later when Avian said to Farthingdale, "The man on the beach had a name."

"What was it?" Farthingdale asked, looking up and tapping his pipe.

"Bloch," Avian said.

———————————

The mornings Bacco reserved for translating Cicero, and Anna reserved for writing. She was adept at Spanish, French, German, Italian and Japanese and Chinese, and often spent time translating work herself. Bacco had never known her to do any original writing and he was quite surprised when she announced her intention to write a pornographic novel, most particularly since she had in mind the high moral purpose of increasing the self-esteem of all those who might read it. This morning she was researching the impact of pornography. He noticed she had been exploring official sanctions and bans, and most recently was studying some United States government report on pornography. This study was conducted with considerable efficiency. She would ring a bell each time she wanted more and a servant would bring in the next section. Anna said it was too thick and imposing to read as one thing, and she could reflect more effectively on it this way. Bacco found it irritating but she insisted on having company while she did this. He had heard no bells for some time now and noticed that she seemed particularly intent. Finally he asked what she had discovered.

"I'm studying the U.S. Commission Report on Obscenity and the relationship between sex offenders, pornography and the rest of us straights," she said, munching earnestly on a Carr's Wheatmeal Biscuit and sipping her lavender tea.

"What have you discovered?" Bacco said.

"There is no difference. Sex offenders and the rest of us, we all react the same," Anna said dramatically. "The trouble is, as far as I can understand the charts," she said looking very studious, "on a scale of one to five, nobody got very excited. The highest score was three point twenty-six."

"A pity," Bacco said, "they couldn't do better than that. What brought it on?"

"Intercourse, ventral-ventral, F over M, was the winner," Anna said, "and runner-up was Intercourse, ventral-dorsal, F over M."

Anna paused, then reconsidered, "Hmm, ventral is front and dorsal is back right?"

"Right."

"So that would be F's ventral, or front, over M's dorsal, or back, with F on top, which would mean," she paused, "his cock would have to bend backwards."

"Exactly," Bacco said.

"Well," she said, "something must be wrong with this chart then," and she proceeded to study it further.

"Look at this," Anna cried, "you see, I knew I read somewhere that pornography was positively beneficial," and she proceeded to read:

". . . not only did subjects become satiated to pornography but there is no evidence that this massive exposure to erotically stimulating material had any major lasting effect upon their attitudes or behavior. What changes did occur seemed to be in a favorable direction and quite minor. Psychological tests given before and after the experience showed that the subjects' opinion of themselves had moved in the direction of greater self esteem . . ." *

"Ohhh," she gave out another cry.

"What is it?" Bacco said somewhat annoyed. He knew she always got very talkative when he was trying to translate Cicero.

"Listen to this, 'Another limitation of the Commission study was that it did not approximate a real-life situation or use of pornography in one's own milieu. It involved a deliberate forced "overfeeding" of pornography for pay. It also meant removing all clothing

---

* Howard et al., U.S. Commission on Obscenity and Pornography (U.S. Printing Office, 1970), p. 182, fn. 29.

176 U.S. Commission on Obscenity and Pornography

sexual and homosexual subjects respond differently to the gender of the model displayed in the stimulus. Several other studies show that unlike heterosexual or homosexual subjects, pedophiles tend to respond to age of the model displayed in the stimulus, rather than to its gender (Freund, 1965, 1967a, 1967b). A recent study of persons with deviant sexual orientation (Goldstein, *et al.*, 1970) found that homosexuals and pedophiles reported more frequent exposure to erotic depictions of nude males and homosexual activity than did heterosexually oriented persons. Transsexual males reported the least experience and interest in erotic materials, and they identified clothing and other items as more arousing than erotic books, magazines, or films.

In an experimental study (Cook and Fosen, 1970), 63 incarcerated adult sex offenders and 66 adult nonsexual offenders viewed erotic slides and rated each in terms of sexual stimulation. Results indicated that the offender groups did not differ in their ratings. The data in Table 13 show that both groups regarded the most arousing themes to be heterosexual intercourse (ventral-ventral and ventral-dorsal), and heterosexual nude petting. It should be noted that these themes are also typically identified as the most arousing by other heterosexual males and females in the natural environment.

Sex offenders appear to be no different from other groups in what sexual themes are preferred or regarded as arousing. . . .

### Table 13: 63 Sex Offenders' Ratings of Sexual Arousal From Erotic Slides

| Content of Erotic Slide | Mean Rating[1] |
| --- | --- |
| 1. Intercourse, ventral-ventral, F over M | 3.26 |
| 2. Intercourse, ventral-dorsal, F over M | 3.23 |
| 3. Nude petting, M hand on F genitals | 3.14 |
| 4. Nude petting, M hand on F genitals, kissing breast | 3.04 |

U.S. Commission on Obscenity and Pornography 177

| | |
|---|---|
| 5. Intercourse, ventral-dorsal, F over M | 3.02 |
| 6. F masturbating | 3.01 |
| 7. M approaching cunnilingus | 2.90 |
| 8. Cunnilingus | 2.89 |
| 9. M and F in underclothes, hands on genitals | 2.86 |
| 10. Fellatio, M over F | 2.85 |
| 11. Fellatio, F over M | 2.84 |
| 12. Intercourse, ventral-dorsal, each on side | 2.83 |
| 13. M over F, genitals on breasts | 2.75 |
| 14. Intercourse, M over F, ventral-ventral | 2.73 |
| 15. Fellatio, M over F | 2.65 |
| 16. Nude F reclined on back | 2.61 |
| 17. Petting, partially clothed, F hand on M genitals | 2.60 |
| 18. F partially clothed, undressing M | 2.37 |

[1]Six point scale: 1=Neutral, not exciting; 2=slightly exciting; 3=moderately exciting; 4=very exciting; 5=extremely exciting.

Note—Adapted from Cook, R. F., & Fosen, R. H. Pornography and the sex offender: patterns of exposure and immediate arousal effects of pornographic stimuli. *Technical reports of the Commission on Obscenity and Pornography.* Vol. 7.

and putting on a loose robe, hooking up one's penis to a condom and electrodes, attaching electrical instruments to both ears, putting a bellows around one's chest, being observed through a one-way window, and sitting in an "isolation booth" for one and a half hours a day for fifteen days.' "

"How extraordinary," Bacco replied, "I'm amazed they got aroused at all."

"What do you suppose it is like to have your penis hooked up to electrodes?"

"I really can't imagine," Bacco said dryly.

"The poor penises," Anna clucked sympathetically, "they must have gotten so confused, it must have been like fucking the rear end of a television set."

---

Farthingdale returned earlier than Avian expected. "You can't imagine what an insane and dotty afternoon I've had of it," he said as he wiped his forehead and sat down in a chair. "First of all I got led to a most remarkable police captain, Lorenzo Martinelli, an extraordinary man given to paranoid fantasies that every other person in Rome is a spy involved in shipping arms to the Middle East. Nonetheless he has a wonderful taste for wines, but is an absolute vulgarian as far as fish soup goes."

"How," said Avian drolly, "did you discover his taste in wine and fish soup?"

"Well," Farthingdale said, "there was lunch after all and we got to talking, and he took me to a friend's vineyard, and the wine, it was after all a north-slope grape, so I knew I would like it, was simply superb. Superb!" Farthingdale said. "It could compete with the best of the French Médocs."

"Tell me, did you find out anything about the murders?"

"Well, not exactly," Farthingdale looked odd, for a moment, Avian noticed, "because Martinelli is so obsessed with the spies. He thinks there are Russian spies, Chinese spies, Egyptian spies, CIA spies, African spies,

Greek spies, and they are all double, and some triple agents. He's capable of thinking there's a double agent working Cyprus and Staten Island. He's quite buggy about the American CIA, I must say, but in any event, I had the most dreadful *zuppa di pesce* I've ever had."

"Where?"

"Some little place in Trastevere. I swore never to touch the stuff in Italy, God knows," Farthingdale said lamentingly, "the French are the only ones who can manage a bouillabaisse, that's because there isn't a damn fish in the Mediterranean worth eating."

"In the entire Mediterranean?"

"Quite," said Farthingdale, "this had in it of all things, shark. Shark. It was full of bones, and that dreadful guarancino."

"What the devil is guarancino, and did you find out anything about the murders?"

"Guarancino is a pitch-black marine monstrosity whose sole distinction is that its name is derived from Greek roots, and no, there didn't seem to be anything special about what he would tell me about the murders. They have one or two clues they're checking."

"What clues?"

DOCUMENT #10

*THE NEW YORK TIMES, SATURDAY, JUNE 17, 1972*

# ARMS NETWORK SOUGHT IN ROME

## Police Suspect Links With Japanese in Israeli Attack

By PAUL HOFMANN
Special to The New York Times

ROME, June 16—The police said today that they were investigating what looked like a clandestine network trafficking in arms destined for Middle Eastern countries.

Police sources also mentioned "suspicions" of possible links between the alleged ring and the terrorist organization that planned the massacre carried out by three Japanese gunmen at Tel Aviv's airport May 30. However, the sources said that so far no hard evidence had been found to support this theory.

Italian investigators asked Interpol, the international police agency, to help trace a German businessman who is suspected of having played a major role in the arms traffic.

He was identified as Christian Karl Ring, 39 years old, born in Breslau—now Wroclaw, Poland—and a resident of Rome for the last 10 years. Mr. Ring, a licensed importer and exporter of foods, left Rome in his car June 4 and has not been heard from since.

**Weapons Are Found**

Yesterday, policemen acting on a warrant issued by an investigating magistrate searched Mr. Ring's penthouse apartment and office in a fashionable neighborhood near the Italian Foreign Ministry and found a submachine gun, two revolvers and ammunition.

The police also found lists of names and Roman addresses and were checking them. The first place to be raided yesterday was a private club, the Diplomat, in a quiet neighborhood in the north of Rome.

The club, which had been patronized for some time by diplomats of Middle Eastern and African countries, was found to be abandoned. An eviction order recently obtained by the Italian landlord was on the entrance door.

A search of the premises proved fruitless. The club's manager, Abu Gheida Yahia, a 30-year-old Jordanian, appears to have left Rome in April. Police sources said there was proof that Mr. Ring had been in touch with members of the club.

"He didn't tell me," Farthingdale said, looking uncomfortable.

"Odd you didn't find out," Avian said, looking at him strangely.

"The *zuppa di pesce* dulled my mind," Farthingdale said. "Oh," he said, looking very sleepy, "I did however find out about Anna."

"Yes?" Avian leaned forward.

"She's very beautiful," Farthingdale yawned and stretched out on the bed, "very smart, an excellent bil-

liards player and her average annual income is nine
million dollars a year."

Before Avian could ask another question, Farthingdale was fast asleep.

Victor slipped slowly up the stairs and slid along
the terrace outside Lola's apartment. He waited for a
few minutes to be sure and then, certain there was no
one in the apartment, lifted the window he had unlocked earlier that afternoon and throwing his legs
over, went inside.

Quickly he went to her desk, sorting through her
papers. Something caught his eye, and he smiled, "Oh
baby, your haiku's all wrong, seventeen syllables,
sweetheart, eight lines," he read:

> *Oh crazy world*
> *You are so wonderful*
> *It makes me happy*
> *Blue is the color of the sky.*

Then he put the poetry back in the blue folder with
the velvet bow she kept it in. In the top right drawer
he found the correspondence. Two letters were air-
mailed to Lola postmarked Cairo. "You bitch," he muttered to himself, "you lousy fucking cunt." He read
quickly through the letters and could see immediately
they must be coded. The codes meant nothing to him.
He photographed the letters and put them back.

Then he stopped. Footsteps. The key in the lock.
He darted behind the heavy drapes, moving a vase in
front of his feet, just concealing himself as the door
opened. Victor could see it was a man, in a raincoat
and a hat. The man walked quickly into the apartment, not turning any lights on, and into the bathroom.
He heard the medicine-cabinet door open. In a moment, the man came back out of the bathroom and
proceeded to the entrance door. He left immediately
and Victor heard the key in the lock turn.

Victor stayed for several minutes behind the drapery, and then cautiously, cocking his gun, he went

into the bathroom. He was sweating from the tension, and his ears hurt with listening for the sound of the front door. He opened the medicine cabinet and searched the bottles. Nothing seemed special. Maybe she was being left a message, or maybe she was being poisoned. He began opening the bottles of pills and aspirin, holding them carefully to the light and sniffing them. On the fourth bottle of cough medicine he thought he smelled something strange and put the bottle in his pocket. Then he went through the rest of the cabinet until he came to Lola's diaphragm. It struck him as odd that she should keep it in this bathroom when there was another bathroom just off the master bedroom. He opened the diaphragm box. The small round rubber ring had been hastily replaced. It rested not quite inside the small raised plastic circle to hold it. He lifted the diaphragm and held it to the light. One part of it read Ramses 80. He paused a moment then remembered, "Oh shit, just her number." Carefully he turned the diaphragm around in the light until he noticed a dark part on the rim that extended for one quarter of the circumference. He held it to the light again, and then probing putting his finger gently under the rubber, he felt something hard. Carefully he lifted the rim and removed a small silver container. Inside was a roll of microfilm. "Goddamn son of a mother," he muttered and putting the film in his pocket, carefully replaced the diaphragm, turned off the light and left the bathroom. He swung his legs out onto the terrace and made his way quickly down the stairs.

---

"I didn't expect you so early," Anna said to Lola as she opened the door. Lola was glorious today in a white suit, right out of the thirties. "You look like Jean Harlow, and your shoes, my God!" Anna cried out, "look at them!"

"Aren't they the best?" Lola turned around in her high-heeled spats with the big bows, giving Anna the full glimpse of her three-quarter skirt, her blue polka-dot blouse and her small white hat with the navy veiling.

"It doesn't suit you I'll say that, although," Anna stood back, "you do look smashing."

"I know," Lola said, "I'm really not a thirties girl, more a twenties girl, when champagne and diamonds and sable coats were all the rage."

"You never do underestimate yourself," Anna said. "Do you want a drink?"

"No, thanks," Lola went to the sofa and sat down. "Is Bacco out?"

"Yes," Anna said uneasily. She wished he would return. She didn't like being alone with Lola.

"You don't have to worry about your delivery this week," Lola said.

"What do you mean?"

"Victor is busily discovering in my apartment that his suspicion that I'm an Egyptian spy is true. He has read my haiku by now," she checked her watch, "which brought a feeling of affection, and amusement to his eyes. If he was smart he got out of the way of my five o'clock delivery, and if he's very smart, he will have found the microfilm in my diaphragm."

"Wonderful," Anna said, "just like in the movies." She liked Victor and did not like how Lola and Caldwell manipulated him.

"You have to have a little drama to keep Victor suspicious," Lola explained.

"What is the film of?"

"Israeli fortifications and attack plans, he thinks."

"Do you think he's working for Hussein?"

"For him, against him, who the hell knows. Every time I talk to them over there there's a goddamn new coup d'état. That handsome bastard's going to have his ass bombed off someday. What a crummy country. I urged him to give it up and come away with me for two years to Nepal and live the life of a meditating ascetic."

"I didn't know you had such yearnings."

"I don't," Lola said, "but two years in Nepal with him would be terrific. He's a fantastic lay."

"I didn't know things had gotten so bad, Lola," Anna said, "that you had to go to Nepal to get laid."

"Something happens to your blood up there, gets thinner, the air pressure or something, I hear it's terrific."

"So take mescaline next time and roll in the snow, it does the same thing," Anna replied rather tartly.

Lola noticed she was getting cross again lately. She went over to Anna, and stroking her hair and nuzzling her neck said, "What are you doing this evening?"

"Some English detective is coming to see me."

"Detective?" Lola's green eyes became curiouser and curiouser.

"About Elmer Lee."

"Oh," said Lola, "what *about* Elmer Lee?"

"I won't know until he gets here, will I?"

"An English detective, how very peculiar," Lola said, as if hearing it for the first time. "Well, sorry you're busy. I thought Plato and I might take you to dinner."

"I can just imagine how far we'd get," Anna said sourly.

"How far?" Lola grinned.

"The back seat of the car," Anna snapped.

"Oh darling," Lola said, getting up and stretching. "You get so annoyed, and yet I must tell you, you clearly enjoy being worked over."

"I love submitting to Plato, I hate submitting to you. Emotionally I hate you. Sexually I loathe you."

"You hate me, but you can't resist me," Lola said in a mocking theatrical tone.

"Stop talking like someone in a comic strip."

"This *is* a comic strip," Lola said. "God, I'm sick of your bellyaching—it's all because," she walked to the windows and turned and stood against rays of the sun bristling through the cracks in the gold-green glass, "you don't like lesbians."

"You're right, smartass, I don't like lesbians. I don't like homosexuals and I don't like transvestites."

"Meet Miss Straight," Lola said. "What the hell do you think *you* are?"

"I'm not a lesbian and you know it," Anna said, the words cracking the air like a whip, "I wish to Christ I was—it would be a lot simpler."

"Well," Lola seemed surprised, "what exactly would you call your relationship with me?"

"God, you *are* stupid," Anna said. "What would I call it? I'd call it incest, that's what. A sweet innocent incest, sort of a mother and daughter routine."

DOCUMENT #11

---

*THE NEW YORK TIMES, MONDAY, SEPTEMBER 11, 1972*

# ARABS IN PERUGIA MEET HOSTILITY

## Rumors Link Them With the Terrorists of Olympics

---

**By PAUL HOFMANN**

Special to The New York Times

PERUGIA, Italy, Sept. 10—This ancient hill capital of Umbria, host to a fluctuating body of more than 2,000 Arab students, has suddenly become tense with suspicions, rumors and fears.

Newspapers in Rome and Florence have charged in the last few days that the Palestinian community and other Arabs living here may be connected with the Black September terrorist group and the attack on the Israeli team at the Olympic games in Munich.

Last night, reports circulated here that 15 to 20 Arab students had been taken out of Perugia and were to be expelled from Italy.

The formal reason for the measure was said to be failure to comply with the rules that oblige every foreigner, except tourists, to register with the police. Implied was the suspicion that the expelled Arabs might be members of conspiratorial networks.

---

Continued on Page 4, Column 4

Continued From Page 1, Col. 3

### Rumors Are Denied

Police officers here deny a rumor—which appeared in the local press—that one of the Arab terrorists who were holding the Israeli hostages in Munich had called a Perugia hotel by phone from Olympic Village.

The police here also discount reports that Arab students living in private quarters in Perugia had been found to have been involved in arms traffic or that some of the local Arabs had left for Munich just before the attack on the Israeli team.

An employe of the Perugia Foreigners University—an institution specializing in Italian-language courses for non-

### 'Exercising Vigilance'

But the duty officer at Perugia police headquarters stated today that "only one or two" Arab students had been expelled. The expulsion order was issued, the police spokesman said, because the student or students did not hold a sojourn permit.

"We are exercising vigilance," the police officer declared. "We are watching the situation, and we have special organs of observation."

The Italian police have lately expanded their services for the surveillance and investigation of suspect foreigners.

Many local people are convinced that agents of the Italian military intelligence service and of the Israeli secret service have lately—and independently of each other — moved into Perugia, which is 80 miles north of Rome. "I'm now getting dinner guests who seem James Bond characters," a restaurant owner said with pride.

Italians—said: "There is always much coming and going of Arabs. They arrive with scholarships or on their own, attend classes for a while, then drop out or take proficiency exams and go on to some other Italian University."

At least 200 of Perugia's more than 2,000 Arabs are Palestinians. Most of them carry passports issued by Egypt, Syria, Lebanon or other Arab nations.

The Perugia chapter of the General Union of Palestinian Students protested in a statement last night against what it termed a "racist anti-Arab campaign" here.

### Slander Charged

The group asserted that it was fighting "the Zionist enemy in occupied Palestine" and insisted that its propaganda activity here was within the limits permitted by Italian laws. It accused "Israeli espionage" of slandering Arabs in Perugia by spreading alarming rumors.

"Get the Arabs out of Perugia!" and similar slogans were scrawled on some walls here during the night. A social worker said: "Two thousand Arabs are a lot for a city of 130,000. Some of them inevitably get into trouble, if only for reasons that don't have anything to do with politics—like running up debts or being over-romantic with our girls."

The local Communist party organization, which controls the city and regional governments, has passed the word around that anti-Arab feeling was being fanned by neo-Fascists.

But an Arab student who said he was an Iraqi and would not give his name remarked: "The people of Perugia have become very chilly toward us"

"Sometimes you actually manage to shock me," Lola said.

"Consider yourself ahead."

"You could go to a psychiatrist if it really bothers you," Lola said nonchalantly.

"*Bothers* me," Ann screamed. "*Bothers me!* You think it's a question of *bother* when you snap your fingers and my head's between your legs?"

"You're so crude, Anna dear," she touched Anna's arm. Anna moved away but Lola grabbed her again. "I think you need a lesson in respect," Lola said stroking Anna's shoulder, "I think you need a very firm lesson," and then taking Anna's head in her hands and rubbing against the back of Anna's thighs, crooning and cooing as she would to a baby and stroking and caressing, she felt Anna's breath catch, then moving her hand between Anna's legs, Lola went to work.

"Did you discover anything else over your fish soup?" Avian asked Farthingdale as he tied his tie and prepared to go out that evening.

"Well," he said, stroking his chin and looking puzzled, "she has the most curious relationship with that little priest, Friar Bacco."

"Curious how?"

"Well, he seems to be a sort of fashion adviser."

"You don't say," said Avian, "How very odd indeed."

"In addition to acting as a sort of chauffeur. The little fellow is an excellent driver, and she goes about only in limousines, even grocery shopping. She does her own grocery shopping; they are often seen at the pier early in the morning buying fish, he is also quite a cook I gather: gather it must be an extraordinary sight, five feet ten of one of the most beautiful and elegant women in the world trotting about with a fat warty little priest, who by the way fancies himself an imitation of Ben Franklin, perhaps because he is forever munching on a roll, a garlic roll unfortunately, as he walks about the street."

"He doesn't sound appealing," Avian said, adjusting his tie.

"Where are you going?" Farthingdale asked.

"I have an appointment to see Anna."

"You might have told me," Farthingdale said, a bit miffed.

"I might have," Avian replied, "but I chose not to."

"What exactly are you going to ask her about?"

"Mr. Lee, the strange Chinese businessman, and his oracle bones." Avian adjusted his hat and bid Farthingdale good night.

———— ————

Anna had a soft black pussycat. Her name was Irene. The cat, long and elegant and yellow-eyed, was, unlike most cats, a veritable insomniac. She never took catnaps, or any other sort of nap, but just purred and paced and meowed like a restless panther twenty-four hours a day.

This was not good for Irene, Anna or her guests who would often, in the wee hours of the morning, be awakened by a small furry black form pacing relentlessly up and down over their bedclothes.

One day, Anna and a friend, an American businessman, brought home the record of the song "Irene, Good Night Irene." This put pussy to sleep immediately. They were so pleased with the result they made a nightly ritual of it, and visitors to the house would often be amused by Anna's putting on the record, and Irene, after only a few minutes, purring contentedly into sleep.

The night that Avian Braine arrived it was still an hour before Irene's bedtime, so when the butler admitted him into the foyer, the cat jumped onto his shoes and began purring against his legs.

Avian bent down to stroke her and the butler introduced them. He picked up the cat and was astonished by her weight. Suddenly the cat jumped from his arms and raced up the stairs. At the top of an elegant winding staircase was one of the most stunning women he had ever seen. She was very tall, dark-haired with blondish streaks, and was wearing a long-sleeved silken caftan that when she descended the stairs revealed a slit all the way up her thigh.

"Good evening, Mr. Braine," she said, walking toward him. He was surprised to find her manner so agreeable and charming.

"This way, Mr. Braine," she said moving toward a room off the foyer, "it's lovely near the garden this time of evening." He looked at her carefully. She was very beautiful, but it was her elegance that impressed him most strongly. She had the manner of a queen, of someone born to aristocratic courtesies and privileges, hardly the manner of a courtesan.

"I've opened a magnum of Château Lafitte for dinner, would you care to have some now, or another sort of apéritif?" she asked him.

"I could hardly resist that invitation," Avian said.

"Good." She rang for a servant and then turned to gaze at him with the most extraordinary eyes he had ever seen, nearly violet, then they looked turquoise. He thought she seemed familiar, and at the thought of that he felt suddenly awkward in her presence. It certainly was unusual. A courtesan with this kind of wealth. He had seen two Picassos in the hall. They were not copies.

She was rather quiet in her manner he thought. She made no attempt to enlist him in conversation until the wine was served. She simply sat there, stroking the cat and staring out into the garden. It was an elegant and impressive Japanese garden and Avian found it very pleasant to look at the shadows falling in it. The silence was odd, but he did not feel like violating it. Finally when the servant left he said to her, "I have a few questions about Mr. Lee."

"Yes," she said, "I know that is the purpose of your visit. Please proceed."

"Was he a," Avian hesitated, "a friend?"

"No," Anna said quickly, "Mr. Lee was a client of

mine. I charge for sexual services, as you must know." She remained completely poised as she continued to stare out the window.

"Was he a good client?"

"He saw me whenever he was in Rome, that is, until recently."

"Is it true that he was impotent?"

Anna seemed surprised he noticed, just for a moment.

"I never experienced it," she said softly.

"Did he ever talk to you about his business?" Avian noticed how graceful and carefully kept her hands were.

"Yes, frequently. He dealt in antiques. Of course you know."

"Did he ever mention the name Harcourt to you, or Covington, Lady Sarah or Silverstein?"

"Silverstein, yes. He spoke of Silverstein the Jew. He lives in Amsterdam."

"Yes," Avian said, "what did he say about him?"

"Only that his prices were high and he didn't like him. Mr. Lee was an anti-Semite," she said. "When I discovered that I refused to see him."

On a chance, Avian said quickly, "Are you pro-Israeli then?"

Her eyes flashed as she snapped, "One does not have to be pro-Israeli to detest anti-Semitism, Mr. Braine. Prejudice in any form is never attractive to me, although I confess I share it," she shrugged.

"In what way?" Avian asked, wondering if she were trying to lead him into a trap.

"I don't like Japanese," she said.

Avian was surprised. "A woman of your cultivation not appreciating Japanese culture? I can hardly believe it, you have a Japanese garden."

"Of course I appreciate Japanese culture. I do not appreciate its military traditions."

"I see," Avian said, "you object to the self-sacrifice of Kamikaze principles?"

"No, it's nothing as morally bound as that." She put

the cat down and drew one leg from under the caftan and stretched it out on the sofa. It was a beautiful, tan leg, Avian noticed, and as she turned to place the cat on the floor, he saw the indentation, the dark line along her thigh, and thought how extraordinarily strong a muscle it must contain.

"It's not the Kamikazes," she said, "I don't like surprises."

"I see," Avian said, finding it as strange as she was wonderful. "You talk like an American on the scene at Pearl Harbor."

"I am an American," Anna said.

After some moments he said, "I don't understand. You have Italian citizenship. Your birthplace is a small town north of Genoa."

Anna smiled. "Forged," she said, "I'm an American. I left that country when I was five. I still maintain dual citizenship, under another name."

"What name?" Avian said, but Anna only smiled. Avian sensed she would tell him nothing more, at least not that evening. "Thank you very much," he said, and put on his coat and rose to go.

"It that all," Anna said, her sheer green silk robe catching in the frame of the door. "Before you go," she continued, "perhaps you'd like to see my garden?" She took Avian's arm and led him through the French doors down the small flagstone steps into the miniature garden.

As they strolled over the white pebbles Avian felt an extraordinary sensation—he wished quite simply to be engulfed by her. As he glanced about he noticed a high picket fence, and what appeared to be another garden.

"Oh, that," Anna laughed, "that's my working garden, just zinnias and azaleas and weeds," she shrugged. "I take out my rages there, pruning and planting." He turned to her, and the way she stood before the pool her green silk gown was transparent, and he could see the very line of her beautiful, extraordinary body, and he stared, unembarrassed, as she suddenly stepped sideways so her legs were astride, her feet boldly four or five feet apart, so he could see even the inside corners of her thighs.

"Sure you wouldn't like to stay, Mr. Braine?"

He was surprised and flattered at the invitation. "I don't pay for my pleasure," he said quietly.

"Don't get sentimental, Mr. Braine," Anna said almost harshly. "There are only two reasons to do anything, one is love and the other is money. Money is far more negotiable."

"I don't understand," he said softly, "why you . . ."

She interrupted him. "I am not a whore, Mr. Braine," Anna said. "I am a courtesan. I have acquired certain techniques and skills for the eliciting of sexual pleasure and excitement, and I have decided to make a profession of it. I am extremely well paid. I select my clients. They come to me. I am not some pathetic streetwalker waiting for some man to decide that I am a worthy recipient for his sperm. I am very discriminating," she said turning to him. "I only take a select few." She spun around and put her cigarette out.

"I don't think you take any," Avian said suddenly. "I think you're a virgin."

Anna smiled. "There are many in Rome who would bear witness to the contrary."

"I am aware," Avian said, "that people have witnessed you in the act of sexual intercourse. Nevertheless you strike me as a woman who is psychologically a virgin."

"What exactly does that bit of hocus-pocus mean?" Anna said coolly. "Despite the fact that he was so close to the English David Hume seems to have had very little effect on the culture. Englishmen seem too fond of tautologies for my taste. Say what you mean."

"You don't seem capable of surrender," Avian said finally.

"That is a military term implying defeat; if that is your attitude toward female sexual response, I suggest you reexamine it."

"It is also a metaphor for the relinquishment of control and power," Avian said quietly. "That is what I meant."

"I surrender control," Anna said brightly, "most pleasurably."

"If paid in advance."

"We all have our terms," Anna said. "I think you should go now," and she disappeared into the next room, calling for the butler to show him to the door.

---

"What was she like?" Farthingdale asked casually. He had decided to wait until morning to tell Avian about the manuscript and the pistol.

"Extraordinary. Provocative as hell, smart, beautiful, rich, and with incredible muscles on the inside of her thighs."

Farthingdale's eyes opened wider.

"I only *saw* them, alas," Avian said.

"It's got to be interesting," Farthingdale said. "All these extraordinary women. When do we see Miss Apricot?"

"Soon," said Avian. Before falling asleep Avian said to Farthingdale in the next bed, "The amazing thing about Anna was she looked so much like the woman on the beach."

"What beach?"

"That afternoon, that dream or whatever it was."

"Oh," he said, and soon they were both asleep. Or to put it more accurately, Avian was sleeping, and Farthingdale was lying half awake, to see if Avian might utter anything revealing.

---

Anna could not wake up. She knew why. She'd drunk too much last night after that detective left. She told Bacco she was worried—"If they're suspicious about Lee, they'll find out about me"—and Bacco reminded her that the system was foolproof, but still even though she knew it was, she felt uneasy. She lay there a few minutes, looking at the yellow roses outside her window. They made her happy. She drifted off again, feeling her mind turn over once again—a problem about mystery and inquiry, and half dreaming and half waking she found herself wishing suddenly that she could bend her head down between her thighs and push it through her vagina and take a look around, to finally confront the space and see that it was space and not "emptiness," which was another thing, but until she satisfied her curiosity, for that was her curiosity, wondering about the inner spaces, and it was always also aborted, she would peek and inquire but she could never pursue, and why not? How could she pursue, for the rest of the dream was that as her head pushed into her vagina and finally burst through her cervix her vagina contracted around her neck, choking her and then finally snapping it off. So then she was headless either end. So much for eternal punishment chastising inquiry, for it seemed to her that was what she was afraid of, really taking a look at herself, not in any profound or philosophical way but anatomically. Why she thought of this this morning she had no idea. The morning was for fun and games. She and Bacco and Santiago were going to buy a new limousine.

She hardly knew what to wear. She got up and decided on a short white wool skirt that Cardin had done for her, and two sweaters from Balmain. And then her beautiful rust soft-as-butter boots, which fitted tightly to her calf and then rolled down like cavalier boots in a large thick soft roll just below her knee. She never wore a bra, but she decided since the skirt was so brief, in some effort to acknowledge decency and her own modesty she would have to wear a wisp of underwear. And that was what it was. A mere wisp. She wanted to feel the cool rolls of the leather or the fuzziness of velvet beneath her when she bounced. She knew the salesmen must think her mad to buy a limousine by bouncing about in the back seat of it, but after all that was half the fun.

"You're getting more and more like the princess and

the pea," Bacco had said to her one day when she complained of the bumps. "Modern streets have bumps and you'll have to get used to them."

She felt grumpy and said, "I will not get used to them, and I don't have to. I will buy a new limousine."

Bacco was calling to her from outside. "Will you hurry, the traffic is going to be terrible, and they're expecting us at the showroom at ten. You know, don't you?" he called to her through the door; he would never come in until she was dressed.

"It's all right," she yelled, and he came in, saying, "You know they're going to try to sell you a Maserati."

"They always try to sell me a Maserati, but I'm going to buy a Rolls-Royce." She paused a moment before her jewelry box.

"What fur are you wearing?" Bacco asked. "I really think that skirt is too short."

"Cardin says it's fine, so it's fine," Anna snapped, "besides I'm in that sort of mood today."

"What sort?"

"I feel like showing off my luscious thighs."

"You have to wear the Norwegian blue fox with that I think," Bacco said.

"Yes, yes light colors, I want all beigy light-looking colors, because that's the color car I'm going to buy." Then she paused. "What am I going to do with all my diamonds?"

"What do you mean?"

"Well, I've got to sell them or do something with them."

"You could try wearing them," Bacco said mildly.

"I have but I hate them. Whenever I'm wearing diamonds I realize why I hate them."

"Why?"

"Because diamonds," Anna said with some finality, "are really very tacky."

———————————

Anna was surprised to see me waiting in front of the house. "Where's Santiago?" she said.

"I'm going instead," I said, "if you don't mind. He had an important engagement."

"Oh," she frowned at this and then said nothing, and settled back among the soft cushions of the car. She was feeling quite chatty and we talked all the way to the showroom. As soon as we arrived Anna dashed out and practically knocked over the salesman, wearing of all things, I thought, for a car salesman, a tail and black tie while he muttered obsequiously, "Yes, madame, we've been expecting you, madame."

"What about this?" Anna said imperiously, standing in front of one of the limousines.

"That is a very fine car, madame," the salesman was saying, "but I thought perhaps a Maserati."

"No," Anna said defiantly, "I want a Rolls-Royce. Now is this the best one?"

The salesman nodded. "One of our finest models."

"Well, open the door," she said to the salesman, pointing to the rear seat, "so I can get in and bounce." The salesman, somewhat harried, opened the door and Anna ducked her head, climbed in and began to bounce on the back seat, a lovely stretch of thigh showing quite wantonly beneath the furs.

"This bounces rather well," she said, "let me try some more," and the salesman led her to another car. Anna bounced again, and as this car was near the window and the street, several gentlemen stopped to take a look at Anna bouncing. Quickly she reached over and slammed the door.

Bacco finally arrived and said to Anna, "Well, what do you think?"

She had bounced in five or six models and although she was enjoying herself, was seeming to have a hard time making up her mind about two of them.

"Well," Bacco said, "what colors do they come in?" He turned to Anna. "Perhaps that will help you decide."

The salesman rushed out with a sample folder of interiors and exteriors. Model A, the first one, it appeared, came in almost exactly the same colors as the other model. Bacco saw that we would be spending half the day there if Anna could not decide.

"Well," Bacco said finally, "what do you call this color?"

"That," said the salesman, "that is Café au Lait."

"And this?" Bacco said.

"That, that is Creamfoam."

"They're the same color," I said.

"Not quite," the salesman said, looking at me as if I were a person of gross sensibilities.

"*What's* that color called?" Anna said suddenly and loudly.

"Café au Lait," the salesman said beaming.

"Oh God, I can't drive a car called Café au Lait," she said, "what's the other?"

"Creamfoam," he said.

"CREAMFOAM," she squealed, "perfect, I've always wanted a CREAMFOAM CAR," and to the salesman's astonishment she took $23,000 in cash out of her purse and paid him for it. As we left she said to the salesman, "See if you can get Creamfoam to me by Christmas, the roads get very bumpy with the snow."

The salesman nodded and retreated. All in all I got the impression he had been staggered by the entire transaction. As we drove home, Anna said, "But I do need a little something to buzz about in myself . . ."

"Well," I said, "you've commented that you love Pinin Farina's designs, and you must know that his Cisitalia GT 1946 has just been accepted by the Museum of Modern Art."

"It has!" Anna clapped her hands. "I'm a dreadful snob but then I must have it. A car in a design collection." Then she frowned. "Does it bounce well?"

"I'm sure," I said, "it bounces divinely."

The minute we arrived at her house, Anna ran in to place her order.

"I've had fresh news from Signor Martinelli," Farthingdale said that morning. "He told me there was a pistol and a manuscript discovered near the body of that Libyan official."

There was a pause. Then Farthingdale said. "You know, don't you, that he was murdered shortly after you arrived in Rome."

"What exactly do you mean?" Avian was tense, and frowning.

"Did you think I didn't know you'd slipped off in Amsterdam?" Farthingdale said, buttering his toast, and nipping neatly into it with his teeth.

DOCUMENT #12

**The Rosedale Manuscript: Classification and Analysis. War Office. Department 008.**
In March of 1941 an unexpected and bizarre incident caused the temporary postponement of SNOW's activity. At this time it was not known whether or not SNOW and ARNOLD each knew the other was controlled, although this office thought by this time they must have well expected it. In any event, SNOW was dispatched with letters from ARNOLD, who was a London wine merchant, to BATMAN, posing as a Portuguese vintner. Under the guise of obtaining quite special prices on the wine, it was agreed that SNOW would meet with ARNOLD on a submarine off the coast of Portugal, and they would proceed to a rendezvous point where SNOW would produce BATMAN. There can have been no doubt in SNOW's mind that BATMAN was acting as an agent of this office but for reasons as yet obscure, sometime during the journey ARNOLD became convinced that SNOW was actually a German agent, and SNOW became equally convinced that ARNOLD was a genuine German agent who would reveal his position as soon as they made contact with BATMAN. Three days before the fixed date of the rendezvous, when the two had been aboard the submarine for two

days, a ship passed by and gave the agreed recognition signal. This only further served to heighten ARNOLD's suspicions of SNOW, and he ordered the submarine to return, while he kept SNOW under guard in the cabin.

Upon his questioning by this office, it was discovered that both men were totally innocent of knowing the other was controlled, a totally unpredictable and largely inexplicable set of circumstances. It was agreed at this point that QUIM should replace SNOW and return with ARNOLD to the rendezvous point, then twenty four hours off.

It so happened that the sea was so thick with submarines at the time and place of meeting that this meeting never did take place. It was some months later when QUIM agreed to meet with the necessary information for BATMAN in Seville.

Avian set down his coffee. "I thought you didn't know," he said. "How did you?"

"Oddly enough," Farthingdale said, "it was a coincidence. I happened to be at the airport checking out Silverstein's locker."

"You never told me he had one."

"No, I know. But in any event, Martinelli didn't want to alarm everyone by publicizing those clues. It makes it more complicated. Either it's the same murderer, or it's someone trying to derail us."

Avian looked up and found Farthingdale looking at him oddly, "What is it?"

"There's one other thing."

"Yes?"

"You do wear a nine-and-a-quarter-size hat, don't you?"

"Yes."

"Well, they found another one. Another bowler near the body. By odd coincidence, it's your size. Did you know?"

"No, and you know," Avian said, gazing at Farthingdale with total aplomb, "I don't believe in odd coincidences."

"Perhaps the murderer will convince you," Farthingdale said, pushing a manuscript across the table.

"Another manuscript?"

"Yes," Farthingdale said with a peculiar look.

"Found where?"

"Next to the body."

"Nineteen century?"

"Not exactly. Rather current. It's about you."

Avian finished the manuscript and leaned back.

"Do you have any real recall of this woman at all?" Farthingdale said.

DOCUMENT #13

I had first met Avian and Richmond at an unlikely party for the press upon their exposé of an international diamond-smuggling operation. I had met a journalist upon my arrival in London who had told me that "two old fogy detectives, private eyes they call themselves, always unemployed, you know, beat up and run down, why, they've cracked this damn thing that's eluded Scotland Yard. Can you imagine. They're having a press conference tomorrow, welcome to join me if you want to come along. They're a pair, I tell you." He paused then looking amused and I said, "Do you mean they're not exactly Sherlock and Watson?"

"Oh my, certainly not," he said. "More like Laurel and Hardy. And yet they are. It's sort of, well," he laughed a bit and then hunching forward in his chair said, "Can't you see? It's like control being played by Oliver Hardy. Yes," he snapped his fingers with great English glee and said, "they're Laurel and Hardy gone to work at Sherlock and Watson." He leaned back savoring his insight. "How bloody marvelous."

When we arrived at the hotel suite we found Avian Braine and Richmond embarrassed by the unexpected arrival of the entire corps de ballet in the nude, through the bathroom. Seems the lovelies had gotten the wrong suite and none of the press minded particularly although Henry Gaddings, my journalist friend, was dismayed at the intrusion of a pair of buttocks in his cucumber sandwich. In any event I noticed then that Richmond had shown up at the party wearing two different socks, I was informed that he always wore two different socks. Not any two different socks, but always the same two different ones. One black, and one navy blue.

"It only shows up in the sunlight," Avian would say, rather sadly, "he has three blue and four black pairs."

If that was the case I wondered why it wasn't true that two black ones never made an appearance on the same day. When I posed this to Avian he said, looking off vaguely into the distance, "It's some sort of rotation system he has I think. It doesn't make any sense, a woman seventy-seven years old, and an old Tory at that, it doesn't make a bit of sense, her taking LSD."

"Maybe she has a young radical boyfriend," I said, "who had turned her on." Avian's brows shot up as predicted and he said, blowing his nose, "Oh no, a person of her station," I nodded agreement until Avian said, "wouldn't date a younger man." Then after a few minutes he looked up at me and said, "Will you be with us long, do you think?" I sensed they would welcome my departure. I said, "I need more material." Avian nodded slowly. "Yes, I see. Will there," he asked, "will there be any photos?"

Avian was referring to a book I was contracted to do on the nature of detective work in ten major countries around the world. We figured, the publisher and I, that if there was any such thing as a national character and a national mind, it would show in the way crime was detected. London was my first stop and the day of my arrival Avian and Richmond had made their appearance in the papers. The fact that I was a woman did not help much. There was a certain tension, although I found it difficult to regard it as sexual.

In any event, although I had not stopped to think about it, Avian Braine seemed singularly uninteresting, and the feeling remained for weeks, so it was perhaps with more than the usual surprise that I noticed that when he arrived at my apartment one evening dressed for the theater, the change in clothes had produced a change in attitude that converted Avian Braine, within a short period of a half-hour's stay in my living room, to an intriguingly attractive man. The most compelling feature of this arrangement as the reader will learn, is that it was in no way the result of a simple technique. He was not a "ladies' man" who performed well with women. It just happened that the two of us provoked in each other a unique sense of enjoyment whose ultimate and intimate base was an uncontrolled sensuality.

It began with the simple suggestion of a cigarette.

"Cigarette?" Avian said, settling back in the cab, his eyes I just noticed the color of gold, brown but with lots of gold, his hair somehow different, and I said yes, and with his long slender fingers, immense graceful, careful hands, he pulled a cigarette from his soft pack and drawing it slowly from the pack offered the pack to me, saying in a new tone, a strained tone, we were both aware in that moment, yes if I could describe a moment, it was that precise moment when I bent my head to receive the cigarette that it happened, that the intense desire began. For what? Dear reader I do not know, but why, you may discover. An intense desire began that remained unmitigated for six months, in my personal history an extraordinarily long time, during which the adventure concerning the embalmed old lady in Trafalgar Square was to cause Avian and me to travel half the globe.

When my mouth received the cigarette, I had no notion of any of this. I knew only that my hand reached out to steady his as he held the lighter for me, and when I had inhaled my first smoke and leaned back against the cab, Avian had insisted we drive through the park, he turned slightly to the side and folded back the edges of the silver foil, folded them back in such a way and in such a manner and then wound his fingers around the pack and put them in his pocket, that I knew we were embarking on something irrevocable.

The air was pleasant, although slightly misty as is typical of London evenings, as the horse clopped through the park, deserted now, it appeared, except for one solitary stroller waiting to cross the road.

"The autopsy," Avian said, surprising me with a return to his professional interest, "showed an overdose of LSD."

"Really? How do you explain that?"

"I haven't," Avian said turning his head in a sudden manner in my direction, then resting his gaze on me for several minutes. "You are very beautiful."

This was said a bit too smoothly and for a moment I became uneasy as I once again reminded myself that I might be, for all I knew, his prime suspect. There was something unnerving suddenly in the situation, for I found myself attracted and excited by a man I thought something of a tired old fool only a few hours ago. I also had the unpleasant idea that I was being manipulated, except that his interest had seemed genuine. I remembered he had made a point of saying that this was an evening solely for his pleasure, when I had offered to buy the tickets and charge them to my magazine.

"Do you suspect me," I said suddenly turning to him as the cab slowed for a light, my tone slightly irritated. Avian said nothing but seemed to be staring at something through the mist of the park. I wondered for a moment if he had heard me, and then as I put the cigarette to my mouth again, it no sooner touched my lips than Avian's hand was over mine, pulling the hand that held the cigarette slowly away, his other hand coming forward in a strange slow manner to take the cigarette from my mouth, which he threw away with a graceful backhand, his eyes never once leaving my face as he bent forward and kissed me. It had a faint professional touch, but although brief, there was nothing casual in it. I wondered momentarily if it were the surprise that had added so to my pleasure. Then Avian said, "I suspect everyone. It's almost second nature with me." He smiled. "There's nothing personal in it."

The cab had entered a rather dark section of the park and the wet trees were hanging down, occasionally brushing very close to our heads. His arm slipped around my shoulders and suddenly I felt his other arm about my waist then dropping down beneath my hip as he slid down one side of the seat to lie on his side and pulled me across him in such a way that I was lying next to him.

"Lie down," Avian said, "otherwise you'll get wet."

He made no attempt to kiss me at this point, an event that altogether disappointed and confounded me and in a few minutes he raised me up again, making clear that the entire gesture was solely in the interests of preventing me from getting wet. Nevertheless his hand had been firm and in some way suggestive as it grasped the upper part of my thigh. I found myself thoroughly puzzled at this lack of turn in events.

"Often, you see," Avian said, puffing on his pipe and looking out into the dark London street just beginning to gleam with the evening light, the people hurrying from taxicabs to the theater, the frequent mist, "people come to us precisely because they are impressed with our manner." I was embarrassed by this because it was clear to me that I had totally misjudged him and he knew this and turned my face so he would not notice the flush. "They think, as you think, as they are intended to think," he leaned back now, I felt his eyes on me carefully, "that we are bumbling incompetents. We are hired, not infrequently, by the murderer himself." He smiled then as my head turned quickly in his direction. It had never struck me that their manner might be a stylistic device to ferret out the culprit. I paused a moment and then I said, "It doesn't appear that you are acting, or pretending anything." I was afraid still of the game Avian played.

"We are not," Avian said. "We have the manner of incompetents. We have the social appearance of fools. It is something, however, I have learned to cultivate as it adds to our advantage. There is no question of pretense involved." He looked at his watch. "It's almost seven-fifteen. I am sorry you have lost your mood for theater." I glanced up surprised and demurred and went for my coat. Avian stopped me and went for it himself. He was right of course, I had lost the mood. I wondered how he knew.

When we entered the theater the curtain had gone up and Avian hurried me down the aisle to our seat. I wondered how he knew the location without glancing at his ticket, and during intermission he explained to me, as we walked a short way from the theater, that he always took the same seat. A necessary precaution, should anyone have to locate him.

He seemed very attentive to the play and we said no more until intermission time when we went out for some air. He pressed my arm firmly as we stepped from the curb, and his hand seemed very warm against my back as we entered a small pub. We could have gotten a drink at the theater but I expected that he wished to be in more intimate surroundings. I had felt the presence of his concentrated gaze throughout the day, and considered myself stupid for not understanding it, although now I found it flattering, it puzzled me, for three days ago no one could have convinced me that Avian Braine was in any respect an interesting man. The strange manner of his suggested a definitely uninteresting man. A manner, Avian seemed to say glancing at me over the dark wood table, is not necessarily the man. I supposed also that a man in his profession would be exceptionally wary, and that my innocence was under suspicion at all time. It was not unlikely, I supposed, that he even thought I was in some way mixed up in the Trafalgar Square affair.

To my surprise, when we finished our drink, Avian pressing my hand which lay on the table idly fingering a salt shaker said, "I'm afraid we can't return to the theater. Come, we'll have dinner." He waited for my demand for an explanation but I decided to wait and simply nodded and said, "Well, if you wish." I slipped into my coat and wondered what had prompted him to leave. When we left the pub, Avian hailed a taxi and directed the driver to the Boar's Head, a fashionable restaurant in London's East End, a Victorian town house converted to a plush restaurant. In the cab, Avian said, "I know you're not disappointed. It was simply not a good idea to return."

Finally my curiosity would not abate and I pressed him for an answer. Avian leaned back in a way that suggested to me a long explanation. He asked me to wait until we had finished dinner as he did not wish to enter into an unnecessarily long explanation just now. Just before we left the cab, to my total astonishment and I must admit by now, to my delight, for the intrigue of his presence had contributed inexplicably to the unique pleasure of that embrace, Avian kissed me.

I do not know to what extent Mr. Braine's superb imitation of a Ronald Colman sequence, and I, in my long gown, stepping from the hansom cab, feeling more than faintly forties, contributed to the flourish with which he did it, but it was, although brief, in no way casual, and I wished by the time I had reached the restaurant door, that we could do away with the formalities of dinner entirely and retire to my apartment. As I have pointed out, three days ago if anyone had suggested that Avian Braine would in any way prove sexually interesting I would have responded with an indulgent smile. Avian sensed my mood I am certain, for just before entering the restaurant he asked me to step across the square to the park.

"You are very beautiful," Avian said, caressing my chin as we strolled beneath the trees, "and you will never be able to understand the English mind." Such a provocative remark naturally brought forth the expected response, to which Avian only smiled and then looking at me as he paused, a short distance from a street light, said staring at me, "The light in the park just now is incredible. Drop the top of your dress." He backed off from me approximately two feet watching my face the entire time. Now, I can't explain this to you in any rational terms, nor should I attempt to, but it was the sequence, and the authority of his command, which removed any doubt from my mind about the necessity of my actions and I was compelled to remove the top of my dress. Ordinarily a description of such actions told by anyone other than myself would suggest a poor imitation of spontaneity, or vulgarity, or plain prurience, but the mood of the occasion was such that I can only tell you it was not any of these, but very much an aesthetic affair, aesthetic and at the same time erotic. If we had been naked, I further submit, there would have been nothing erotic about it. Slowly I removed the one strap and then the other and then putting my hands behind my back, still staring at him, I let the dress drop to my waist.

Avian looked at me, a faint change of expression on his face and then very softly whispering said, "Step back one step. Only one." I did and emerged into the full glow of the street lamp. Far down the path I could see a couple emerging. Yet I dared not move. I stood there as Avian looked at me with an intensity I cannot describe.

He stepped toward me as I stood there in the light from the lamp overhead, unable to speak, enraptured by the mood broken only by my anxiety regarding the couple approaching us on the path.

Avian stood a foot away from me now, his arm reaching out and caressing my breast gently, discoveringly.

"Someone is coming," I said.

"Don't move," Avian said, his face revealing slightly, only slightly his pleasure as he continued to caress me. The couple advanced. My eyes did not leave Avian's face. They looked at each other, I sensed their movement, the quickness of their steps. They hurried on. No one had seen anything. That was the agreement. Immediately after that Avian hailed a cab. We did without dinner and hurried to my apartment.

Perhaps it was the propriety of his English gentleman's attire and the manner in which he discarded it, perhaps it was the way in which he stroked my thigh briefly in the cab, pressing the thin white silk gown firmly against it, wrapping my leg tightly in it, pressing his mouth through it. I do not know. All I know is that after that evening, which we spent in agonizingly slow sequences before the fire in my apartment, I lost all interest in analyzing it. It was the only time in my life when sexual desire was mingled in such incredible fashion with an overwhelming sense of the unbearableness of time. Sequence was a torture. When his mouth left mine and began a slow, undulating, pleasurable decline behind my neck, behind my ear, down across my chest, I wanted nothing but that his mouth should return to my mouth, and that it should remain upon my breast, when his lips began a soft brush across my belly, a slow soft brush as his hands circled my buttocks, and the full hairs on his chest seemed to finger my nipples . . . Even his hair. I remember perhaps more than anything else, the full thickness of his hair, the odor of his hair, something close to burnt leaves, some faintly acrid aroma, combined with the incredible thickness, the softness of it, the brown curls thick in my hands as my legs wound slowly carefully over his shoulders. It was the only time I was savage in my pursuit to end an insanely unbearable pleasure, and yet I could not pursue it, I could not bear to relinquish the pleasure in pursuit of the greater pleasure. It was not simple excitation but some perverse (this I freely admit) joy that was determined to break me in half, I felt buried by some intolerable weight of pleasure, some branch grown thick and heavy and aching with the weight of flowers, thick with the smell of blossoms and scent, until I was groaning from the weight of the pleasure and I begged him to break me. And he did.

But there was no ending of it. All the satiation in the world would not have satisfied me. There was only one ending to our union, and that was physical exhaustion. This also seemed impossible, for our happiness only excited me more, and I had, or was possessed by the most astonishing energy that had ever penetrated my blood. We slept perhaps fifteen minutes that night and in the morning we walked about the city, made love at noon in a Soho hotel, had dinner at a seafood restaurant, managed fellatio in a deserted metro, had dinner in London's best restaurant, fondled each other in the opera house, had supper at the Carlton club, and made love in the park.

Our theater date was Thursday. Avian and I did not sleep until Saturday morning when at 11 a.m. finally we fell against each other after a breakfast of muffins and wine in the park, and we slept for eight or nine hours, for when I awoke the sun was beating down feverishly upon us, and the wine, which had spilled on the blanket, sent up a faint vinegarish smoke beneath my nose, and I was surprised to see that even when sleeping, we did not sleep as one does after making love, loose and relaxed, but closely wound around each other, in fierce possession, his legs even relaxed, pressed firmly around my thigh, my head just above the smell of his hair, warm from the sun. We slept not like lovers, after loving, but like those interrupted in the heat of their pursuit, like those quick deathbed lovers locked in sudden entombment in the lava at Pompeii.

Avian said very quietly, "No. I don't think this ever happened. There are two possibilities: it happened and I forgot it, or it happened to the other Avian Braine. Richmond was his sidekick. He died a week after Avian died."

"Of a heart attack also?" Farthingdale asked skeptically.

"No," Avian said. "Someone murdered him. We never found out who."

"But the old lady in Trafalgar Square," Farthingdale said. "That was just two weeks ago. Why put them together as if they were all part of the same time?"

"I don't know," Avian's voice was very tired. "It could mean anything. It's like a dream. I'm prepared to believe anything. Including that *you* wrote this," he turned to Farthingdale. He did not say this in jest.

Farthingdale said, "And that I am the murderer as well?"

"Not necessarily," Avian said. "That would be a separate question. People will often go to insane ends to prove mental superiority."

"I see," Farthingdale said.

When breakfast came, there was another note in another fortune cookie. It said,

"In the dream, at its edge, witnesses know what is missing."

Farthingdale said he was going out for air, and Avian lay down on the bed. He was very tired.

# BODY III

## THE

## AND THE
## SCHLONG

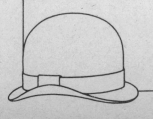

# 1

Anna leaned back against the seat of the train, her heart beating from the run. She had done it, she was sure she had not been seen. She checked her watch, it would take her eleven hours to get back to Rome. She dreamed, full of the memory of one man, yearning with desire for another, lonely, long cut off, suspended between two destinations, steadily rocking on the train, rocking toward, mind backwards, full of Hitchcock movies, murder and mystery and intrigue, she felt she had been on the train forever in a nineteenth-century dress, in a sweet chemise of the twenties her lips bowed through the thirties, and the forties all shoes and platinum blondes, from then until now she felt herself take on the presence of all ages, sitting in a train, eternal woman, contemplating murder.

"Who do you think this murderer is?" Avian said.

"It could be you," I replied, "you had amnesia."

"The diary?"

"Even the diary could be you."

"Wouldn't I recognize the thoughts . . . ?"

"No."

"A long amnesia that prevents you from recognizing yourself in the past? It's possible."

---

"Where will he kill next?" Bacco asked.

"I don't know" Avian replied "I am on the track of systems, or murder by thought, so to speak. Only thought can prevent it. This is definitely an intellectual contest. This murderer wants to be defeated by thought. Somewhere there is a rosetta stone to his system," Avian said thoughtfully, "and I had better find it soon. This murderer is brilliant and I suspect," Avian said, his mouth twisting oddly up at the corners, "physically beautiful as well."

In Seville, an official in Franco's government was walking home from the government offices when a single bullet penetrated the base of the brain. The revolver, found by his head, was inlaid with diamonds and pearls, and in the cock were three blonde hairs.

There was no evidence save the gun and the manuscript, but if eyes could say what they had seen just before they closed, investigators would have understood the presence of the smile on the dead man's lips, witnessing a beautiful apricot girl running across his dreams.

---

Everyone was talking about the murder in Seville. For reasons unknown, this time the manuscript found near the body had been made available to the newspapers, who revealed it was not a nineteenth-century document, but an eighteenth and more than that, it was written, the newspaper said, by a woman.

"That's too bad," Anna was saying, "about the

century. I much prefer the nineteenth century. I would have loved to have been a nineteenth-century man."

"A nineteenth-century man and not a woman?" Avian asked.

"Well actually," Anna said, "I would have loved being a woman until eighteen thirty when the salons closed. That would have been superb. After that, a man."

"You would have had to change sexes in order to get through the century then," Lola said.

"Yes," Anna said, looking very secretive, "what an interesting idea."

No one said anything for some time after that. Farthingdale sat, thinking. It was a queer afternoon. He could not imagine why Avian had decided that afternoon to make the news of the murders public. Other than that Avian found Anna to be a prime suspect. In any event, Farthingdale was glum. His idea of a good afternoon was not to be sitting around a swimming pool discussing erotic manuscripts with a courtesan, her girl friend, a suspected Egyptian agent, and her two sidekicks, who passed themselves off as a rabbi and a priest. Bacco, he noted, was interesting at least as far as his taste in food was concerned. He privately thought that later he might attempt to engage him in some further conversation. But the rabbi puzzled him completely. He had a beard and sharp dark eyes and was magnificently trim. He must work out three or four times a week, Farthingdale thought. His short body was tan and sinewy, and he was, by all accounts and his performance in the pool, an absolutely marvelous swimmer. Anna clearly adored him, and it appeared that they were fast friends. He claimed he was her Hebrew teacher, but Farthingdale thought they must have a sexual arrangement since Anna had introduced the rabbi as my sexy little rabbi, Rabbi Fennerman. Rabbi Fennerman's trunks were extremely brief and extremely tight, and left no questions about the delineation of his genital anatomy. Privately Farthingdale found it a bit shocking, but publicly he simply acknowledged the introduction and tried to avert his eyes.

They had come to the pool that afternoon at Santiago's invitation, or rather both Santiago's invitation and Anna's insistence. They had met her on the street, and Farthingdale had to admit he found himself quite charmed by her. Quite. Indeed more than charmed. Not only was she beautiful, she was alive in quite an extraordinary way. And endearing. He found he had a quite spontaneous affection, as well as an erection, in her presence.

And her concerns were most curious indeed. She had announced upon her arrival that she was bringing portions of her own erotic manuscript, and she intended to enlist the aid of the entire group in order to formulate some sections more precisely. All of this with a great air of mischief, he thought, while this dreadful murder in Seville had taken place. Farthingdale always found murders dreadful. His aim was always to capture the killer as quickly as possible and then have a good dinner. Avian, however, had lately become intrigued with the nature of the motivation to such an extent, Farthingdale thought, that he lost track of the savagery of the crime. Avian, on the other hand, thought that Farthingdale this time, in his eagerness not to miss a meal was spending too little time in pursuing motivation and association. This particular series of murders presented an interesting conflict. Farthingdale was in a hurry, and Avian, although profoundly disturbed was almost basking in the mystery of it. Farthingdale had figured most of the basic premises for himself already. Clearly Avian's control from World War II was alive and well and at large and possibly, Farthingdale also thought, living in Argentina. It was clear to Farthingdale that everyone was after the Impressionist paintings the Nazis had confiscated—Anna, Avian #1, Avian #2, Santiago, Silverstein, Harcourt, and of course, for his own reasons, himself as well.

He stopped musing for a moment when he heard Anna talking loudly about Iraq and oil.

"I've told you, Mr. Braine, I'm a fence. An oil fence, it is true, but nonetheless a fence. Iraq has absolutely no place to sell her oil, so I'm handling some delicate negotiations. I'm founding a company in Spain, and selling it to the United States. If the American business community should ever find out they're buying Iraqi oil it wouldn't do at all, would it? That's what I was doing in Spain."

Farthingdale sat up. So Anna had been in Spain. And the official in Seville had been murdered. He glanced over at her and noticed that she seemed much too relaxed to be genuinely concerned about the murder. Lola, however, he could not help but note, was continuously crossing and uncrossing her legs. Perhaps he thought she was just one of those people who became highly stimulated in the groin at the sound of murder. Or perhaps not. He made a note to watch her carefully the rest of the afternoon. It was only a few moments later when Anna began to read aloud from the manuscript found near the official's body in Seville. ☞

"Now that you've all gotten the feel of it," Anna said, "you can help me write mine," and she leaned down and picked up a rather large-looking brown envelope and extracted from it what she called her new erotic novel.

"Now everyone," she called, clanking on a glass, "pay careful attention. First we have to define terms. Now we need terms for the male and terms for the female. The first question is, is the dirtiest word dirtier than the euphemism, and which is better for arousal?"

"Certain words," Anna said, "we know are dirty, i.e., prurient. They are: spread, if you follow it with the legs; if you follow it with peanut butter it's okay; squat, usually, licked, usually."

"Sucked?" someone asked.

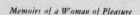

*Memoirs of a Woman of Pleasure*

I, struggling faintly, could not help feeling what I could not grasp, a column of the whitest ivory, beautifully streak'd with blue veins, and carrying, fully uncapt, a head of the liveliest vermilion: no horn could be harder or stiffer; yet no velvet more smooth or delicious to the touch. Presently he guided my hand lower, to that part in which nature and pleasure keep their stores in concert, so aptly fasten'd and hung on to the root of their first instrument and minister, that not improperly he might be styl'd their purse-bearer too: there he made me feel distinctly, through their soft cover, the contents, a pair of roundish balls, that seem'd to play within, and elude all pressure but the tenderest, from without.

But now this visit of my soft warm hand in those so sensible parts had put every thing into such ungovernable fury that, disdaining all further preluding, and taking advantage of my commodious posture, he made the storm fall where I scarce patiently expected, and where he was sure to lay it: presently, then, I felt the stiff insertion between the yielding, divided lips of the wound, now open for life; where the narrowness no longer put me to intolerable pain, and afforded my lover no more difficulty than what heighten'd his pleasure, in the strict embrace of that tender, warm sheath, round the instrument it was so delicately adjusted to, and which, now cased home, so gorged me with pleasure that it perfectly suffocated me and took away my breath; then the killing thrusts! the

78

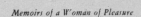

*Memoirs of a Woman of Pleasure*

unnumber'd kisses! every one of which was a joy
inexpressible; and that joy lost in a crowd of
yet greater blisses! But this was a disorder too
violent in nature to last long: the vessels, so
stirr'd and intensely heated, soon boil'd over,
and for that time put out the fire; meanwhile all
this dalliance and disport had so far consum'd
the morning, that it became a kind of necessity
to lay breakfast and dinner into one.

We had now reach'd the closest point of
union; but when he backened to come on the
fiercer, as if I had been actuated by a fear of
losing him, in the height of my fury I twisted
my legs round his naked loins, the flesh of
which, so firm, so springy to the touch, quiver'd
again under the pressure; and now I had him
every way encircled and begirt; and having
drawn him home to me, I kept him fast there,
as if I had sought to unite bodies with him at
that point. This bred a pause of action, a
pleasure stop, whilst that delicate glutton, my
nethermouth, as full as it could hold, kept
palating, with exquisite relish, the morsel that
so deliciously ingorged it. But nature could not
long endure a pleasure that so highly provoked
without satisfying it: pursuing then its darling
end, the battery recommenc'd with redoubled
exertion; nor lay I inactive on my side, but en-
countering him with all the impetuosity of mo-
tion I was mistress of. The downy cloth of our
meeting mounts was now of real use to break
the violence of the tilt; and soon, too soon
indeed! the highwrought agitation, the sweet

79

"Oh, that one," Anna said, "depends on how you use it," and with that she leaned back, smoking a lollipop.

"Now is penis better or dork better?"

"Dork?" Lola said. "Ugh, is that a word for penis?"

"Yes," Anna said, "it rhymes with pork, that's what I don't like about it."

"Scratch dork," Lola said. Anna agreed. They sat for a while around the pool enjoying the cool breezes. Finally Rabbi Fennerman said, "What about schlong?"

"Schlong?" Anna asked incredulously, "Don't you mean dong?"

"No, no schlong," the rabbi insisted.

"I like that," Anna said, writing it down, and then she read the sentence out loud, "He put his schlong into . . ."

"Wait," Lola said, "put is too aggressive, try something more delicate, like place."

"Place," Anna said, considering it. She looked around, taking a vote. Bacco nodded. So did Rabbi Fennerman. It seemed that they agreed that place was the thing for schlong.

Anna started again. "I think we're going to write a very good pornographic novel. Now listen to what we have so far, 'He placed his schlong into . . .' "

"No no no," Bacco said, "place is *too* polite, schlong has a very pushy quality."

"I think that's an anti-Semitic remark," Rabbi Fennerman said.

"No," Anna said, "I don't like pushed his schlong into."

"Wait," said Lola, "it's not so aggressive if you change what he's pushing it into."

"What do you mean?"

"Well, if you have him pushing his schlong into her cunt, that's very rough."

"Well, what do you want it in, her ear?"

"No, some euphemism. How about pushing his schlong into her velvet glove?"

"I don't like velvet glove," Anna said, "it sounds fuzzy."

"You're right," Lola said, sitting back and thinking it over. "If anything is velvet it should be the schlong."

"What about rose," said Bacco.

"Perfect," said Anna, reading out loud, "He pushed his velvet schlong into her rose . . ."

"No no no," Lola said, "you can't say that."

"You can't? Why not?" Anna asked.

"You can't because," Lola said simply, "people don't go around pushing things into roses. At least certainly not decent, honest, hard-working people."

"Well, he's got to do something to it," Anna said, "maybe pry. What about 'he pried open the rose'?"

"That makes it sound like a tin can," Bacco said. "Um."

There was silence for a moment and then Lola said, "Maybe the rose could do something to him."

"Like what?"

"Embrace," Bacco volunteered.

"Embrace?" Anna said questioningly.

"Yes, good, good," Rabbi Fennerman said. "The rose embraced his velvet schlong."

Anna was busy scribbling it down and asked him to repeat it.

" 'The Rose and the Schlong.' You know, that's not a bad title," Bacco said.

" 'The Rose and the Schlong,' " cried Anna, "yes yes, it's absolutely perfect." And so they all agreed.

"There's one little problem with your little erotic tale," said Bacco, moving his chair so as to get out of the shadows and into the sun, "and that is that you have no strong narrative drive."

"A strong narrative drive," said Anna, getting up and moving his chair back into the shade and admonishing him about sunburn, "is not compatible with the theme—love and murder."

"Murder?" said the little priest. "I thought you said it was going to be an erotic novel."

"Of course. Why do you think I need the murders?" Anna replied, coating herself with another layer of oil.

"Well, whatever it is you're doing you can't have a tale, I don't care what it's about, without a beginning a middle and an end. You can't have a tale without a narrative, erotic or not."

"All narrative does not necessarily come in a line," replied Anna.

"Bah, mere sophistry," Bacco complained, "how can you tell a tale without a narrative?"

"Perhaps," said Anna opening that Renaissance eye very high and very wide, you dissemble."

"But, but, but," the little friar went on, working himself up into a lather, "the dissembling will end at the end. You must have an end, even if there is no beginning and no middle."

"There are certain dilemmas," Anna said, patiently, as if speaking to a child, "which are inappropriate to resolution."

"Did you ever notice that in the nineteenth century," Lola said, "they called cocks machines?"

"Machines?"

"Yes," Anna said, "it's so quaint. I think it must have been because of the industrial revolution, anything that connoted power."

"I always knew the industrial revolution was sexier than those historians were willing to make it out," Lola said.

"Oh for heaven's sake," Bacco said in an irritated tone, "the industrial revolution wasn't sexy."

"You certainly get some strange views of history around here," Rabbi Fennerman said.

"Is the purveyer of the schlong short or tall?" Avian said suddenly.

"Short, tall," Anna and Lola said simultaneously.

"Short?" Lola turned to Anna. "Why short?"

"There is something very exciting about short men," Anna said. "Like the center of their sphere is their genitals and the shoulders and legs revolve around that like some huge bright magnificent ball bearing gleaming in the light, and the body moves around that. They must be well proportioned of course. They must be broad-shouldered and have magnificent forearms. There it all lies. Then they must be hard like sculpture."

"Well, not for me," Lola said. "I like tall, medium tall and medium thin."

"Thin?" Anna said. "Thin is no good—I need fleshy or muscles—thick I need."

"You need fleshy," Lola said sarcastically. "You need whatever it is that whoever it is that's turned you on happens to have."

Anna paused. "Mmmm—you might have a point, except about Plato."

"Plato," Lola sighed, "don't get into that."

Avian sat there listening, and wondering if Anna would talk to him about Plato. He would see her privately tomorrow.

After a few moments, Bacco suddenly excused himself explaining that he had a spontaneous and uncontainable lust for francillon salad. Farthingdale's senses started at this and before he could stop it he heard himself saying, "I'll come along if I may—I have by the way some extraordinary mustard seeds from Israel in my car . . ." and the two of them talking excitedly trailed off toward the kitchen.

"Do you cook yourself at all?" Avian inquired politely of Anna.

"Yes," Anna said smiling, "but only when I am happy, and I am usually happy only once a month."

"Why so regularly?" Avian asked unthinkingly.

"That is when I menstruate," Anna said with no embarrassment.

"Oh." Avian almost felt himself blushing.

"Do you *like* to menstruate?" the rabbi asked in a tone of amazement.

"Yes!" Anna said. "I feel fantastic. I feel heavy and full, like a tree, my breasts grow like fruit— I could eat them myself—they are so bursting and luscious—I feel all of that—thick and heavy and full of the blood"—she turned to the rabbi—"You could never shut *me* away for that—I love the blood—to me it is the first of first, a new beginning again and again, the sign the body is reborn." She smiled then lying back, and stroked her abdomen then, circling it, spiraling across it with the suntan lotion, making patterns across the light blonde hairs of it, designing ornate mazes, adorning herself like an ancient warrior, with the promise of invincibility.

They sat there then the four of them, the sun going down slowly and the cool evening breeze beginning to lift. Anna smiled to herself. The shame, the shame about blood. She could not embarrass them and tell them she menstruated now, she would be content with the feeling itself. She felt, in these times, serene. If one could be both serene and enchanted, that is what she was. Enchanted by the pleasure in her own body now, at the extraordinary centering that fixed her to the earth, that gravity in her body as if her womb were her direction, and by some enormous magnetic field emanating from it had made her part of the earth. She felt full of silver circles, smooth and glittering, joined and glowing with a secret power— a confidence—a rich and heavy confidence that transcended contradiction—an earthbound airiness of the spirit.

## 2

The next day Avian discovered that the official murdered in Seville was an importer of masks from Uganda. He made the connection, he wasn't quite sure how, and decided he must find out more about both Plato and Caldwell. As far as he could ascertain, only Anna and Lola had ever seen Plato. Caldwell was another matter. It was clear, Farthingdale said, that Victor and Caldwell were working together for various Arab and African Liberation fronts. Lola seemed to be working for the Egyptians, but that information was less secure.

---

"You got the horses," Lola said that afternoon to Anna strolling in from the garden, "so why can't we do the robbery?"

"I don't want to," Anna said, annoyed that Lola had interrupted her.

"But I do," Lola said sweetly, "and so you will."

"Yes, I suppose I will." Anna absolutely hated Lola, hated Lola because she loved her and somewhere she knew in her crowded brain she thought love was unflagging obedience. She detested this in herself.

"Actually I've thought about it," Anna said, turning to Lola, "and there's only one genuinely destructive emotion."

"What?"

"Love."

"Are we at that point in our lives where we believe everything Genet has to say?" Lola said coyly.

"Sooner or later, one reaches that point." Anna walked into the living room, sat down and lit a cigarette.

"If you haven't committed suicide by the time you're

forty, you're forced to stealing—you need it for the excitement," Lola said.

"You're infatuated with theft," Anna said to Lola.

"And you with suicide," Lola replied, changing the subject.

"With *women* and suicide," Anna said. "I don't understand Plath, you know. She had children. I've always thought that if you got to the point where you could bear something—something actually growing and being nourished in your wounded hide, you'd be too *victorious* to kill yourself. Triumphant, you know."

"That's because you have this simplistic biological scheme—anything resembling an explosion—any excuse for adrenaline—you see as psychic victory."

"You ever see anyone depressed in the presence of adrenaline?" Anna said dryly.

"No, but you're going to burn out."

"I don't care about burning out, it sounds terrific to me, I just want to be sure I catch fire."

When Lola left, Anna felt good again. She got up and went into the kitchen. When she was happy she took great pleasure in cooking things. Today with the sun coming through the window in the late gold light of the afternoon, and the breeze still with the salt in it coming from the sea, she stood by the stove turning the onion translucent in the large black iron pan, turning clear like soft glass and then quickly she chopped thinly the red-skinned potatoes, added the thick bronze olive oil and turned them until they were brown. And then the green leaves of the escarole, a brilliant young green, soft curled edges flashing, and covered with onions, and the occasional thin red-skinned edges of the potatoes. She spun the escarole around in the pan hissing and steaming and she loved it. The colors, the smells, were glorious. She turned the gas off and squeezed two firm large yellow lemons fresh from the tree over the vegetables. She cracked the pepper with a rolling pin, sprinkled some on, coarse and fiery, and sat down with a glass of wine.

The breeze was coming up strongly now. The sky had darkened suddenly. It was going to rain. She felt at peace.

---

There were days when she cooked, when she walked she felt a slow knitting together of the fractured parts of her soul. I am healing, she would think, I am getting stronger, stronger and stronger and very very interior. It was a quiet unseen process but she felt it, it gathered like a force in her, concentrated and attentive. On days like this she did not wish to talk. She would speak to a friend that called, or call one, and she would chat with shopkeepers, but she could not give in the talking, or take either. She could chat, she would not be engaged. Those times for her were times without words, waiting for a time with new words. Sometimes if she thought she might be recognized in Rome and felt the need for a walk she would take a bus, staring out like an invisible observer, an uncrowded bus swirling through Rome's streets at midnight, it made her feel like the Flying Dutchman, circling the world from some unseen perspective. Then she smiled. It never lasted more than one or two days. But it required that she be alone. Her sanity was dependent on it, and that was sometimes a perilous thing. In two days she would go to Malta.

She suddenly realized the time and went upstairs to review her portfolios. By tomorrow she must have her argument and her position clear. Mr. Dilani was due, and that would require that she spring like a tiger.

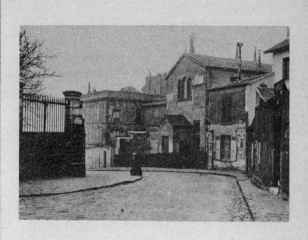

## 3

"What are those you have there?" Farthingdale asked Avian at breakfast.

"These? Photos. They just arrived in the mail."

"From where?"

"I don't know."

"From whom?"

"I don't know."

"They just arrived?"

"Yes."

"Addressed to whom?" Farthingdale furrowed his brow.

"To me," Avian said.

"To you, here at this address?"

"Yes," Avian said.

"But who could know? We signed in under a different name."

"I know," Avian said, a shadow forming on his face, "I know we did. But I found them this morning on my breakfast tray."

"Was it written or typed?"

"Typed," Avian said, tossing the envelope in Fathingdale's lap.

Farthingdale frowned, folded the envelope and looked at the pictures. "All nineteenth-century again," he murmured.

"Yes," Avian said, "and in each one, there's a face that you can't see."

Farthingdale remarked that he was going out.

"Oh," said Avian, "there's one other thing."

"Yes?" Farthingdale turned around. Avian handed him a photograph. "Oh," he said, "it's you."

"It's taken in front of the embassy in Seville," Avian said.

"I see," Farthingdale replied. "Were you there yesterday?"

"Of course not," Avian said.

Farthingdale put the photograph down on the table. "It's not a good likeness," he said. Then he went out, closing the door behind him.

Avian lay back on the bed, feeling one of the horrid, dreaded headaches that periodically assailed him, coming on. Oh God, he thought not one of those, and reached hastily into his valise for the pills.

The pills were missing.

---

Anna could not concentrate on the portfolios— some ancient feeling had swept in on her that day— and at such times the strongest experience she had was the ever present lustful all-encompassing wish for nonbeing. This was not the wish to die, but the wish to live, and yet, have the living done for you, the wish to simply be, to float, and observe, to experience dimly, from a distance, like a semicoma to swallow a wave and fall backwards beneath the sea, to float and dream, or not perhaps even dream, for it was the wish to have even the dreaming done for you and to float, simply float.

Simply float. Not to fly, as Santiago would have it, but to be sinking and be buoyed up, to be buoyed up by the sinking, to displace and surrender, to be engulfed and surrounded to be in the sea and of it, not on it, to be the surrounder and surrounded. To dwell. Yes, perhaps that was it, to dwell in the water. The enormity of this passivity alarmed her. In ways she could not understand she knew it had everything to do with being a woman, female, that passivity, she thought, and yet, it was a curious sexless state, a way of not feeling, and not being a woman. The point at which these understandings contradicted themselves was the point at which she gave up understanding them. That perhaps she thought was the point of the contradiction, for her to give up. That was of course what contradiction was: the surrender of meaning, the meaning being the release. No one ever solved a problem.

Somehow the wish not to solve it was simply overcome. She believed that, and turned then from sipping
her strawberry soda to the latest Batman comic, which
Santiago had procured for her. She loved to read the
Joker, opened the package of raspberry licorice Bacco
had brought from Cannes and in between panels of
the Joker wondered if Hegel had had an insight regarding the dialectic or it was really the dry run of a
hack novelist who believed that resolutions clarified
things. When she got bored with that, she strolled
around the yard and then called Santiago. When she
was bored, she got hungry for him.

---

"The murderer is working on your mind, Avian,"
Farthingdale said at dinner that evening.

"And he's succeeding." Avian pushed away his
plate. "I can't."

"It isn't you, Avian, you haven't murdered anybody," Farthingdale said simply. "He just wants you
to." He stopped seeing that his companion's fists were
clenched so tightly the knuckles were turning white,
and the veins in his forehead were thick.

"My pills were taken from my suitcase," Avian
said.

"Perhaps you mislaid them."

"No. But I looked for them. And I found them."

"Where?"

"In your valise."

Farthingdale, startled, took a sip of water. "What
prompted you to look there?"

"I don't know," Avian said. He clenched the water
glass so tightly it broke in his hand cutting his palm.
He wrapped a napkin like a tourniquet and excused
himself.

"I'll see you at the hotel," he said softly.

Farthingdale nodded, sat back and ordered a cognac.
It was going to be more troublesome than he originally
suspected.

Santiago rode over her slowly, softly, the sweet resilience of his balls caressing her, the soft fullness of his balls and cock surrounding her covering her, she rose to a sweet exhaltation and then, then only would he slide back, slide down and back his wet cock over her clitoris, the folds, a long, slow slide back and down he would make until he got to the edge of her vagina and then slowly, oh so slowly, it seemed to her he would take hours tooling his way into her until he reached the very heart of her, which beat fiercely and gently like the pulse of a small bird, and then the release—the soft feathery flight and yet she would not let him go, needed him to lie there inside her, feeling the small constrictions of him, until finally he would drop out. Anna was always amazed after being in bed with Santiago. It was full of a sweet slow pleasure, and yet it was over quickly and she was startled. It was not like Plato where in the heat of her exhaustion and at the peak of her pleasure she felt full of savage destruction, a destruction she wished to go on forever, she wanted to come forever then, with Santiago it peaked it rose, it floated, exploded and was over. Afterwards she would find herself looking at him and thinking that she felt as if she had just awakened.

---

"You received some additional photographs in the mail this morning," Fathingdale said to Avian, and he slipped one across the table.

"Oh," Avian said, "it's a lovely one. Henri Lartigue, I know it well and love it."

Farthingdale said nothing.

"Where was it postmarked?"

"Rome," Farthingdale said.

"What do you make of it?"

"I don't know. The woman has an x on her dress. I presume that means she's marked in some way."

"Marked? How? This photograph was taken in

nineteen eight. Even if this woman was twenty then there'd be scant chance . . ." he paused. "Lady Covington?"

Farthingdale nodded. "Perhaps."

"What on earth do you suppose he means?"

Farthingdale shrugged. "He's making it difficult for us, that's all I know."

"I think I have to see Anna again," Avian replied.

"About what?" said Farthingdale.

"Oh, just a hunch about Plato."

"Yes well," Farthingdale said, "I've got a hunch or two myself—one that requires I check out a World War Two agent by the name of Snow."

"Snow?" Avian asked with some astonishment.

"Yes. He's alive and well, and if my information is

correct, living in Iran. I thought he might give me some information about Quim and Bun."

"I see," Avian said, "and anyone else?"

"Did you really think he was dead?" Farthingdale asked.

"Yes. When are you going?"

"Later this week. This morning I'm going to the Libyan official's apartment—are you coming?"

"Yes," Avian said, "wait for me downstairs. I'll be along in a minute."

Farthingdale excused himself and Avian remained quietly staring at the photograph.

DOCUMENT #15

**The Rosedale Manuscript: Classification and Analysis War Office. Department 008.**
Certain problems arose in late 1942 in connection with SNOW. Late that year it was arranged that SNOW should go to Amsterdam to meet General Green and that he should take QUIM with him. The purpose of this arrangement was that 1) QUIM could therefore report on SNOW's position abroad, as well as 2) on the German espionage system in the Netherlands, and 3) then if possible enter Germany, penetrate the GERMAN SERVICE and bring back what information she could.

The specific details of QUIM's assignment are coded into Chapter 14 of The Rosedale Manuscript under the key word BUN.

What exactly transpired in this strange affair will forever remain unknown. We know that SNOW arrived in Amsterdam first, where he was flatly accused by General Green of a double-cross. As he later admitted, SNOW then proceeded, in the hopes of saving himself, to turn over the transcription of his wireless message to us. According to

QUIM's account, upon her arrival SNOW failed to mention any of this activity. Consequently when she finally entered Germany, she was subjected to a month of intensive interrogation which by virtue of her brilliance, she survived. Several months later SNOW and QUIM returned to this country carrying new sabotage material in the form of fountain pens filled with detonators, and the sum of four hundred thousand dollars. This was a totally puzzling turn of events to this office. Several questions remain unanswered. Did something pass between QUIM and SNOW that remains forever untold? If SNOW had in effect told the Germans everything, why was QUIM not executed on the spot? This meant that possibly QUIM had gone over to the enemy, something which considering her special personal history, we knew to be extremely unlikely. And what of the $400,000? If SNOW had, as he claimed, been "rumbled," why did he not warn QUIM before she entered Germany? SNOW incidentally claimed that he did warn QUIM but she took no notice of it as she became, to use his phrase, "enamoured" of a German officer.

The exact details of what transpired between QUIM and SNOW on this particular mission remains a mystery.

"Have you spoken to Victor?" Santiago asked her the next morning.

"He doesn't answer the phone."

"That means he's writing."

"So he doesn't answer the phone?"

"Well, he's in the bathtub."

"The bath? You mean he writes in the bath?"

"Oh," Anna said, daintily drying her foot, "I thought

you knew. Victor can only write when everything but his head is under water."

"That's a little difficult, isn't it," Santiago said, "considering the composition of paper?"

"Oh, the paper's not in the water, silly," Anna said. "He's got a table over the tub. I guess he keeps his arms free." She bent over, busily rubbing some cologne into the flesh around her toenails. Santiago lay back on the bed smoking, watching her curiously. He noticed that Anna did not take baths the way she used to, as something to get over quickly, but now she anointed herself slowly. He'd asked her once about this and she had said, "The ancients had a point, you know, with all that anointing with oil. Showers are the death of civilization. This way you remind yourself you have a body. You touch it constantly. You touch your own body."

"You seem preoccupied with that," Santiago said.

"I am a courtesan, what do you expect?" Anna thought, lying back in the tub. "I think only that I am a person lying in the tub, there is the shower curtain, there is a towel, this is a tub full of water and I am a person in the tub, but what I am thinking what I am experiencing has nothing to do with the idea of a shower curtain, or a towel, or a tub full of water."

She had said this and Santiago had replied, "Or that you are a person."

Anna found these conversations difficult. She pinned up her hair once again and, brushing some salve across her lips, walked quickly to her closet. She had to meet Dilani in an hour.

# 4

"Maybe nobody did it," Farthingdale said of the Libyan customs inspector.

"What do you mean nobody?" Avian said, peeved. "If nobody did it, he wouldn't be dead, there wouldn't be a murder if nobody did it, or a pistol or a manuscript."

"He could have just died," Farthingdale said.

"Just died?" Avian was fuming now. "Just died with ten pistol shots in the chest and back from this gun, his neck and legs tied together? Just died. Really I wonder where I found you sometimes."

"I think that was done later, after he was dead," said Farthingdale. "I think he had a heart attack."

No one said anything for some time."

Avian turned to one of Martinelli's lieutenants. "Did the autopsy look for a heart attack?"

The policeman looked confused. "I don't know."

Avian turned and said, "Find out," and went down the stairs. I caught up with him outside.

"What are you doing here?" he asked.

"I'm very curious about murders," I said. "Now whatever gave Farthingdale such an idea?" I said.

Avian shrugged. "I should have known. Whenever he says anything genuinely preposterous, that kind of thing happens. His most ridiculous comments are inevitably his truest."

I cornered Farthingdale later at the corner drugstore eating homemade spumoni.

"How did you know?" I said.

He shrugged. "Sometimes I just know."

"But how? Aren't you curious as to what in the room gave you the clue? Something tipped you off."

"Of course," Farthingdale smiled. "I found a vial of Dilantin in the medicine chest. If you're going to murder somebody it's rather peculiar to do it halfway in and halfway out of the bathroom. I mean there was no forced entry, the visitor wasn't a surprise. He was going to kill him of course, he just didn't act fast enough. Poor bastard had a heart attack on the way to the medicine chest."

"But you guessed," I insisted. "You weren't sure."

"One is never sure," said Farthingdale.

Avian walked back to the hotel and then dialed Anna. She was home and would be glad to talk to him about Plato, but she had a brief engagement and could he come in an hour?

He agreed.

_____

"You are quite late in your payments, Mr. Dilani," Anna said rather coolly.

"Quite so, I realize," Mr. Dilani said, "but as you know I have several ships that have all met with mysterious disasters."

"Yes," she said, crossing the room and taking a seat in a large armchair behind a desk, "perhaps it is a sign from God."

"What kind of sign?" Mr. Dilani said, nervous and alert.

"A sign that perhaps the import quotas on Iranian oil might be changed by trade regulations in the United States."

"I see," Mr. Dilani said, "blackmail. I thought it would be subtler than this, madame. Despite all your trapping of high culture, you are cheap and uncivilized."

"Uncivilized, yes, but not cheap," she said. "You must remember, Mr. Dilani, that civilized behavior is suitable only to civilization."

"I thought that was what I was a member of," he said dryly and was about to go on when she interrupted.

"I can't imagine how you support such illusions. I told you at the beginning, Mr. Dilani, that these transactions have nothing to do with civilization." She smiled at him in total condescension. "This is the oil business."

"If I don't use my influence," he said, "to make it easier for Iraq to dump their oil . . ."

"The authorities would find out how much you pay those who work your wells, not to mention your interests in Rhodesia. It wouldn't sit well for a member of the House of Lords . . ."

"Your methods disgust me."

"Good. They are your own. Perhaps it is a sign of progress."

Mr. Dilani picked up his hat and turned to go. He stopped in the doorway and stared at Anna. She was beautiful, but he found her ruthless and impossible. He couldn't understand, he'd never paid for a woman in his life and when he offered her a small fortune to spend the weekend with him, she turned him down.

"I don't like you, that's why," he remembered her saying. And now he didn't like her. Oil was a man's business. And so was billiards. He noticed the game room to his left. He had heard of her reputation at billiards; he was not inclined to believe it.

He nodded toward the room. "Billiards is a man's game," he said.

"I'm sure that's not true," Anna said. "I'm sure I play as well or better than any man."

That was precisely what he wanted. He would ruin her easily. "Let us play," he said.

Anna stood up and smiled. "I never play for less than twenty thousand dollars a ball," Anna said, "and in your condition . . ."

"You are the best in Europe, I have heard," he said.

She nodded. He nodded too. "And I am the best in the world," he said.

"So I've heard," she said softly.

"Billiards," he said, "a million dollars a ball."

"How could you pay me?"

"Call your attorney. We will play for the four wells."

"I'll call my attorney, Mr. Dilani," she said, loving the idea of wiping him out, "My place or yours?"

"My place," Mr. Dilani said, "at six."

"Have all the papers," Anna said, not looking up as she rang for a servant to show him to the door, "and don't worry about me, I bring my own chalk and cue stick."

---

"Plato is many things to many people, Mr. Braine, but to me he is a pimp. That is, he is a pimp who works for me. Procuror I believe might be a more accurate phrase, although less colorful," Anna smiled.

"Someone told me he has a long and disgusting history."

"Yes. His brother Armand is one of Europe's most trusted political murderers. Very adept at the training of assassins. It's been a family business. From Sarajevo on down they are responsible for most of Europe's political murders. They disgust me," Anna said, her eyes full of the green light they got when she became furious. "Terrorists and assassins, who would shoot a man in the back in the name of liberty."

"But a tyrant, Anna," Lola interrupted. "The only way to overthrow tyranny is through terrorism and assassination." Lola bit daintily on some stuffed celery as she said this, catching the long strands between the very tips of her teeth.

"Tyrant? Who is the tyrant? Anyone who shoots a man in the back. Tyrants and cowards at once. Those terrorists who shoot civilians in the name of freedom, who bomb homes in the name of liberty, who decide on human sacrifice for political ends. Who believe that politics and freedom can finally coexist in some ideal state. They are infants. Dangerous infants. I hate them. I will do whatever I must to extinguish them."

"Why do you tolerate Plato then," Lola said.

Anna shrugged. "He gives information that may be useful someday."

"Why do you say things like that," Lola said to her, suddenly looking around at Avian, "when you know that all of Rome whispers that you may be a spy?"

"So they will continue to think so."

"Isn't that dangerous? You might get assassinated yourself."

"I might and I might not." Anna shrugged. "You worry too much."

Lola left then and Anna said to Avian, "I don't know why Plato should be of any interest to you. Plato is stupid, ultimately; irritatingly stupid."

"Why do you put up with him?"

"He has the biggest, blackest prick on God's earth," Anna said.

"There must be other things a woman of your cultivation needs, sensitivity, an exacting mind," Avian said.

"Sometimes you need other things," Anna said, "but most of the time when I need, I need the biggest, blackest prick on God's earth."

"And he gives it to you?"

"Not gives exactly."

"What exactly?"

"He forces me."

"If you want him, why does he force you?"

"I don't want him," Anna said, "but something in me wants him, the minute he touches me . . . He rams me, bangs me, and then he stuffs it down my throat so I gag."

"It doesn't sound appealing."

"Oh, it isn't," Anna said. "It's forceful all the way, but I scream, I lose my breath as well as my mind, he bites my nipple and I scream so all of Rome can hear me, I scream when he bites my lip, I scream when he puts that thing in me and comes three times in a half-hour until he can't get in I'm so full of his jelly."

"And then what happens?"

"I can't get enough. I told you I need psychiatric

help. Three times with that damn flagpole and I'm just getting started."

"How long has this been going on?"

"With Plato? Since I was nine."

"Always with Plato?"

"Except once," Anna said, looking at him carefully. "I tried it once after he'd fucked my brains out in a barn I was ready to explode, he just couldn't fill me, and I ran out and got a horse and wound my legs around that horse and fucked the blazes out of a stallion."

"Wouldn't a stallion be too large?"

"It was fantastic," Anna said, gazing at him directly, her eyes luminous. She was impressed with his composure. "He was ten times the size of Plato, so of course he split me."

"Is that what finally stopped you?"

"The split? Yes, it hurt, but I always need to hurt." She watched him carefully, very composed indeed. And then she said, "I'm the kind of woman who needs to be busted open." And then, in not a very different tone, she said, "Would you care to stay for dinner?"

"I would like to, but I have one or two things to do."

"Come back then," she said slyly, and so he agreed. But first of all he was going straight to Lola's.

It was clear to Avian that Anna was trying very hard to shock him. He did not know how much to believe about what she felt about Plato and was suspicious of asking her anything else. She would guess he would ask Lola the same questions of course, but he thought there was something to be learned anyway. And as he drove toward Lola's apartment he hoped seriously that his suspicions were confirmed.

He had arranged to meet Lola before he went to see Anna and she had only grudgingly agreed to see him. So he was surprised that she seemed so cordial when she greeted him at the door. These women, he thought, noting her dress, a sheer mauve gauze that went magnificently with her red hair, were endlessly provocative. She invited him in, asked him to sit down, and went straight to the point.

"You've been to see Anna about Plato, she told you incredible stories, and now you've come by to corroborate." She took a sip of her drink, a drag on her cigarette and said, "She and Plato are absolutely mad. Probably a lot of what she said was true," and then she smiled, "and a lot wasn't."

"Have you ever slept with him?"

"Several times. Anna doesn't know."

"Is there anything special about him?"

"Yes, there is a lot special. For one thing, he is very tender."

Avian watched her face closely to see if this were some sort of joke. It wasn't.

"Physically speaking, is there anything special about him?"

"He's beautiful," her eyes shone, "an absolutely perfect body, large forearms, a very large chest."

"Anything else?"

"What *else* do you mean?"

Avian hesitated. "His penis, is it notable in any way?"

"His penis?" Lola seemed surprised. "Well, it's a terrific penis, just fine."

"And extraordinarily large?"

"Large?" Lola said her eyes opening wide. "I wouldn't say especially so, it's a normal average member."

"I see," Avian said.

"Mr. Braine, don't listen to Anna about Plato. I mean, she needs him sexually but she doesn't see him or understand what he is at all. I suppose she told you he was black."

"Yes," Avian said startled. "Isn't he?"

"Perhaps," Lola shrugged, "and perhaps not."

"Don't play games," Avian said annoyed.

"That's all I know how to play," Lola said turning to him, "you ought to be grateful I'm willing to play anything at all. In any event, you ought to know Plato loves driving her crazy." Lola looked strange. "He really does, you know. I mean with me, we have a good time, but them, they lose their minds in bed, takes them *hours*," Lola was quick then, "but that's all, they don't give a damn about each other, or know each other, or anything, they've been going on for years and they know nothing of each other. They're just fucking machines."

"Machines don't lose their minds in bed," Avian said quietly.

"No, I suppose not," Lola said. "I don't know what you will ever find out about Anna. I've known her forever and I see nothing but parts that don't fit together. She seems crazy and sane, independent and seducible all at the same time." She turned to him. "Of course you know about Anna and me."

"I have heard," Avian said.

"It isn't anything I do," he was surprised to hear Lola add quickly, "I don't wield the power over her, she gives it to me, when someone gives it to you, how can you not use it?" She looked at him, with a surprising vulnerability then, something he did not expect to see in her beautiful but nonetheless guarded face.

"Well," Avian said, getting up, "I think I've gotten everything I need for the moment."

"You'll be back," Lola said, walking him to the door, "you'll go crazy trying to piece this all together."

"I suppose," Avian said.

Lola held his hat in her hands turning it round and round, examining the brim. "Oh, you wear nine and three-quarters," she said suddenly. "What a coincidence."

Avian felt his body grow rigid. "In what sense," he said, turning slowly toward her.

"So does Plato," she said, "It's an unusual size, a

rather large size even for a man." She handed him the hat. He could read nothing in her eyes. He walked out the door and slowly down the stairs. An odd coincidence, he thought. How very odd indeed.

They began with a fine, light red wine, which Anna explained was "a Mouton, I prefer it actually to a Lafitte, at least to begin a meal with. They have never awarded it a Grand Cru but that is due to the traditional politics of France. It is the first of the second growths, technically, but equal to the first in quality, many times of the year. In any event, I adore Phillipe Rothschild, and Ellie too, but you can't drink Lafitte every day, after all."

"How well do you know Monsieur Rothschild?" Avian asked.

"We've met several times," Anna said. "I was seriously considering buying his vineyard, at one time."

He noticed that at his place and all along the table as centerpieces were small jeweled animals. He thought he recognized them.

"Are these Fabergé?" he inquired.

"Yes," Anna replied. "Aren't they amusing? And lovely?"

"And expensive."

"Yes, I have acquired expensive taste. Well, after all, one doesn't have to live cheaply on nine million dollars a year."

"That's quite obvious," Avian said. "A rather expensive collection of art for a courtesan, if that is in fact what you are."

He was served a cold soup, he thought it the best avgolemeno soup he'd ever had.

"Bacco does most of the cooking," Anna said "although on his day off I have an excellent Chinese houseboy. I couldn't bear to eat Chinese food more than two days a week, and Bacco knows all the European cuisines so well. He's not bad even for one or two Indian things." She sipped her wine and glanced coolly at Avian on the opposite side of the table. He couldn't figure out what color her eyes were. He thought at first they were green, and now they looked purplish, almost violet.

"Your eyes seem to change color," he said finally.

"So people tell me," Anna smiled. "Would you prefer champagne instead of a sancerre with your cheese, Mr. Braine? I find it a refreshing change."

"A dry champagne would be lovely." Anna nodded to a servant. "Do you serve only French wines?" he asked her.

"Oh, no," Anna said, "just for this evening I chose French." She smiled at him, in what he was forced to regard as a totally captivating way. "I'm so delighted you could come to dinner, Mr. Braine. I've had a difficult day and needed some distraction. I'm having quite a time with my petroleum portfolio."

"Do you own a well?"

"Several. Two in Iraq, one in Syria, one in Lebanon, one in Egypt, and as of last night," she smiled, "I've acquired four more."

"Why on earth," Avian said, "do you take money for going to bed with men? Clearly you don't need it."

"I need it to maintain my sexual identity," she said, then quickly and more sharply, "sexual expertise is my profession, Mr. Braine. It is troublesome to require payment for it only if you think there's something basically dirty about money. Most people who think money is dirty think sex is dirty; not infrequently they are my clients. I am happy to report, however, that I do not suffer from that confusion. Money is money, and sex is sex, and I am expert at managing both."

"Nevertheless," Avian said, "the classic view is that a sexual encounter requires some portion of the soul."

"Soul? I don't believe in the soul. If you're talking about the emotional complexities of passion, I couldn't agree more. We don't know much about it. It doesn't present me with problems," she said looking up at him directly. "I don't make arrangements with a man if he isn't attractive to me in some way."

"There's been some talk about a German industrialist."

"Carl Werner? Why him? He's physically disgusting you think. I put that out of my mind. He has an extraordinary gift for finance. That made him interesting."

"That made him *sexually* interesting to you?" Avian asked in amazement.

"Why not?" Anna said smiling. "I tried to explain to you I am physically and psychologically adept at sexual arousal and pleasure, but for myself I am interested in making explorations of the mind."

"You talk in circles," Avian said, suddenly losing his appetite. He wished he did not feel so provoked by her himself.

"Circles are lovely shapes, you shouldn't be so prejudiced against them," she said playfully.

"They're not good shapes for thinking, my dear."

"Thinking follows the natural contours of one's body I've discovered, I'm sure yours is logical, powerful and at the moment, hard."

"And yours," Avian said ruefully, "of course is full of circles."

Anna smiled. "Bacco is making sole duglere. You'll like it. I tried to persuade him to make partridge, but he wasn't in the mood."

Avian seemed not to hear her. "Who are these men?" he asked.

"What men? My clients?"

"Yes . . . men of vast power and wealth, they can have all the women they want . . . you are beautiful," Avian said, "but why you?"

"Why not me?" Anna said. "I am beautiful. I have had the good luck to be something of a physiological freak. I am perfect. Some are curious about that."

"How perfect?" Avian said.

"Oh, things like distance between ankle bone and calf, length of thigh, waist indentation. My breasts are actually too large to be considered perfect, but actually they're large and perfect, and my teeth of course, I've never had a blemish, never had a cavity, and my hair," she pulled at it, "naturally shining and full of bounce." She shrugged. "Face it, I'm perfect."

"You are perfect," Avian said.

"So some are curious, but most you know want a special kind of sexual excitement. Their mistresses require an emotional involvement, like it or not, and eventually this seems to get in the way with most people. With me they sign contracts, and it's different."

"Contracts?"

"Yes, for the more expensive ones. For smaller campaigns, I use the major credit cards," Anna said and rang the bell for the servant, who appeared immediately and silently began to clear.

"You seem too perfect to be true," Avian said wryly as he sipped a cognac.

"My clients think so. I can talk about anything from art to wine to football to cars to finance. I can pretend I'm dumb if I sense they need that, I can overpower them if they need that. I can seduce them if they need that."

"Anything to please."

"I'm not pleasing them," Anna snapped, "I'm doing my job."

"Which is pleasing men."

"I'm paid for it."

"That's different?"

Anna smiled. "That's very different. I have simply made a profession," she leaned across the table emphasizing her words, "I make *money* doing what women do by instinct—catering totally to the wishes of men."

"But the *money*, isn't it . . ." Avian hesitated.

"What?"

"Degrading?"

"Money degrading?" Anna's eyes opened wide. "You must remember, Mr. Braine, just because the pound has been devalued does not mean the currency in general has been maligned." She got up and walked toward the door. Avian hesitated a moment, then followed her.

"I hope you don't have any primitive capitalistic hang-ups about money," she said, "predicated on the assumption of a nineteenth-century sweatshop. We shall never get along if you do. You know I quite agree with Mr. Shaw that the only people you can trust are selfish people."

"Are you?" he said, paying careful attention as he walked slowly down the halls with her.

"Usually," she said, turning toward the marbled hall that led to the library.

"You are perfect and you are liberated, so," Avian said, opening the door to the library for her, "you must be happy as well."

"I prefer not to discuss happiness," she said, and turned on the record player. "You'll have to excuse me, Mr. Braine," she said checking her watch, "I have three or four calls I must make within the next hour. This is an excellent library. I'm sure you can find something to interest you." She drifted out the door then. Avian was sure she was up to something quite different from phone calls, and when he saw her turn down the end of the hall he decided, quite spontaneously, to track down Bacco in the kitchen. It was a fortunate time for Avian in that Bacco became terribly loquacious when chopping parsley, and when Avian wandered into the kitchen, he happened to catch Bacco furiously preparing parsley for a *vitello al tonno* he was preparing for the next day. Avian thought that there was an extraordinary amount of parsley being chopped and Bacco explained that it was the one stage of the cooking process where he got completely carried away. In between Bacco's enthusiastic lectures on the nature of the veal and the tuna he was using, Avian was able to elicit some information about Anna.

"Anna loves Lola," Bacco said.

"And you, do you love Lola?"

"No," the little priest said, quickly sautéeing some garlic, "Lola gets anything she wants."

"Doesn't Anna?"

"Anna doesn't want anything, or rather she wants absolutely everything and absolutely nothing, but she goes after it, most of the time not so much because she wants it as because she's afraid not to have it. Here, taste this," he said, sticking a coated index finger in Avian's face.

Avian did. "A bit bitter," he said, "it needs something."

"Yes, so glad you agree. That was quite what I thought." Bacco stood for a moment, one hand on his hip in total concentration.

At that moment Anna came in through the door. "Mr. Braine," she said in a surprised tone, "there's a call for you."

Avian turned. "No one knows I'm here."

"Someone does," she said. "You can take it in the library."

Avian set down his glass and excused himself. As he walked toward the library he had the uneasy feeling that she must have set this up for him. He opened the door cautiously, saw the phone off the hook and picked it up.

"Hello, this is a person-to-person call, is this Avian Braine speaking?" The voice was metallic.

"Yes," he said. "Who is this?"

"This is a recorded message from the murderer, i.e., the killer, the voice has been put through a computer so you are not hearing my voice, but the computer's voice over my words. On April eighteenth,

October eighteenth and November third, three murders were committed in the year eighteen ninety-eight. I suggest you check out the source, balance it against *Das Kapital*, find the underlying structure of Either/Or, and you may save a life in Córdoba. You have two weeks." And then unexpectedly, "Cheerio."

"Who was it?" Anna asked when he hung up.

"The murderer," Avian said, turning to her.

"Oh," she said, "What did he say?"

"He said 'cheerio.'"

Anna stood and crossed to the French windows. A breeze lifted the curtains, exposing the gold petals of the sunflowers outside the door. She smiled, clapped her hands and called for Irene. The cat jumped into her arms and Anna bent her head down into the cat's soft belly, listening.

"I thought the cat went to bed earlier than this," Avian said.

"When there's company, she stays up later," Anna said, settling down comfortably with her.

"I see." Avian glanced around the library. The number of Impressionist paintings he noticed was extraordinary. "You have a special interest in Impressionism?"

"Yes," Anna said "a very special interest."

"So many were confiscated by the Nazis."

"Yes, I know."

Anna looked at him. He felt the time had come to leave. "Well, I must be going now, I thank you for a lovely dinner."

"You must come again," she said, moving ahead of him through the doorway to the hall. He watched her silk form swaying around him across the black and white marble tiles on the floor. At the door he turned to her and said, "I learned a great deal."

"No more than I intended," Anna said. She smiled. He tipped his hat and they said good night.

Anna felt desolate after he left. When she wasn't distracted these days, she was gloomy and brooding. And yet she had been unaware of it. Bacco had to *tell* her that she was in a severe depression. She knew her birthday was coming. Perhaps that was it. Bacco had to explain to everyone that there could be no celebration. She knew no one understood her on this, that she could not celebrate being born. The fact of the matter was even on her best days, she found it no cause for celebration. There was no pleasure in it yet for her, no real deep abiding pleasure. She did not wish to die; it was not that. But given the choice of coming alive or never knowing it, she would choose never knowing it. There was no question about it to her. Life was the one thing that was more trouble than it was worth. Intellectually she supposed her attitude about this horrified her. But what could she do? She shared none of the currently popular notions of suicide—as some romantic choice of the will over the life force. A lot of crap. Suicide was violent; fury going the wrong way. She envied that part of it. Her attitude toward life was essentially deader than that: whether one lived or not didn't really much matter, she just didn't want to truck with it.

Some days, walking along the beach, full of mood and tensions, she would kick the sand, feeling the hard packed ridges ride up through the muscles in her legs along her thigh. Her thighs were like granite; shaped like a woman's they were as steely as a man's. "I'm getting musclebound," she thought. Then she sat down and stared at the sea. Why did she hate to live so much? What was it that she resisted so that Bacco said she had to be dragged, kicking and screaming into life. Why? What was it? She lay back, remembering a day when she was twenty, so full of life she sprang from her bed and raced a mile through the damp, fresh, fragrant morning, through the trees and past the fields and houses, jumping the small brook and racing panting up the enormous hill, the cold air in the back of her throat, the smell of the new day like a taste on her tongue, the beginning of the sun coming through the morning clouds, it was all a glorious moment of heat and light and power, the power in her body as she sprang up the hill, the excitement of her own physical well-being, the thrill and exuberance of being alive.

Then something happened. She never felt it again. Something terrible happened to her in her twentieth year. The fat man in the white suit with a letter. Everything that had been strength, and light and yearning turned to its opposite—weakness, despair, and impotence. Like a sadistic operation that trimmed off only the nerve endings, she lost her capacity to feel pain and pleasure and began a long slow torturous process of turning to stone, and like a once-resilient tree with a million years condensed into days, by the time a year had passed she felt she was solid, petrified wood.

She wandered then out through the garden to the sea. She was perplexed—some days her feelings changed—but at the thought of her birthday she became very distressed. She walked along the beach—out toward the promontory. Silverstein, she knew, was out there, waiting for her. Then, as she sat on the high white cliffs, staring out to the sea, she wept. It was an old familiar weeping, it was not the kind of crying that racked her with pain; she had known that too, and there was a kind of relief in that, a relief even in feeling the pain. But this crying, this slow slipping of the tears down her cheeks was surrender. The tears of defeat, of knowing that no matter how she examined, how she endeavored, how she strove, how she tried, all of those experiences allied to effort or will would finally be of no avail to her. It was as if it were up to the grace of God, and God had not decreed it. She smiled at her own metaphor, even when I'm telling the truth I'm lying she thought. No, she could not believe in God, nor his grace, but she was finally a harsh if reluctant determinist, things were as they were, a person was what he was, and what she wished more than anything, and what she knew was so impossible was that she could not expunge her own outlook from her soul. And that was what was required. She looked at the small ships moving across the horizon. She would never win this battle. Something had been stolen from her, some gift for being had been taken, and she would never have it again. Some arch betrayal had seized her instead. In these moments she was up against herself, an adversary that denied her pleasure and feeling in life, that turned only bitterness and envy and smallness and deadness into her path. She thought sometimes she could turn it back but she was resigned now. The stink of nihilism, like some ether, was invading her soul, and try as she might, she knew how puny indeed was her valor, for the ether would paralyze her, offering only moments to wake from it, which she could resist feebly while it worked its way into the very fiber of her being, distilling putrefaction and defeat, rotting her to the core.

It was a relief to think that tomorrow they would commit the robbery.

"Did you know, by the way," I said to Santiago as we drove to the beach, "that Silverstein had dealings with Friar Bacco?"

Santiago slowed the car. "No, of course not. That warty little priest?"

"The very one. And you ought to be careful calling him a warty little priest. She absolutely dotes on him. They go everywhere together."

"Don't remind me. I can smell the odor of his garlic breath every time I walk into one of the rooms in her house that he has just left. He's always around, the gardener, the cook, the chauffeur, the doctor, God knows there is nothing he can't do."

"Yes, well I thought that Silverstein thing odd."

"How do you know?"

"I noticed, it was just by accident really, that there was a ring in his ring case, you know, with a seal on it, that read *Ex Libris*, a red seal."

"Yes?"

"Well, that's the same ring that Bacco wears. It signified his order, he told me."

"The famous order that no one can seem to find."

"Oh, I did find it. There are four of them in some collapsing old grain mill north of Florence."

"Are they Catholics?"

"No, they're drunkards. No one seems to know what they are. They're offshoots of an offshoot. Since there are only four priests in the order, and they are all over sixty-five, the Vatican isn't going to worry I suppose since the order won't be in existence much longer."

"Did you ask Silverstein about it?"

"Yes, and he said that he'd picked it up from a dealer in Rome, some graverobber type I gather, and it is true that one of the friars in the order did die some months ago."

"So it sounds quite plausible," Santiago said.

"Except it sounds like a coincidence."

"And you don't believe in coincidences?"

"Not really," I said. "Do you?"

"I believe in love," Santiago said, stopping the car and leaning over to me. He was about to kiss me when suddenly he reached over and unlatched the door and shoved me out, and we rolled interlocked down an immense hill, which was soft with sand, and some occasional sea grasses, all the way to the sea.

"We've left the sandwiches in the car," I said, annoyed, at the bottom, "and I'm full of sand. Really, your impulses," but Santiago was not listening he was still on top of me very still and looking straight toward the hills.

"What's the matter?" I said, suddenly sensing that he was frightened.

"That," he said pointing and as I raised my head and turned to look I saw running in silhouette along the top of the ridge a figure in a hat carrying what seemed to be a longrange rifle. In a minute it was out of sight.

When we returned to the car there were two bullet holes that had smashed the windshield.

We found the bullets and Santiago put them in his pocket.

"Who and why?" I said. "I never heard a sound, did you?"

"I sensed it. It was uncanny," Santiago said, "I just sensed it."

It was not until later that evening that he admitted to me that he had been shot at twice in the last three weeks.

"So," I said, "they know who you are."

Santiago shrugged. "Someone knows."

"Perhaps we should pay a visit to Harcourt," I said.

"Perhaps."

All of Rome was talking about the robbery. It seemed it had been quite wonderful and dramatic, the girls escaped on white Lippizaner stallions, and as they rode they threw their clothes into the street until they were naked and then jumped off the horses, running naked into a huge balloon, stationed in a field, which had a piano player playing honkytonk piano in it. And as soon as they climbed in they cast off into the sky, waving to everyone below, the music from the piano floating off into the clouds. Everyone agreed it was all quite magical, and very well done and all of Rome saw it because the robbers had thoughtfully sent a videotape of the entire event to every TV station in the country. Avian, who did not watch TV, did not see it and was at this moment down discussing the matter with the local bank manager:

"Anna, Lila, Lola and Elaine, to the tune of 'Mairzy Doats.'"

"They sang that?" Avian asked disbelievingly.

"Yes, sang it, sang it, damn it, sang a song in my bank, the four of them, wearing net stockings and platform shoes, red silk garters and pearl-handled revolvers, picture hats with flowered veils and short skirts that barely covered them, indecent," Ricardo said, "it was close to being a night club act."

"What else?" said Avian.

"They wore red taffeta slips that rustled under their skirts and velvet bows on their platform shoes, they wore white silk blouses the décolletage my God, they were gorgeous, simply gorgeous," Ricardo wrung his hands, "the dirty little bitches, and they shot my dog."

He burst into tears, and everyone looked away.

"Why his dog?" Farthingdale said later, "a pointless cruel senseless sadistic thing."

"He was nipping at my heels," Lola said, "I didn't want to trip and tear my stockings." She pouted.

"You're a fool," Anna said, "and a pain in the ass and an amoralist, none of which I find either interesting or useful. That's not why you shot the dog."

"Okay, okay." Lola got up from the couch and went to pour herself a drink. The bright red lipstick matched the color of paint on her fingernails. The bangles circling her arm gleamed in the late afternoon light.

"Okay," she said, stretching her long silky legs back on the couch, propping a pillow behind her long gold red hair, "that isn't why. You know damn well why, Anna," she smiled brightly. "A dog is a dog and he got in my way. Besides I just felt like shooting something."

"You always shoot things that get in your way," Anna said disgusted by Lola, by her enchantment with her.

"Don't be stupid," Lola said, "I'm not a murderer. A dog is a dog." She took a long sip, her throat working in long waves, framed like a serpent in its undulations as Lola drank, and the sun went down its russet shadows playing in the tall windows behind her.

Anna turned on the TV set. The film of the robbery looked rather good.

Everyone in Rome was willing to think it all a marvelous entertaining game, except for the dog.

"Lola would fuck it up," Anna thought nervously.

"Are you really going to donate the money to Save the Children Federation?" Lola asked Anna.

"Well, do you have a better idea?"

"It sounds too close to a moral gesture to be genuinely appealing," Lola said, "but no, I don't have a better idea."

I said I was disgusted by moral issues and suggested we smoke opium for a while. The air was cool and dense and I enjoyed it. Only Anna was seriously concerned with becoming addicted. It seems that Ezra Han, her Japanese friend, had frightened her by telling her that opium addiction was inevitable—he'd been addicted for seven years.

It was about four o'clock in the morning when I saw Anna get up and leave the house. She had not smoked very much, if anything. I knew she went hunting for Santiago. I did not think much about it, since I was in a dreamlike state myself, until the next day. I was to meet Plato, he said he had important information for me, and so at three o'clock I went to the appointed place. I hesitated because there was a man in a bowler hat standing on the corner. He approached me wordlessly as I stood there and wordlessly handed me a package. I opened it. It was a large white clock. I waited. The clock chimed. Plato did not arrive.

---

Anna liked to awaken next to Santiago, soft, silky skin slow waiting. Anna liked to awaken feeling hot, the slow warmth, then the slow sucking in of him next to her, he was soft and fleshy, dense and smooth, then hard inside her, plumbing.

Anna's eyes were plump and green today and misted over, yet with something azure just beneath the mist, like a blue olive. Perhaps she was sad, I thought, for we were going to see Lola's boyfriend, Caldwell, for the express purpose of flushing him out. Anna wanted to know his political connections more exactly she told me, as she felt Victor was in danger from both Lola and Caldwell. She also told me she thought Caldwell was responsible for the murder in Seville. I for one thought this spy business all rather silly. Murder was one thing, that was always interesting. Spies, of course, were colorful, and they had their uses. I had often been intrigued myself with the idea of totally purposeless murders, with an allegedly high degree of motivation. Agents, particularly double ones, would be especially good as victims for this purpose. And I was intrigued with finding out who agents really were. It was always true that spies, detectives, secret inquirers of all kinds were always revealing themselves as they sought to expose their enemies. It is impossible to discover the real and original purpose of anything so complex as murder—which is always assassination, always a political act, a terrorism of the soul, always ideological in the sense of a desperate thrust against an insurmountable power. A purposeless murder, certainly, would keep everyone infinitely guessing, and misled by their own justifications for it. Of course, I only thought about such things, I was not given to violent acts.

---

"Tell me," Anna said, her voice cool and dry as we walked over the cobblestones, "which is it you meditate on, Mr. Caldwell, your penis or your navel?" The remark was quick and clearly left its mark. Caldwell has done too much bragging of his philosophical concerns.

Caldwell surprised us when he replied after some time, "Neither. I study my back through the reflections in the mirror."

"Oh," Santiago said, picking up Anna's mock seriousness, "you think it is the spinal column that will liberate us?"

"No," Caldwell said, "the back. You see, Santiago, that is the difference between us. We stare at the same space; you are concerned with the message transmitted, I am concerned with the weight it will bear."

Anna winked when we reached the restaurant and deftly shuffling the cards she always kept with her and lining up the chips, she ordered her drink and then said, "I'm told you cheat at cards, Mr. Caldwell, do you think you can cheat me?"

"That depends," Caldwell said, taking out a fine Cuban cigar, "on who has the more accomplished systems. You deal."

It was at that moment that it first occurred to me that Caldwell might be the killer.

After Anna had won several hands of poker, we turned to the business of food. Perhaps that prompted the philosophical discussion, I do not know, I only know I had never expected Anna to get into a conversation regarding the endless body and mind controversy. I knew that when she and I had discussed it she told me that she had thought that when she left the room, the chairs and table remained, she had never bought the Berkeleian argument, but that now she was convinced they disappeared. We discussed it one afternoon and had concluded it definitely revealed an increase in ego. It was odd therefore to listen to her discussion with Caldwell now.

"Do you mean to tell me," Caldwell was saying, "that you do not think the mind is within the body?"

"No," Anna said, "of course not. It floats before our eyes; that which we see, that is our mind."

"That is a function of the mind, but the brain is the mind."

"The brain is the receptor for the mind," Anna said.

"What is it like, this mind," Caldwell asked impatiently. "Can you describe it?"

"Yes," Anna said, "it is like a placenta. It feeds and is fed but belongs to neither party, and is discarded upon death being of no use to anybody."

"You mean," Caldwell said nervously; "discarded upon birth."

"Birth, death, whatever," Anna said, "I shall have to think about it. For some of us in many ways those events are remarkably similar." Anna stared at Caldwell for some time, studying the lean, planed face. He was not adept at philosophy she felt sure. Nor was she for that matter. Her feelings did not subscribe to any school. For actually, Anna knew if she were really going to be honest, she thought the mind was in the belly. There was no questioning that in her reflective moments, in her attempt to capture the authenticity of a present, or her feelings about herself, in her attempts to capture herself, so to speak, that fleeting ghost and hold it fast, she had to go the way of yoga, down and back and into her center, but past and below her solar plexus, past the breathing center, to some masticating continuance, some undulation, some peristaltic place where things ruminated and were rethought, and constantly modified, and it was back, a mood, back and down, never forward and up, back and down and withdrawal, a kind of turning around in a tunnel or a slow backing down, like regaining speech by having one's tongue unfasten and slide slowly back and down, down. Sometimes she thought of her own belly, perhaps it was a womb, perhaps it was the visceral space between, slung in some vacant spot in her own torso that she played. Her childhood seemed contained there; a lonely place, that childhood, but one that forced its own amusements, with blocks and letters and singing to herself, an infant nearing two who roamed freely now through Anna's body, Anna's own body the labyrinth, not of spirit, but of mind, body, mind, all one in Anna.

Anna set down her glass. "I don't feel well," she said, thinking, It's like being pregnant with oneself.

---

It was clear to both Avian and Farthingdale that Anna of course, had engineered the robberies. They did not know why, although they each suspected she did it as some sort of derailing device. "She probably thinks we're stupid enough to think that anyone who robs banks doesn't engineer international murders," Farthingdale said.

"Do you really think she thinks we're stupid?" Avian asked, genuinely curious.

"It's a possibility we must bear in mind," Farthingdale said. They did not see each other much these days, or talk. Avian knew they would meet sometime near the end of the week and, if no new clues had broken, would circle carefully around each other in total suspicion.

Avian had thought hard about the man in the bowler hat. At times, the focus came in very sharply for him, and then quickly faded away. He felt he knew who he was, he felt some strange mysterious connection to the figure in the hat. But the sound distressed him, suddenly walking into a room, turning a corner in his car, and hearing some planted cassette go off and that metallic voice eerily egging him on, "Tit for tat in my photographic hat . . ."

That night when Avian put his head on the pillow a slow winding sound began, very far and distant. He was nearly asleep and at first did not hear it, and then faintly heard, "Tit for tat in my photographic hat." He sat up, and hurled the pillow and the wires across the room and through the windows. He was sweating heavily.

He managed somehow, with several Seconals, to sleep. In the morning it was not better, however. On his breakfast tray were two new documents.

DOCUMENT #16

When staying in a seaside resort in August, 1886 I received a letter one day and upon opening it, found to my amazement that it contained three photographs in which I had no difficulty in recognizing myself. . . . it cannot be denied that the three exposures were a true reflection of what had happened two days before. On investigation, I found that a good friend had availed himself of the opportunity of making several photographs of me, and had done so with the aid of a photographic hat.

**Victorian Inventions,** p. 112

If they knew what I wear when I walk in the street,
It should be quite a terror to the people I meet;
They would fly when they saw me and ne'er stop to chat,
For I carry a camera up in my hat.
A Herr Luders of Gorlitz, has patented this,
And I think the idea is by no means amiss
With a hole in my hat for the lens to peep through,
And a dry plate behind, I take portrait or view.

I admire say, a sea scape, or else chance to look
With the eye of an artist, on picturesque nook;
There are plates in my hat, if I pose it with skill
That will take any beautiful view at my will.

If I'm stopped in the street—that may happen you know—
By a robber whose manners are not comme il faut,

His identification should never be hard,
There's my neat little photograph in Scotland Yard.

So we'll all wear the hat made by science complete,
With a camera, lens, and a dry-plate en suite;
And take views in the street with its bustle and
traffic
With the aid of this German's strange hat photo-
graphic.

—**Punch,** 1887

DOCUMENT #17

On 9th July, 1874 the Belgian de Groot fell to his
death with his famous parachute. For years he had
been working on an apparatus intended to emulate
the flight of the birds. For this purpose he constructed a device with bat like wings. The frame-
work was made of wood and rattan; the wings,
spanning nearly 40 feet, were covered with strong,
waterproof silk as was also the 20 foot long tail.
The machine was controlled by three hand operated levers. His first trial consisted of jumping
from a great height on to the Grand Place in Brus-
sels. It ended in complete failure. Fortunately de
Groot escaped unharmed. During the past summer he came to London, and there, standing in
his apparatus, he was taken aloft by Mr. Simmons
in his balloon and released from a height of 450
feet. He glided down safely landing in Epping
Forest.

On the fatal evening of 9th July 1874, de Groot
planned to descend into the River Thames with
his parachute machine. Having first taken him and
his apparatus aloft to a height of 4,000 feet, the
balloon descended to 1,000 feet whereupon de

Groot, floating just above St. Luke's Church, released his machine from the pannier of the balloon. However, instead of bracing itself against the wind pressure, the wing frame collapsed and whirled down, dragging de Groot to a fatal fall.

Due to the suddenly diminished weight, the balloon rose quickly. Mr. Simmons, the balloonist, swooned in his pannier when he saw de Groot drop to his death, and did not regain consciousness until he was floating above Victoria Park. He landed on a railway track in Essex just in front of an approaching train, the driver of which managed to stop in the nick of time, thus avoiding a second accident. Such deplorable events as this serve to prove that the path of the inventor is indeed strewn with thorns.

—Death by Parachute:
Leonard De Vries, **Victorian Inventions,** p. 46
Original from **La Nature** (1874), p. 143

"I have to go to Damascus," Anna said.

"When?" Bacco asked.

"On the next plane," she said, getting up and putting the papers on the table. She was reading her British agent's report on the original Avian Braine.

DOCUMENT #18

*THE NEW YORK TIMES, SATURDAY, NOVEMBER 25, 1972*

# British Paper Reports Bormann Alive

Special to the New York Times

LONDON, Nov. 25—The Daily Express said today it had "incontrovertible evidence" that Martin Bormann, Hitler's deputy who has been long sought as a war criminal, was alive in Latin America. It described Bormann, now 72 years old, as a prosperous business man who had evaded capture thanks to the protection of six South American presidents, governments and police departments.

The Express did not say where he was living now, but it asserted: "We know precisely where Martin Bormann is living—at least until this Daily Express story reaches him."

"He will go on the run again, of course," said The Express

writer, Stewart Steven. "But this time we who took part in the hunt have insured that his boots will be forever lined with lead."

**Writer Is Credited**

The paper gave credit for the discovery to Ladislas Farago, the Hungarian-born American writer who has written widely on intelligence.

The article did not say that Mr. Farago had seen Bormann, but indicated that at great peril he had "systematically infiltrated" the secret services of several Latin American countries that had carefully documented every move that Bormann made within their territory. It cited Brazil, Argentina, Paraguay, Chile, Bolivia and Peru.

It said these Bormann records had been smuggled out of South America and were now in safe deposit boxes in the United States and Europe. Most of this material is to be published in a book by Mr. Farago to appear in the spring.

There have been conflicting reports for years that Bormann died in Hitler's bomb shelter in Berlin as the Soviet Army closed in. Hitler himself committed suicide there on May 1, 1945.

Bormann was sentenced to death in his absence as a major Nazi war criminal by the Nuremberg Tribunal, after the war. He is still wanted for murder by West German courts.

According to the Express, he escaped from Berlin to South America "thanks to the protection of the Vatican, former Argentine President Juan Perón and some of the most powerful politicians and financiers in South America.

The paper said he had "bought" South American presidents, governments and police departments with the proceeds from gold and precious works of art smuggled from Germany to Argentina by submarine before the war ended.

### News to Publish Series

The New York Daily News, in this morning's editions, published the London Daily Express article and said that starting on Monday it would publish a five-part series with documents and pictures "proving that Martin Bormann lives."

The Daily Express writer, Stewart Steven, gave credit for finding Bormann to Ladislas Farago, a Hungarian - born

**Martin Bormann during World War II.**

American author who was said to have made six trips to Latin America in the search for Hitler's deputy.

Mr. Farago, a former correspondent for The Associated Press and The New York Times who became chief of research and planning for the Office of Naval Intelligence in World War II, has written more than a dozen books on the war, events leading up to it and wartime espionage, in addition to numerous magazine articles and book reviews.

His books include "Burn After Reading," on World War II espionage; "The Broken Seal," on breaking the Japanese secret code before Pearl Harbor; "Strictly From Hungary"; "War of Wits"; "Abyssinia on the Eve"; "Behind Doors," and "The Tenth Fleet."

He also wrote "Patton: Ordeal and Triumph," which was the basis for the movie "Patton." Mr. Farago's latest book, published early this year, is "The Game of the Foxes," on German espionage in Great Britain and the United States during World War II.

# *THE PERISCOPE*

## THE WATERGATE FIVE: CHAPTER II

A Federal grand jury is digging hard into the case of the "Watergate five," who were nabbed rifling the Democratic National headquarters in Washington, D.C. The quintet, which included four ex-CIA men, is about to split five ways, with each looking for his own lawyer. (One, James McCord Jr., an ex-CIA agent and a consultant to President Nixon's campaign headquarters, wants F. Lee Bailey, defender of the Boston Strangler and Lt. William Calley.) The government also is showing great interest in E. Howard Hunt, another ex-CIA man and a White House consultant, whose name was found in notebooks on the Watergate burglars.

## ARAB VS. ARAB

Syria's efforts to get back five high-ranking officers captured by the Israelis have caused new tension with, of all places, Cairo. Jerusalem insists that, in exchange for the five, it wants not only three Israeli

pilots held by Damascus, but ten other Israelis in Egyptian prisons. Syria wants to deal but Egypt, its partner in the United Arab Federation, refuses. The reason is that Cairo has been fighting with Damascus over a Syrian officer it claims was running a spy ring in Egypt.
**Newsweek, July 10, 1972**

---

"I hate Christmas," Anna said as we made our way to the airport. We were detained briefly when Anna insisted on stopping to help a truck driver fix his engine. She was an excellent mechanic, although the truck driver was as huffy as he was appreciative, particularly when, since we were in Italy after all, she told him she could only accommodate him temporarily as he was in desperate need of new points. I thought she carried it too far, however, for after she had fixed the engine, she left it running and asked him to hold together two wires, which it was clear made absolutely no sense to the poor driver at all, but he did it nonetheless, since his engine was running, and while he did that, she ran around to the back and changed the tire. He couldn't let go of the wires, and stood there looking a bit baffled and helpless. Once we were in the car again, Bacco admonished her for showing off and said she must .review the provocations and conditions for hubris.

"I hate Christmas," Anna said again when we got out of the car. The airport was strewn with colored lights and signs, and trees. Then she sighed, "No, I love it. It's like everything else I suppose, the absolute exaggeration of all of our ambivalences—I love its promises, I hate that they don't come true."

"You don't believe in God?"

"No," Anna said smiling mischievously, "only magic."

As we made our way through the airport, Anna commented that God was all over. There were not only jingle bells and Christmas carols, the floors of the airport were strewn with beggars and those too ailing to make their way to the long ramps without stopping. At one point we passed a man whose black hair was sticking out in all directions and who was leaping about strewing pamphlets everywhere. As we got closer, he began to shout, "BELIEVE IN GOD AND OBEY HIM," as he enthusiastically attempted to convert anyone who passed. Anna of course was in her typically irreverent frame of mind and did not protest when suddenly he grabbed her and put his face close to her and said somewhat fiercely, "Believe in God, Obey Him!"

Anna kept her composure completely as she took his head in her hands, surprising him, and said softly, "No baby, you've got it all wrong. When you really believe in God you don't have to obey him—because it would never occur to you to disobey, he becomes you, you become him. It's all one glorious stream of truth."

He gazed at Anna stupefied. "Who are you?" he asked finally.

"Me, honey?" Anna said picking up her bags. "I'm the Almighty herself all dressed up in mortal drag!" The man reeled back against the wall and poking a long dirty hand at her said, "Sinner!" She turned to us, her face expectant. "He doesn't believe me. It's even harder for me than it was for my brother, Jesus," and she gathered up her bags then and went on.

Anna kissed Bacco and me goodbye at the gate. and she told Bacco not to worry. "Please," she said to him fondly, "try to think of something for me to wear to Hussein's party. I know Lola will look absolutely smashing, and I can't bear to think she'll outdo me."

"She won't," the little priest said. And then he said, "What about Irene?"

"She'll be all right until I get back. Be sure to keep the music going. I'm not expecting anything new for some time now." She picked up her bags and her cue stick and strode quickly toward the plane. Bacco did not wait to wave her off. Goodbyes made him sad. He could see already that her thoughts were in Damascus.

As soon as Anna's head touched the cushions of the plane, she felt herself relax. Damascus. Perhaps, you never knew, she might see Abraham. He was sometimes in Damascus. She felt herself dozing off, and then she woke suddenly, as the plane lurched from the ground in a very badly executed takeoff. Her eyes glanced around the plane and she noticed the man sitting opposite her. A man in a bowler hat. He seemed vaguely familiar to her. Then he turned his profile toward her and nodded. Anna drew back. He was wearing lipstick.

She did not turn his way again. Any form of transvestism made her uneasy. But a man in a derby, in formal attire. It was odd. She thought no more about it. Perhaps he was an actor, perhaps he . . . she didn't know. She was very tired and lay back to sleep and dream. She fell asleep dreaming of the party in the palace of the King . . . she would be beautiful and witty and charming and enchanting and wise and wonderful and rich and they would love her for none of these things but for herself alone, and as she dreamed thoughts of Abraham came into the dream again, she would perhaps dance with him at the palace of the King, her dark-haired dark-eyed mystery lover whose face barely emerged, and the music would be sweet, some gay melody, some folk peasant tune, high and lilting mixed with an almost Vivaldi intensity, it was all a wonderful dance, and dance she did, she danced and waltzed and dipped and swirled in the arms of her phantom lover and was happy, oh God, she was happy, she had never known such sweet happiness, her lover gazing down at her, she could not quite see his face, his arms locked around her waist, his face bending down to her, she was spun at that moment into the universal heartbeat that had always bewitched the spirit of young girls, she was Natasha and Kuragen, she was every passionate woman and her dark lover who promised that night to steal her away, and she would go, knowing that he was bad for her, knowing she would have to go, her veils flying from the carriage, he would press her close and kiss her fiercely, her heart beating wildly, and then to the dance again, the music ending, her lover bent, and a kiss fell upon her lips as gentle sweet and small as a slip of morning dew.

She woke up. Who was he? She was drenched with perspiration, with thoughts of the lover, who was he though? She searched her mind, his face would not emerge. She remembered Lola saying, for she had had the dream many times, Lola saying, "It's probably your old man."

"Who?"

"Your father. Papa. The basic oedipal fixture."

"Oh, don't be ridiculous," she had said. "I don't remember him. He died when I was two."

"You remember him," Lola said, and Anna had stalked out of the room.

Later she said, "I'm going to find him whoever he is. I think it may be Abraham."

"Abraham may be part of it," Lola said. "You're always meeting him in the midst of gunshots and intrigue and hasty partings. All the trimmings are right."

"How come suddenly you're so wise and wonderful?" Anna said to Lola.

"It's just becoming so obvious," Lola said, "you're going to turn into one of those broads who spends her life panting after the Mystery Man, Brenda Starr and the Orchid King, Narda and Mandrake . . . uh uh," Lola said, "not Narda and Mandrake, actually Narda and whoever the big black buck in the lion skin was."

"Lothar?" Anna said. "Don't be ridiculous, Lothar was a eunuch."

"Not in my funny paper," Lola said, "We didn't recognize eunuchs in Scarsdale."

Anna smiled. Thank God Lola had a sense of humor. She was trapped by her, ensnared by her, she liked to think of Lola as the incarnation of the forces of evil. But Lola was not the incarnation of evil, nothing as simple as that. She was human and mortal and a spy, and she would kill her, Anna knew, someday Lola and Plato would try to kill her.

She lay back, smoking a cigarette. Unless she got to Silverstein first. She herself had a deal, a promise to elicit from Silverstein. But he would kill her too. Kill her by torturing Bacco, or something else equally horrible. She was sorry she had ever done it. The KGB. A short stint in the KGB, and Silverstein on her tail for life. "We have to kill him," Bacco had said. "Or he'll kill us." She knew it, she had ordered executions before. It was nothing new, particularly. Except that she would have to do it. She didn't want to do it. The KGB had been smart, using a Jew. No one would suspect him of being a Soviet agent. Oh well, the party at Hussein's would be interesting. Every political hack on the continent would be there, selling his wares. She was aware something was happening to her. She was losing her interest in politics. She thought these days periodically wild crazy romantic adolescent thoughts, like falling in love and having a baby. She had driven Bacco wild with it. He told her she was regressing. All those Frank Sinatra records. It was marvelous. She did love them. She smiled looking out the window. They were approaching land. She would call Abraham the minute they landed, or perhaps in the way he found things out he would be there to meet her. She smiled remembering the summer he came to visit her, and he said to her, "You have not yet begun your life as a woman, you have a lot to live yet, before you can be with a man," and she had needed him, in some deep primitive hungry way she had needed him those hot wet August summer mornings, needed him and yet she had nothing to give him, she waited like a hungry child for those large soft and callused hands to move over her body, shaping her, stroking her stroking her again and again, the big smooth hands moving down her thigh, caressing her back, the hands over her breast, shaping and smoothing, she lay there feeling she had nothing to give, could not be anything for him, but there, waiting as his large hands gave her breath, his kissing deep in her throat, as though he molded her from clay breathing the breath of life into her lungs, making her first woman, first child from the earth, the union of the two shaping her, strengthening her until she was awake and wanting, alive and trembling, astonished by her desire, she who had been dead, a stillborn lump of clay, hopeless, defeated, feeling she would never feel desire again for anything, or hope or feeling, would never want in any way, she awoke then, trembling, amazed at the strength of this new body, this body alive and moving, wanting, despite her, wanting him desperately, then pushing for him, grabbing, taking, reaching, placing, she would dive toward him, grabbing his thighs, her nails digging into his buttocks, pulling him into her, over her, please, ah, please, he could not be fast enough for her, waiting, the rushing, the pulsing, needing his penetration, he was too much and never enough for her, never far enough, never long enough, never enough and too much pounding her until she was new and breathless the breath, the worn spirit driven from her and her eyes opening suddenly.

---

I said that I did not understand why Santiago should love Anna so, and Santiago indeed himself did not understand it any better. The thing that I noticed was how eager Santiago was to protect her. He had already made one call to Damascus. An uncharacteristic and generous impulse, or perhaps she was the only one who permitted it.

"I remember," Santiago had said, "one day when we were walking along the Via Veneto, and suddenly there had appeared an ice cream truck. It was an American thing, and Anna said 'Ooo, how I should love to have a chocolate milkshake!' " And Santiago seized her by the hand and made her go and get it and it was I knew because Anna these days so rarely desired anything, and he wanted so for her to have it because she wanted it. Santiago had said once that he did not know how Anna lived sometimes, for she had no desire for anything.

When I said this to Bacco he said it wasn't true—sometimes she wanted everything, but there was no middle ground, she either wanted absolutely everything or absolutely nothing.

---

"Everyone's looking for something—eventually they come to me," Harcourt said as he sat in his English club in his English chair, which surrounded him like a pouch. "I've been to Japan," Harcourt said, tilting a cigar into the ashtray with precision. I thought immediately of exotic sexual pleasures and found it unpleasant. The thought of Harcourt in any degree of abandon whatsoever was distinctly unsuitable. Abandon? No, Harcourt was too fat, too rotund, too English for that. I looked past the drape and concentrated on the rain gathering on the sill.

"Your napkin, sir," the waiter insinuated his long aquiline face insulting. Santiago looked up but did not move. "You need a napkin, sir."

"Goddamnit, the man knows what he needs," Harcourt said. The waiter retreated. And retaliated. It was at least a half-hour before he brought our drinks and the ice had melted. Harcourt propped his feet up on a footstool of green faded velvet and clearing his throat said, "God, it's a hell of a time to be in London." Harcourt I concluded briefly was a man who must have a secret life because he certainly didn't have an open one. I mean the one that he led wasn't really a life at all. It wasn't informed by vision or desire or even habit. It was a random series of circumstances that he happened to latch on to, or rather that latched on to him, drawing him in where they could; like a dog wandering aimlessly through a field, Harcourt went, gathering burrs and bugs, dandelions, daffodils in his coat, a nit biting his hind leg sending him east, a gnat sucking his back sending him west. Eventually he crossed the field but one route would have been quite the same as any other. Therefore I concluded Harcourt had no life. That is, there was no series of circumstances to which it made any difference at all or that was influenced in any way by Harcourt's character. This was because Harcourt had no character. No character, no life, I concluded as we left the club to hail a taxi in the driving rain. I looked across Trafalgar Square feeling quite good. The afternoon I thought had been productive after all. There amidst Harcourt, stuffed chairs and the hunting magazines of an old men's club I had managed something. I had come to an idea. Harcourt, I thought, yes you must have a secret life.

Santiago said back at the hotel that it was conventional to base my reasoning on the a priori conclusion that there was such a thing as life.

"Well," I protested, "not even social habits, then he hasn't even that."

"That is not necessary," Santiago said.

"Harcourt eats and Harcourt shits," I said. "That is all he does in his life, therefore he has no life, therefore he has a secret one, since he is not dead."

"Eating and shitting," Santiago said leaning back, spreading his legs, "are almost all that is required. Please," he said, "don't become religious."

---

Silverstein waited in a submarine off the coast of Comino. Comino, not far from Malta, was a rocky uninhabited island ideally suited for snorkling. Anna swam there often. He had gotten word she would not be long in Damascus.

---

When Anna arrived home it was early evening, and the fog had begun to roll in. Bacco hurried to meet her with a small lamp.

"Where have you been? Your plane's been in for hours. I was worried half to death."

"I've been with Frank," she sighed.

Bacco frowned, "You're not going through that again, are you?" he asked nervously.

"I've got him under my skin . . ." Anna began to sing.

"Hush." Bacco said. "You have a visitor."

Anna looked surprised. "Who?"

"Armbruster. He's a nervous wreck. He keeps belching and calling for more Brioschi."

"Armbruster . . ." she said. "I haven't seen him in years, show him to the yellow room . . . I'm certainly not going to entertain him tonight . . . whatever can he want?" She was puzzled Bacco saw, and so was he. It was not usual for them to have uninvited guests.

The yellow curtains blew softly when Anna entered the room, closing the door behind her.

The chintz coverlet flickered in the breeze. Anna lit a small lantern she kept for foggy evenings, and turned to the visitor in her chair.

"And so, Mr. Armbruster," she said softly, "what is it?"

"If," he coughed, this strange Swiss businessman, "a man were not a father, but only raised a child, it wouldn't be incest, would it? I mean it wouldn't be a crime, it wouldn't be indecent, do you think?"

"This is not a class in moral philosophy, Mr. Armbruster. What is it you wish to know?"

Perspiration broke out on his forehead. His hands trembled. Mr. Armbruster turned his face away from Anna as he said, his voice remaining somewhere in his throat, "My daughter, she is not actually my own flesh. I adopted her at the age of three, she has expressed a desire for me I find hard to resist." Mr. Armbruster burst into tears. "I cannot help it. I am overcome."

---

It seemed to Anna it was hours before Armbruster had composed himself enough to leave. She was exhausted and turned toward the staircase to prepare herself for bed. She stopped dead. Plato stood there, waiting at the top.

Bacco was hurrying in from the garden when he saw Anna standing transfixed at the bottom of the stair. Trancelike, she seemed for several minutes absolutely unable to move. He knew that expression, knew then Plato was near. She was terrified of Plato, and Lola too. Why, Bacco didn't know. Fearless in almost every other way, they nonetheless held her, like a magnet holds steel. He knew there was nothing he could do now; already she was moving slowly toward him.

# BODY IVTH

## AND THE WATER-REPELLENT MIND

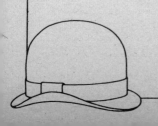

# 1

"Well, Farthingdale," Avian said as they sat down to dinner, "I've figured a lot of it out. Would you like to hear?"

Farthingdale knew Avian had been in South America. "I've traced the connection with one of the messages in one of the fortune cookies," Avian said. He slid a piece of paper across the table. "It's from Lorca, the words were changed in the fourth line to 'In the dream, at its edge':

> "*Words stay under the water*
> *Over the crest of the water*
> *A ring of birds and of flame.*
> *In the reeds and the sedge*
> *Witnesses know what is missing*
> *A dream without any north,*
> *Hard as guitar's dark wood.*"

"A poetic streak, do you think," Farthingdale asked, "in our murderer?"

"So it would seem," Avian said, "although I don't think he's a poet."

"What do you think he is?" Farthingdale said.

"I think he's what you think he is," Avian said.

"Aha," Farthingdale said, taking a sip of water. "In that case, I'd better tell you what I have on my mind."

"I was hoping you would," Avian said.

"Of course, it's another detective," Farthingdale said, "and the way I've figured it out," he took a napkin and began making notes on it, "is the following. During World War Two, Spy A, probably Quim, possibly Bun, hid, in various erotic manuscripts, the clues to the entire British espionage system, including code and place names. Consequently somewhere in that manuscript is the final destination and total activities of both Quim and Bun. That's why whoever it is that is after this murderer wants the manuscript. That party clearly knows that both Quim and Bun were double agents, and it was to their care that Martin Bormann entrusted the information concerning the paintings confiscated by the Nazis, now worth several million dollars."

Farthingdale cleared his throat. "Part Two, as I see it, and do correct me if I'm wrong, involves these dildoes, which we are supposed to think are valuable as remnants of Chinese oracle bones, but which we know," he took a sip of wine, "from our friend Silverstein, must be of something more than historical interest."

"So far," Avian said, "we're in agreement."

"Good," Farthingdale said, "then I will proceed. It's good, isn't it," he said raising his glass, "not to have to surmount intellectual obstacles." Avian raised his glass in return.

"Well, then," Farthingdale said, "concerning the bones. Actually, the bones are fake oracle bones which are valuable because they have coded in them two curious artifacts of the war: one, the name of

German double agents, and two, the location of valuable and as yet undiscovered oil deposits in the sea off the coast of Japan."

"Anything else?" Avian said.

"Well," Farthingdale said, "I have as yet an unformulated third angle."

"Do tell me," Avian said.

"Well, thirdly," Farthingdale said, "someone Harcourt knows is after these manuscripts for a third coding, which has something else to do with the Nazis. What as yet I cannot discover. It might be Anna who is after them or it might be an ex-Nazi. Anyway, whoever he is, he worked through several agents in Yemen, and as far as I can determine is probably living in Cairo. He'd be arrested if he went back to Germany, and he's agreed to help Al Fatah if they promise to help him get whatever it is he wants. It might very well be the paintings he's after as well."

"Quite," said Avian, "do you know who he is?"

"Any day now," Farthingdale replied. "Have I missed anything?"

"Only one thing," Avian said, "as far as I can tell. Quim had a child who is alive and well and living in Rome."

"Oh yes," Farthingdale said, "silly of me to have forgotten to mention that. Anna is Quim's daughter, of course."

They raised their glasses together then, in total salute, each still wondering privately to what extent the other was trying to cover details the other one had not yet discovered.

It was some time later when Avian said, "Do you think Anna knows that Quim is her mother?"

"I doubt it," Farthingdale said. "The Gestapo finally killed Quim and Bun in August of nineteen forty-four. Anna was living with a foster American family then. She only knew Quim and her father during the first year."

"Yes," Avian said, "I don't believe she knows her father was a Nazi, however."

"In any event, she doesn't know which Nazi," Farthingdale said.

"Do you?"

Farthingdale took a long draw of smoke, then looked at his pipe and tapped the tobacco down in the bowl. "Yes, I know," Farthingdale said.

———————

Each time with Plato it was the same with her. Quite suddenly in the midst of the languor, the floating, the eternal losing of ground was the hard pounding presence of his violence. At the moment when she thought she had, through some incredible sensory state, *lost* all sense of her body and through her lost body lost all her awareness, beyond feeling to floating, sensation a sweet anguished memory, just at that moment he would reach into her, into some long-fought-off part of her being and begin to scratch it to the surface. It came forth then, bleeding and torn, scratched and wounded, biting and tearing. She felt the violence begin to proceed up from her belly like a storm, like a ripping, gnashing wind. She would consume him in her violence then; they would meet in a fury of a passionate destruction that wanted to consume and enfold, to eat. She wanted to swallow him and be swallowed by him, to be torn and shredded, mutilated, violated, engulfed, transformed, pure ether. Air. And that was how the afternoons went, between the violence and the particularness of it and the endless floating pleasure where she thought she would lose her mind. She knew then why men were violent, and women were afraid. Women were more willing to go crazy. Violence kept you sane, for even in the midst of its uncontrollableness, it was the guarantee of control—a chance at the upper hand. It was surrender, and the lust for it in women, that drove them mad.

It was after being with Plato, Bacco noted, that Anna ran straight to Santiago. "He's refreshing," she had told Bacco. "He is what he is; he has no mythic dimension." Bacco privately thought this an overly intellectualized view of the actual motivation, but that was unimportant to him. He just wished she wouldn't spend so much time with him. She was upstairs with Santiago now.

"I am bored bored bored!" Anna screamed, "with this reality and illusion, reality and illusion, it is BORING! It is as old as Pirandello and as BORING, as intellectually flaccid and BORING!"

"It is as old as Plato, my dear, and no doubt as old as man himself. I don't find it boring," Santiago said.

"You tell me what happened on the beach did not happen on the beach. Then you say what happened on the beach did happen on the beach. Well, all I want to know is did it or didn't it? I thought it happened. I felt something. What did I feel, a memory or a dream? And what of the hut, the umbrella, the little man in your film?"

"In the sense that all dream is memory, I suppose in some way it did happen," Santiago said. "Nevertheless the details were somewhat altered, no doubt to suit your convenience, and that of your deam."

What kind of detail?" Anna turned now, her eyes brooding. When the rage surfaced in her periodically like this Santiago saw that her lips were almost a purplish hue.

"Only you know that," Santiago said. Anna clutched the hairbrush. There were moments when she wanted to kill him. Instead, she threw open the sash of the window and gazed out into the wine-dark sea. A small white boat, its sail tilting along the horizon, its hull cast almost on its side, glistened and moved along the water. That small craft, like the cast of certain aspects of her mind brought her a curious comfort. She plopped into a yellow chair, gazed at the wallpaper and wondered if she resembled at that moment any of the ladies of Matisse.

"You can't see yourself," Santiago had said, "except as the way in which I see you. I am your mirror. Without me, you are nothing."

Anna thought him crazy, drove off and bought a pineapple and returned home, brooding, where she argued with Bacco over what was the best way to cut it.

In the midst of the pineapple fracas, Lola strolled in and said, "It will be fabulous, I hear. I think he's going to do it like Queen Victoria's Crystal Palace."

"Ah," Anna said, "It's going to be simply super," she exclaimed, "and waltzes they are going to have waltzes, can you believe it I adore to waltz, I always knew I would fall madly in love with some man who waltzes extravagantly well," Anna said. She smiled.

"You read too many Russian novels," Lola said, "I want somebody who can frug."

"That's because you think everything can be communicated through the pelvis," Anna said defiantly.

"Not everything," Lola said, "I wouldn't say everything, but," she looked skeptical, "certainly everything that counts can."

Anna asked Bacco to cook some lunch. She was going upstairs to take a nap.

"Where was this found?" Avian asked.

"It was delivered to police headquarters," Farthing-dale said.

"By whom?"

"An unidentified messenger, covered in black who exposed herself to the police sergeant and left."

"Our friend from the park?"

"I presume it's the same one."

"Did this one grin like a jack-o'-lantern?"

"No—you're dealing with Italians here—he said it was *magnifico*."

"Of course there's no way of identifying anyone by their genitals . . ." Avian trailed off and Farthingdale was finding it hard to control his laughter.

DOCUMENT #19

"Tell me more," I said, "about the original Avian Braine."

"He's dead," Avian said annoyed at my sudden interest. I paused a moment and then quickly said, "You don't know that. You don't know if he is or not. I don't think he is. I think it's him." There was enormous silence in the room for several minutes. Avian got up and walked to the window and lit a cigarette. It had begun raining now, and the wet wind blew back the smoke into the room, circling me insidiously as I stood there in silence.

"Yes," Avian said, his voice strange, "I began to think so just this morning."

"It occurs to me," Avian said, "that there has

never been a satisfactory way of describing social acts in terms of cause. Brilliant sociologists like Marx and Weber formulate a theory which is brilliant in its internal logic. However, when one arrives at the real basis of social movement, of group to group, of opinions and responses to war, it becomes difficult to isolate factors, or cause. That is why I am drawn to this work. In a murder, you know the death of the victim was 'caused' by the murderer. What 'caused' the murderer to do it can, in certain cases, be effectively known.''

"Avian Braine was a buddy of mine when we were in World War Two," my lover said as we sat in the living room, his usual amber skin wan. He looked exhausted. "He was working for British intelligence at the time, which I discovered, quite innocently, on my own. He had been impressed with the rather extraordinary quality of my associative ability," Avian paused and took a sip of his drink, "and persuaded me that I could render invaluable service to the cause of the Crown, et cetera, et cetera, and could in fact make a good deal of money. In addition to which," he said, "it's a lousy life, but you don't exactly get bored."

"So you became a double agent."

"Yes, and he was my control. It was extraordinary, how precisely alike our minds were. We were very valuable. Then Avian died, quite unspylike, of a heart attack. He had given me instructions that if anyone should ever inquire I knew nothing about him. He had by that time left the service, if one ever leaves it." Avian smiled wryly. "It was three months after he left that he suffered a heart attack in my presence on a Paris street. He was dead on arrival at the hospital. I **thought** I had effectively disposed of the body. And then I took his name. I told intelligence I would help them if they would grant me his identity and leave me free to practice as a private detective. I don't like being bound in, you see. He had no relatives, no friends, so the transference was simple.''

"Wouldn't someone have tried to kill you?"

"Avian Braine was of no use to any intelligence service at that point in his life. He'd performed all the missions he could manage."

"And you?"

"As I say, I have this extraordinary ability, which you have noted. Avian and I had a series of horrendous experiences, but sometimes there are those who are going to lead you to hell and you go willingly if you are sufficiently mad, which any seeker of the truth is, you go willingly because he has promised you will glimpse her on the way."

"Is that why you went, to glimpse truth? You went to hell in the cause of philosophy?" I asked.

"Not exactly," Avian said. "In the cause of lust. I heard she was good in bed."

"Why the absent-minded, dowdy professor routine?" I asked. "What's the point of that?"

"It makes me appear harmless," Avian said. "The only way I can be free to exercise my ability is to keep my accomplishments hidden. Scotland Yard, Control, whoever I help never makes it known. I'm just a dumb flatfoot who inherited some money, a washed-up former spy to anyone who might be interested."

"Rather like Batman, your disguise," I said.

"It's not a total disguise," Avian said, "there are aspects of me which are very comfortable in that guise."

"Really?" I said, catching the new tone in his voice.

Avian only nodded then and said, "From time to time I may have to go away, quite suddenly, quite inexplicably." He paused and took another drink. "I'd rather not discuss it with you other than to say, my extraordinary brilliance costs me a very high price."

I sat very still in the chair. He could not discuss it with me—who knew everything? I felt cheated. "How long, how long do such periods last," I said softly. I was not surprised, surely he knew that.

Surely he knew I had divined something other than an effective theatricalism between his two personalities, something close to schizophrenia. What the nature of it was, I don't know. But it had the stamp of genius that such illness can sometimes deliver.

"Usually three months," Avian said. "Once every ten years." He paused then. "Anytime now something could happen to separate us for three months."

"I could see you," I said.

"No." That ended our discussion.

The next morning Avian called me from his office at 10 a.m. and told me to pack. "We're going to Madrid."

"I think Avian may be alive," Avian said to me on the plane. "He's alive and trying to see if it is possible to commit a murder and not have it discovered by your own mind, which is mine, so to speak."

"Do you really think the motivation for murder is philosophical?"

"No. It is never philosophical, but that isn't what's determinant here. What's determinant is that **he** thinks it's philosophical."

We were sitting in Anna's house in the midst of a heated discussion about the Israeli situation when the servant announced the arrival of Farthingdale. Anna shrugged. "There's nothing to do but let him in," but it made no difference for suddenly there he was standing in the living room. The record was playing "Goodnight, Irene, Goodnight," and Anna did not have a chance to turn it off. Clearly he wished to surprise us. At the moment, however, he saw only Anna. We remained in the garden.

"It's a little early for the record, isn't it?" Farthingdale said to Anna, making no apology for his rude entry.

"She takes naps," Anna said.

"That record is in the key of G. The other night it was in the key of E," he said.

"You have an extraordinary ear, Mr. Farthingdale," Anna said, walking to the record player and switching it off.

"You needn't interrupt little pussy's nap time," Farthingdale said.

"Oh, she's on her way," Anna said. "I think she's heard enough."

"Just the first four bars?" Farthingdale said. "That was hardly a refrain."

"It was enough," Anna said.

"Why was it in a different key?" Farthingdale said walking to the windows.

"Cats are very sensitive to pitch. She seems to like it. I try to give her a little variety."

"The G sets off one set of signals, the F another," Farthingdale said turning to her. "You would know never to play a key of F record during the week. Only Saturday and Sunday. The notes are different. And with good reason. That cat contains a radio transmitter. The major moves of the entire war in the Middle East are being broadcast from your little furry pussy." He heard a click and turned around to find Anna and us.

"It would be stupid to shoot me," Farthingdale said, "I have information that may prove useful to you."

We listened. All four of us.

"I think," Farthingdale said at breakfast the next morning, "that Hussein's house party is going to be rather revealing in regard to the murder."

"You do?" Avian said surprised. "You think he'll show?"

"Yes, I do."

"So we will attend, of course."

"Of course," Farthingdale said, reaching for the mushrooms he had taken to eating with his eggs in the morning.

"Have you arranged it?"

"I have."

"Do tell me how."

"We're going as Anna's guests."

"How very appropriate," Avian said, quickly buttering his toast, and ordering more tea.

---

Silverstein waited. No swimming for several days. Perhaps she was onto him. She was going to Hussein's party. If all else failed, the plan would go down. Silverstein smiled, right in the middle of shark territory. The submarine would surface just in the nick of time. She would have to be glad to see him. He began moving toward Gibraltar.

The day we were to leave to go to Hussein's party, a number of events occurred, which when we put them together later made perfect sense, but at the time went totally unnoticed. First of all Bacco decided not to fly with Anna, Farthingdale, Avian Braine, Lola, Santiago and me in Hussein's private plane. He said on second thought he really did not wish to be in attendance as Anna's wardrobe assistant until she totally retrieved herself from her adolescent state. It was true, I noticed it myself, that Anna was going on and on these days about waltzes and parties and generally had a rather moony quality. I found it odd but rather charming. Bacco, however, said that it agitated him terribly, but he was confident she would soon be over it. So, when he decided not to come, no one thought a thing about it.

Then, the day we were to leave, the pilot called in ill and said that he would make arrangements and find another pilot to fly us tomorrow. This was agreeable to everyone but Santiago and me, as Santiago needed the time to check on the photographer shopkeeper who had been murdered by General Amri in Libya several months ago. Consequently, Santiago and I decided to leave on a commercial jetliner that very afternoon. I preferred this anyway, as Hussein's private plane was stopping for additional guests in Cairo.

This left Avian Braine, Farthingdale, Lola and Anna to go by private plane. As I understand it, things happened in the following way:

Anna was very excited about the party as they boarded the plane. Bacco was quite loaded down with hat boxes and dress boxes and jewelry boxes and was yelling at the attendants to keep everything in perfect order. Lola was there, looking quite chic in a black leather pants suit, and grumbling about how tired she was. She was so whiny that Anna finally ordered her inside and told her to curl up in the back of the plane and go to sleep. Farthingdale and Avian seemed to be thoroughly enjoying the occasion, although Farthingdale remarked that he too was tired and retired to the rear part of the plane. Anna pouted at this and said she would have no one but the boring pilot to talk to and insisted that Avian ride up front with her. This he seemed delighted to do, and I was not surprised when I heard it for I had already formed the opinion that he had privately submitted to her charms and was quite as in love with her as the rest of us.

In any event, before they took off, Anna glanced in the back to see Lola and Farthingdale totally covered with blankets and trying very hard to sleep. She left them alone and went back to the front and ordered the pilot to take off. Bacco, stalwart as always, waved at them from the ground, dabbing at his eyes with a handkerchief. When Avian asked why he was crying, Anna said, "He always cries when I leave. It's nothing special, he just hates goodbyes. If you don't say goodbye, he's quite all right, but I forget and always say it. I said it once on my way into the supermarket and he absolutely dissolved in tears."

Avian smiled, his first smile in the entire week. He was aware of an extraordinary passivity that possessed him. He was simply letting Farthingdale take over. He knew why. He was terrified to think that the real Avian Braine was the murderer, and even more terrified to contemplate that it was himself. He did not let himself think too much these days of his suspicions about Farthingdale. Whatever it was, whatever had happened in his mind in these last weeks, it was quite beyond his control. He had decided simply to give himself over to events. To events, and possibly to Silverstein. If his sources were right, Silverstein was after Martin Bormann, and would lead him to several million dollars' worth of paintings. He knew the other

Avian Braine, if he was in fact real and not a figment of his imagination, would try to beat him to Bormann. He sighed. He didn't know whether he would make it or not. Perhaps he was getting tired.

Anna leaned against him as the plane sailed into the clouds. He felt the softness of her hair against his neck and thought how good it would be to make love to her. And then, it happened. That strange, over-powering sensation. He was convinced in a minute that he had. And when she started unleashing her belt he was in no way surprised, it was all quite familiar as she slid her panties off, lifted her dress over her head and bent down to remove his belt, his tie, his shoes, nibbling the front of his neck, his hair, kissing and tonguing until they were both naked and perspiring and making love on Anna's Norwegian blue fox coat, never noticing that the temperature in the cabin had dropped to almost 38 degrees.

It was a short flight. When Anna saw the time she got up, got dressed and went to the rear of the cabin to wake Lola and Farthingdale. She nudged Lola first. The blankets where Lola had been sitting collapsed. No Lola. She pushed against Farthingdale; another tent of blankets collapsed. No Farthingdale. Anna screamed.

"Bail out, bail out, get the parachutes," she cried, realizing she'd been trapped, but it was too late. There was a great explosion, and the plane, Avian, Anna and the pilot exploded into a million pieces over the Egyptian desert.

Anna woke up in the snow. The sun was bright, hurting her eyes, and she turned to her side. There were rocks and some few trees ahead of her. She lay there a few minutes, listening. She heard nothing. She remembered now. She sat up, carefully. She wondered how long she'd been there. She looked around. There was no sign of the plane, no smoke, no debris. She was in deep snow. She looked at her body. It seemed incredible to her, she bore not a scratch. Just on one arm. She raised her sweater and saw one long scratch from where some weight had pressed on her silver bracelets. She shook her arm. The bracelets rang. She felt her head. She felt dizzy. Somewhat dizzy, but all right. She looked around. Thank God it was daylight. Below her, what seemed very far below her was the desert, stretching out in miles of sand, iridescent in the noonday sun. She thought for a moment. There was no sign of the plane. She must have been thrown clear. If she stayed near the mountains, she would have the snow, and the water. If she went to the desert, she would have no water. Yet here she would freeze. Tonight, she would freeze here. She looked at the desert. Or there even. She would freeze there tonight. Either way.

She was frightened in a way she had never been frightened before. She felt the tears well in her eyes. The fear of no alternatives. She would choose one, take one, she must. She had no idea where she was going. She knew no one could survive the desert. Slowly, tears falling down her cheeks she made her way through the rocks and down to the sand below.

She was being watched.

The horseman rode toward her on a small black horse, a beautiful fine-boned Arabian horse, seemingly out of nowhere. She stood quite still. She could see only the eyes, dark and squinted beneath the robes. It was strange, she thought, for a man out here to ride alone. He dismounted and came toward her. She tried to gesture about the plane, she tried French, she tried all the languages she knew, he spoke some rare dialect, she tried several Arabian dialects. He pretended not to understand her. He tied her hands and her feet and put her on the back of the saddle. She did not fight him. He would give her shelter and food, rape her, and possibly kill her. She didn't care.

The horseman's tent was made of skins, it was at the bottom of the mountains near some water. He untied her and gave her something to drink. He said nothing but stared at her and in a few minutes began to make a fire. She was exhausted suddenly and fell back against the straw matting in the tent. She decided it would be safe to sleep. It was some time later when he wakened her. She was naked beneath some fur and he was naked over her. She recognized the eyes in the dark bearded face over her, the face that removed the fur covering her. And he took her then and rode her in the high cold air, her round hips turning on the straw, the soft shadow of her pelvis, scooped out in dark circles by the fire, the slight rise of her belly soft against his bristling hair, her hips rolled her thigh tensed as he took her whiteness and moved into her, his force and weight surprising her and she rolled, to her surprise to his pleasure they rolled in some strange somersault, over and over to the edge of the tent, to the edge of the straw and the hard cold sand, and he moved into her again and again and the snow began to fall light and soft as she writhed beneath him, chest to chest bodies wet her red mouth and the silver bracelets ringing on her arm.

He shot a desert animal and dragging it over the cold hard ground threw it into the blazing fire. And they ate.

When the police arrived with their stretchers, they

found only a dead pilot. No cargo, none of Anna's furs or jewelry, and no Anna and no Avian. The Bedouins had been there first. "At least that means she's alive," I said.

"Oh Christ," Santiago said, "what the hell do you think they're doing to her?"

"Not to worry," I said. "She's not fat enough for a harem. Probably the most that's happening is that they're feeding her. Bacco is beside himself. I told him there's nothing he can do. He's taking a ship at three."

"A ship? Why a ship? A plane takes forty minutes." Santiago was angry at Bacco's lack of urgency and walked irritatedly about the room, crashing into lamps, emptying ashtrays, smoking again, and perspiring.

"Bacco, in case you have forgotten," I said, "likes, whenever possible, to travel by water."

"What you mean to say," Santiago said, "is that he's afraid of flying."

"No, I don't mean to say that, I mean to say he loves to travel on the water. Did you ever hear of anyone going from Rome to Paris by boat? That's how he goes, all the time. It turns him on."

"Turns him on?" Santiago shrugged and leaned back on the pillow. "What the hell are we going to do. How can I find her?"

I shrugged and began filing my toenails but Santiago did not see me for he was dreaming now of Anna and wherever he looked in the room former images of her arose.

"Yes, it turns him on. He swears to me that in the middle of the night he takes off his clothes and walks around the ship. Around, not about. He walks out on the waves and feeds the gulls and keeps pace with the ship. He swears it."

"Why is everyone I know absolutely crazy?" Santiago said. "Do you know, I don't know a normal person. I really don't. All of us, we're all mad as hatters. Walks on the water. Jesus Christ."

"Part of it, no doubt," I said.

Victor Hugo was writing, Renoir was painting,
and Mumm was the word.

Lola explained to Bacco that she had been kid-
napped by Victor's agents, and just barely managed
to escape. She arrived breathless at the door and told
him he must warn Anna. Bacco wanted to kill her.
Yes, Farthingdale had already been there, told him,
yes, Lola had been forced off the plane at gunpoint
at the last minute, and Farthingdale, suspicious of her
kidnapping, had rolled off as the plane went down the
runway and then followed.

Forced off at gunpoint, but somehow Farthingdale
suggested it had all been planned, so that in case
anything went wrong with Anna's plane, Lola would
be covered. In any event, Farthingdale was convinced
the plane's real aim was to destroy Avian and himself
as well.

Bacco pretended as though Lola were innocent and
explained that Anna was probably alive, although they
might never find her. Lola was either an excellent
actress or actually distraught. He couldn't tell and
forced himself to offer her some lavender tea while
they decided what to do. Lola said she would take
the next plane and go help search for Anna. Bacco
said that would be fine. He did not wish to let her
know his own plans were for going by boat. He had
never trusted her, never would trust her, and hated
that Anna loved her. Why he would never know.
Whatever it was that should make you love another.
But if it weren't for that, he thought, Anna could
leave her clutches. He sighed. Anna loving a woman
who would kill her. It made no sense. But the little
priest had no time for complex reflections. He was
sick with anxiety. He thought to himself that he would
die if anything happened to Anna.

The third day Hussein's army joined the searches.
Not a trace of Anna could be found, but they did
come upon Avian Braine who was severely injured

and quite incoherent. At the news of this Farthingdale remained at his bedside and listened attentively.

I said to Santiago that I was sure Anna would never miss the party, and he remarked that she certainly wouldn't since both Lola and Victor would be there, not to mention Caldwell, who would be wearing a cape of peacock's feathers, diamonds and mirrors.

For reasons I do not understand I remained fairly calm about Anna. I was sure she was all right. Bacco and Santiago were quite frantic, however, and Bacco had discovered some strange man—a veteran of two world wars who seemed not to know the last one was over. He had somehow gotten hold of a tank and equipped it with recordings and loudspeakers of war songs and spent his days in the tank eating K rations and playing "Hang Out Your Washing on the Siegfried Line" as he went tooling over the Egyptian desert. Bacco had been out with him for several days but they had turned up nothing.

---

Anna was sure he would kill her. She didn't know when, but eventually. Or perhaps not. In any event, he clearly would not let her go and she would never be found here. She thought the horse would take her if she could get away far enough and fast enough before he called it. It was an extraordinarily well-trained horse, she noticed, and she would have to be very careful. That night when the man's breathing was even and deep, she slipped out shivering and led the horse away. She swung herself on and jabbed her bare heels into its sides. He had taken and hidden her shoes. The horse darted forward and Anna gave it its head. It was pitch black, there wasn't a star in the sky and riding into the night wind was like diving into a tunnel of dark water. She pressed her face down to the horse's neck and prayed it would not go in circles.

It seemed to her that she had ridden several hours when the horse stumbled, fell and she lost her balance.

In a second she was in the sand, and she could barely see the horse standing not far away. She went over to the animal, standing on three feet and could see immediately its leg was broken. Her feet were cold in the sand. It was crazy but she'd have to leave the horse and keep walking. She knew she'd go in circles, but she was lucky. After what seemed to her several hours, she unexpectedly hit a group of rocks and stopped. They might shade her in the day; at least a plane might spot them. She lay down, thinking snakes or no snakes, and went to sleep.

Four days later she was still at the rocks and delirious from neither food nor water. The nomad's robes had protected her somewhat, but she was dangerously ill she knew. She was visited by sweet phantoms in her daze; she dreamt of angels in long white dresses as she longed to be wrapped up, to be coated and misted over, adrift and dreaming of a beauty so spectacular, and so private and now gone forever, lost in some secret garden of the mind. She remembered Bassoni wrote, "In order to understand this life, you must die at least once," and DeSica put them on bicycles and in white dresses and made a movie. So she dreamt of bicycles.

There were moments when her thoughts were clear and she prayed that she would live. The rest of the time she drifted, hallucinated, felt her weakness, and slept. The helplessness of dying made her angry, and then it made her laugh. It was funny, dying. It was funny that when you finally began to lose your senses, the thing that had always terrified her, it actually became quite agreeable. They would never find her here; the vultures had begun to circle. She might have three or four days. She knew she hadn't moved very much. She knew she was almost infested with fantasy; she had seen troops moving before her just the day before, and she knew they were not real, but she ran after them anyway. Then she crawled back to the rock.

It seemed to her it was several days later when she heard the music. Music so clear and real she was forced again to stand up. There was a tank coming toward her and she heard the words as clearly as from a phonograph:

> Kiss me goodnight Sergeant Major
> Tuck me in my little wooden bed
> Kiss me goodnight Sergeant Major
> Sergeant Major be a mother to me

As the tank rolled toward her she lurched from the rocks, barely able to stand, and waved feebly. A new song rolled forth:

> Hang out your washing on the Siegfried Line
> Hang out your washing Mother Dear
> Hang out your washing . . .

She stood, not believing the tank could not be real. It stopped several yards from her, and yes, it was the small round form of the little priest, Bacco, Bacco was running toward her. Her eyes were disbelieving, it was Bacco. She tried to run as some huge force in her leapt toward him. Then she felt his hands. He was not a mirage. Bacco was real. He was bending over her, with some cool sweet water, his tears splashing on her face, holding her head up as he muttered, "What are you doing out here without a hat. It will do the dickens to your skin."

That was the last she heard. When she woke up again, she was in a hospital: Bacco was fluttering over her arranging some flowers, Farthingdale was sitting in a chair smoking a pipe, and Santiago was pacing the floor.

Avian awoke. He remembered. Avian Braine telling him about Charlie Fatah. He remembered the description carefully. Charlie Fatah was Harcourt. He had been after the paintings for a long, long time.

When Farthingdale brought him the document Avian said yes, that was the original Avian Braine. He had simply forgotten to tell Farthingdale that he, too, was subject to amnesia.

"When do you think the document was written?" Farthingdale said.

"It makes all the difference, doesn't it?" Avian said.

"Quite," said Farthingdale. "I'm beginning to think Silverstein has planted all these clues and documents in an effort to convince you that the original Avian Braine is alive. So convinced, you would know you had to beat him to Bormann in order to catch him, and of course you would feel compelled to catch him. That way Silverstein gets led straight to the treasure."

"I don't know," Avian said, "I simply don't know."

DOCUMENT #20

When I wake up in the bottom of a gently rocking boat somewhere outside of Cairo and as I look over the rim of the oarlock I see that the sky is beginning to turn the color of puce. I become aware of a tremendous pain at the rear of my head, and it occurs to me that I have the sensation of something quite stiff and sticky on the top of my neck. I attempt to move it and it is then I realize I am numb. I am in the bottom of a rowboat and I cannot move. The head, perhaps. I try, with what seems to be an overwhelming effort, but it only creaks slightly, and then there is a terrible tearing pull. **God damn you, Charlie Fatah, you nearly got me killed.** It is very quiet then for the next few minutes. The boat has stopped rocking and the sun appears in a brilliant flash and I feel that I would like to close my eyes against it but I cannot. I cannot close my eyes. My lids are numb.

In a minute a black watersnake pulls itself up over the side of the boat and begins a slow undulation over my belly. I begin to vomit, at least my viscera are working, and as I do so, I feel a lacerated pinch in the center of my gut. It feels as though somebody has been shaving my tummy, from the inside.

Then the sun turns black. My eyes do not close, but it is night.

The next thing, it seems several months later although Charlie Fatah is telling me it was a dream, I am in a hotel in New York City, somewhere on the Upper West Side. Charlie Fatah is trying to explain to me that I made the mistake of walking into a room of hooch smugglers and they let me have it across the back of the neck. Charlie said he found me down in the alley, the blood on the back of my neck being licked off by some pussy-cat. It occurs to me to tell Charlie Fatah that I am not as stupid as I look and that I know we are in Cairo. Al Khairah has a smell if you've ever been there you do not mistake it for the equally foul, but totally different East River. I begin to say this but before I finish I know the room has changed.

Charlie is looking at me as I sit up in bed. We are in Cairo and I ask him how long it has been since he has been in New York. Charlie appears concerned. He shakes his head. "Never."

"That's a lot of bull, Charlie," I try to say, aware that somebody has taken the trouble to starch the right side of my head.

"What is your name?" Charlie says, looking at

me unsteadily with that damn toothpick he keeps working at his mouth. I am surprised suddenly that I do not seem to know because I have no sensation of having forgotten anything.

Ten minutes later I say, "I don't know. I know your name is Charlie."

He nods. "Who are you?" he asks, and once again, with no sense of having lost anything I reply that I haven't the faintest idea. I know, however, why I am here.

"Why?" Charlie says.

"I'm after Braine, someone named Braine. We're after some double agents. We had to come to Egypt."

"What agents?"

I pause and take some water that is sitting there looking warm under the night-table lamp. "I don't know."

"Who am I, Charlie, a spy?"

Charlie looks at his hands and shakes his head. "No." He gets up then and walks to the windows.

"What year is it? Why am I an amnesiac?"

Charlie says nothing, just stands in his white suit puffing on his white pipe, staring out to sea.

## 9

"The King has postponed his party, in order to accommodate the inconveniences of his guests," Farthingdale announced at breakfast the next morning.

"I must say, he certainly seems considerate, considering he has his own problems."

"Yes, there seems always to be a coup threatening on the horizon."

"The way I hear it," Farthingdale said, packing up a few things, "is that his most trusted generals are not in fact to be trusted."

"Where exactly are you going?" Avian asked.

"Me?" Farthingdale said. "Oh, I'll be back for the party. Only going for a day or so."

"Where?" Avian seemed very nervous Farthingdale thought.

"To Teheran."

"What for?" Avian said.

"I find myself having an overwhelming lust these days for Beluga caviar. Also," Farthingdale said, puffing as he dragged his valise from the bed, "it is the season for sturgeon."

"You won't find Snow," Avian said suddenly, "unless he wants to be found."

"I have it on the highest authority that he's in Iran."

"Harcourt would lie for Snow. He wants the paintings too."

"Harcourt says there's a daughter."

"Impossible. Snow was injured during the war. He can't propagate."

"Harcourt swears there's a daughter . . ."

"Don't be too sure of anything with Snow. Remember that he is an expert at disguises. So expert," Avian said, looking at Farthingdale, "there have been moments when I thought you were he." Avian got up then and walked toward the balcony.

"You didn't tell me he was a gun collector," Farthingdale said.

"You won't find him," Avian called back, "unless he decides to be found. He thinks I'm the murderer, so he might."

"Are you sure he thinks that."

"I would, if I were he," Avian said, and turned to gaze toward the sea.

Farthingdale left, leaving Avian alone in the city to cope with Anna, Lola, Bacco, Santiago and the various free-lance political murderers and assassins on hand in the city for Hussein's international ball.

It was not long after Farthingdale left that Avian got a call from Anna asking for him. When he explained that he had gone off to Teheran, she sounded positively stricken, to his surprise, and then asked him if he would mind coming and staying in her hotel.

"What seems to be the problem?"

"I'm very worried. Victor was supposed to be here, and no one's heard a word from him in days," she said. "Not only am I worried about Victor, but if Victor's in trouble," she hesitated, "so am I."

Avian was surprised she would allow him that much information and wondered if Farthingdale had made some secret arrangements with her. In any event he agreed to show up at her hotel in a few hours, and in the meantime he would check on Victor.

It was quite possible, Avian thought, walking through the city, that Victor was simply hiding out. He hardly thought Victor would want to show up at what was going to be on one level a meeting of a lot of power-hungry guerrilla fighters all claiming to liberate the people. From what he had been able to put together about the political situation he knew he for one would never attend the ball in anything less than a bullet-proof vest. If he could have figured a way to manage it, he would even have considered wearing a helmet.

By the time he got to the hotel, he had enough information so that he knew he would have to tell Anna something was definitely not in order. Victor had not been seen by anyone in Rome for several days. When he told Anna this she seemed calm enough and quite ready to believe that Victor was simply hiding. Since Victor worked in complete and total opposition to what Avian knew Anna's commitments were, he was surprised at her attachment to him.

"Victor?" she said. "Oh, I adore Victor. He is the only innocent in all of Rome. He thinks he saves the people; he is not a terrorist," she said to Avian, "he is too sweet to be a terrorist."

"How long have you been working against them?" Avian asked quietly and directly.

"Against the terrorists?" Anna said looking his way, "as long as I can remember. I hate them in any of their forms, they destroy the innocent in the name of politics." He was surprised at the ferocity with which she said this. "But I am getting tired now, we are near the end. I have done enough."

"Perhaps," I said, interrupting the conversation, "perhaps you should settle down and get married."

Anna laughed. "To whom?"

"Perhaps to Victor," I said, "you seem to like him so much."

"Not to Victor," Anna said, "I could never marry a man with a bad prose style."

At that moment Lola swept in in a white fedora and a pinstriped suit with, of all things, a purple satin tie. The skirt came just above her knees, and she was wearing what appeared to be a black and white tie shoe that looked like spats.

"Oh, you look wonderful," Anna said, "that old thirties look again."

"Hussein likes it," Lola said turning around, "I'm seeing him for lunch."

"He must like to live dangerously," Anna said, but Lola only smiled in the dazzling way she had and asked of us what we were doing.

"We're just sitting around trying to get Anna married off," I said.

"Anna?" Lola turned to me surprised. "Anna can't get married until she finds her father."

"Oh God," Anna said, "you read one or two psychology books and you suddenly think you've been given divine inspiration. Look, I don't know what this is all about, since I have told you I am not in love, I do not believe in love, and in any event, marriage is a capitalist institution and I have no interest in it whatsoever."

Lola seemed to ignore this defense entirely and launched into a pseudoanalysis of Anna's condition, which, although extremely superficial, I nonetheless found highly interesting.

"The problem, you see," Lola was saying, "is that everyone talks about the son's rebellion against the father, but no one talks of the daughter's rebellion."

"She's supposed to rebel against the mother," Anna said somewhat impatiently.

"No, that's just not so," Lola said, "it's in the nature of the father to be rebelled against, it's part of the paternal authority, so it manifests itself either as the daughter falling in love, in very rebellious daughters with the father's competition, or in very very rebellious daughters with the brother, and," she looked at Anna, "in daughters afraid to rebel, or daughters who have never found the father to rebel against, in never falling in love at all."

"Perhaps you should have these little formulas printed up on cards, and drop them from airplanes, so people will know that all this blessed insight comes from the Heavens themselves." Then she turned to Lola, "And now for your problem, dearie."

"My problem?" Lola looked at Anna. "Mine is so complex you'll never understand it. Mine is betraying, to the point of murder, those closest to me. I will die young," she said, putting her cigarette out in an ashtray, "and soon."

"Do you want to?" I asked, thinking that this was all a little too dramatic for my taste.

Lola shrugged. "It's inevitable."

"That means you want to," I said, but before I could go on Lola turned to me fiercely and told me to shut up.

Anna walked toward the windows, and gazed out at the long rolling desert sands. Perhaps I should have stayed with my nomad, she thought. She knew that Lola, in her own crazy, demented sick and horrid way, had just given her fair warning. Lola was out to kill her.

# 10

The night of Hussein's party Anna had spent simply hours getting dressed. To me, she looked more beautiful than ever, surrounded by white mink stoles, wearing a gold lamé sheath, which she was positively poured into and over which had been sewn, at great cost and effort, millions of tiny little diamonds. She absolutely glittered, and glittered in waves. She looked staggeringly beautiful, although I must confess, if I were being an absolute purist about it, a bit torchy. Nonetheless when I put that to her she said we were in the Middle East and not in Washington, D.C., so torchy was as refined as understudied might ordinarily be.

I lost her as we walked over the beautiful grounds to the King's palace, with limousines pulling up and

gorgeous ladies greeting and laughing and very handsome gentlemen surrounding Anna at every turn. Hussein himself had taken Anna's arm, something which I
thought left Lola feeling a bit miffed, although I had
understood at dinner that Lola was sitting next to him.

I wandered into the palace and then into the upstairs rooms. It was there I had agreed to meet Santiago.

As I walked about through the palace I was impressed by the fidelity with which the theme of the
Crystal Palace had been executed. Down to the finest
details, everything was absolutely perfect. Perhaps the
only thing that drew away from the perfection of the
décor was the presence of the military stationed in
windows and doorways, supposedly unobtrusively.
Some of them were in full evening dress, others not.
On the second floor I found Santiago as we agreed, in
the appointed room. He had the tapes going and his
transmitter.

"What time is it set to happen?" I asked.

"Just before midnight," he said, and then turned
away. I could see he was having difficulty monitoring
the call, whoever it was. I knew there was bound to be
trouble, leaving so much evidence inside that silly cat.
But Anna had been insistent. It was true, the cat was
not likely to be discovered, but if Farthingdale figured
it out, there was no telling who else had. In any event,
I could tell by Santiago's face that he was seriously
worried about Silverstein.

I decided there was no point hanging around there,
and went downstairs again in search of Anna. It took
me some time to find her, but when I did, I found her
enchanting a rather large group of people, and in the
midst of a conversation that seemed quite intense. I
approached her.

"We are trying to decide," Anna said, explaining the
impasse to me, "whether love or money is the most important thing in life."

"I see," I said, wondering how such simple-minded-
ness could amuse her, "and what have you decided?"

"Neither," Anna said. "Money and love are causes. They are not events. The most important thing, i.e., event in life is," Anna turned a bright flashing smile toward her audience, "is products."

"Products?" several people said in unison.

"Products," Anna said dramatically, waving her arm gracefully as she began to circle the room, "things, objects, manufactured material, that which has passed through a man's hands, and often his financial empire in order to appear somewhere, tempting you to part with your money, for most people the most profound spiritual encounter they can ever hope to have."

"Products . . ." muttered someone thoughtfully.

"Without products, where would we be?" Anna went on. "How would we know ourselves? By what means would we assess ourselves? How could we value ourselves, realize ourselves? Think of the desert of our experience without products!" Anna said this last quite passionately, and when she was done there was a stunned silence, during which she made a dramatic exit. Then everyone buzzed, quite seriously about how seriously she was to be taken, but by the buzzing I can tell you they took her very seriously indeed.

I caught up with her as I wanted to be quite near her during the dinner hour. "You do love putting people on, don't you," I said. "Personally, I think it's a trifle silly."

"I wasn't putting them on," Anna said striding beside me down the long main hall. "If I don't get some food soon I'm going to die."

"You won't die. I thought your stomach might have shrunk out there on the desert. It would have done you some good, heavens knows, you are putting on a pound or two."

"You're getting awfully bitchy," Anna said to me. "You'd better start being nice to me, Lola's trying to kill me."

"Don't be so dramatic. She doesn't need to kill you," I said stopping and trying to get a piece of celery from a waiter who walked too fast for anyone to seize anything from his tray. "Silverstein's the one you have to watch out for."

"Why don't you tell me something I need to know sometime," she said.

"Why are you so grumpy?"

"Because," Anna said, "I'm looking for romance. I know almost every man here. I have to find a new one. There's not one of them of any interest to me. I want to be swept off my feet."

"You're getting more romantic every day," I said, "what is going on?"

"I don't know," Anna said, surprising me by turning around and looking at me directly. Then she excused herself and walked toward the terrace.

---

Anna wondered what to do. She felt confused somehow—at first she thought she missed Plato and then she didn't know. She desperately wanted a man. But a man who knew what to do. She had looked them over. They seemed too eager to prove themselves. She sighed. She wanted someone who knew what to do, knew how to come in and take over, to take care of himself and meet her at the same time, she did not want some polite, cordial dope to come in and mickey mouse around twiddling her nipples, she wanted a man who would put his hands over her and then plough her, plough into her like a DC-6 strafing a minefield. Clumps of dirt, and spurts of blood. That was how she liked it. Or that was how she used to like it. Something had changed in the desert. She didn't know what she felt any more.

She took her drink to the far end of the terrace and waited. In a few minutes, a man came over and introduced himself. Oh come on, she thought, let me see something so I know. She looked him directly in the eyes. She just couldn't tell. She didn't want to guess wrong, because if she guessed wrong there would be no pleasure in it for her. If he wasn't the right one, there would be nothing she could do, because the rest of them, you just couldn't let a man know you wanted him to deliver, because they'd melt away on you, most of the time you couldn't let them know you would match them stroke for stroke; it scared the blazes out of them, and so she would lie there holding herself in until they got near the end and then she would let it rip, twisting and pulling and turning and screaming. Men were afraid of passion in a woman, she concluded. They always called it violence, and seemed surprised.

She turned back to the party. Anna loved parties because the women showed their arms, which were soft and long, and some were fat and some were thin, and their breasts, small birdlike fluffs and big swinging tits, and large soft immense mountains one could sink into, and the women walked and their hips swayed out, and they crossed their legs and lifted their glasses, and one saw in every way they were women. As one saw the men, with the hair on their arms, some light some dark, the shape of the jaw, the chest heavy and the thigh thin, and the walk, the way a man put his weight forward on his foot, and the voices. The voices of the men soothed her like a balm. She loved parties; she loved anywhere where one was surrounded by the presence of sex, sex pushing itself forward into what it was, sexual difference, and sexual subtleties; there were men and there were women. She retreated into the security of those differences like Hegel into the confines of a mental system. When Anna heard the laughter of a woman's voice, saw a braceleted hand shoot forward felt the presence of a beard brush her cheek in a kiss, felt it all sure and sound, it seemed destiny itself was secure, had been battened down and made comforting, that life would go on reassuring and implacable, that anatomy was indeed destiny, in the most profound and curious sense. She wondered that she could feel all this at a party—as if the very core of humanity had been met and sanctioned by the most seemingly superficial of events.

"Did you ever sleep with your father?" Lola asked me as I met her on the patio, biting daintily into a small canapé.

"No," I said.

> *No it is not possible*
> *And yet it is possible*
> *And no it is not possible*
> *And yet it is possible*
> *And no and yes and*
> *yet*
> *It seems*
> *Possible.*

That I was in fact on the patio biting daintily into a small canapé.

---

Avian had gotten the message and returned to the hotel to meet Farthingdale.

---

Anna had not expected to see Abraham here. She had not found him in Damascus, and had been glad. The word had been he'd left the Service completely, and become something of an alcoholic. The thought of seeing him in any sort of weakened condition made Anna sick. Years ago when she first met him she had found him attractive, strong and virile, a young boy enjoying his manhood. He was on top knowing he was good and loving it. And then the others they told him, he was not on the real top, and the real power lay elsewhere, and so he left to do other things, things he wasn't equipped to do. He was a measurer, an observer, he was a man who could tell stories about money, he could not manage it, fly with it, lose it and spend it and get it again. He was lost in the new race, and his nerve and his spirit with him. He lost badly over those years, and now at the bottom was "making a comeback." A comeback at thirty-eight turned

Anna sick. She saw him now, he had gone soft, soft in the face and belly, soft the way men do when the spirit goes out of them like that. He drank a lot. He was an alcoholic, trying valiantly to defend himself against it, drinking Bloody Marys by the gross. She looked at him across the room, and she knew then she would take him, felt the presence of the old love for him, the passion and compassion, the pity and the longing all filling her until she knew she would take him and restore him if she could, and she took his hand and led him then, sweet looking, so sweet, she saw him now all boy before her, full of an innocence where there should have been fury as she led him gently up the stairs, through the pressing bodies, "Hey Abe, here Abe, hi." The secret laughter at him now, soft; the way he drank. She led him in and sat down, he had no awareness yet what she would do, and surprised him when she took his glass away, took it away in her hand, and put one hand behind his head, looked at him surprised and unsure now, and put her hand behind his head and moved her body into him and he resisted his back tense but she moved again until he kissed her lightly faintly, barely there, thinking then she knew more of the drink she'd taken from him, "I'm no good at that any more," he said but she pulled him in, she went kissing and stroking until she felt him then, felt him as his arms went tight around her, it would be all right if he didn't cry, felt him grow like a wet cord around her tighter and harder as she undressed him, moved his hands while she dropped his pants, looked away from her as she pulled his shirt over his head, made his hands push the dress from her shoulders felt the warmth in his hands on her breasts and led him then to the bed where he fell against her like a dull, hot weight, his head near her shoulder on her neck, tears falling against her chest wet lying next to her, as she stroked his head, rocking him, nibbling his neck, waiting for the force to come, if it would come, waiting for the transformation, feeling him small and loose inside her, rocking gently she felt for a moment he was getting smaller, rocking, smaller and smaller as if he would shrink to the size of his phallus, like a small desperate fetus straining to implant itself again like some aborted promise about to drop and then, then it happened as she felt the heat coming from him, felt the strength again and felt him growing in her, she bit then heavily into his shoulder as he cried and rolled her over, she had done it finally, awakened it, the former hate in him, the anger, the fury amid the tears, the wet eyes, amid the broken man he was over her now, pressing her head into the bed, his thumbs in her neck like a knife, pounding her looking at her with fury for awakening in him that forgotten spirit, causing him pain, pain and glory, immeasurable pain, and then he was overcome, overcome as he pounded relentless until she felt the sudden breaking like a soft petal losing folds of itself, like the soft fallings of mimosa, taking forever to drift to the ground, she taking all her pleasure in that moment when he screamed, he screamed like a man who'd been murdered, and they lay still for a long time after.

Anna returned to the party, late, and transformed. They had bid goodbye. That was that. He had turned to her after he was dressed with something new, and raw, in his eyes. It had cost him, that feeling she had pulled up from his bowels. It had surprised her. She hadn't expected that, didn't know she was going to be the conjure woman for all his lost aspirations, his lost ejaculations. Always it had been the other way around, always his saving her, giving life to her, and she, nothing for him. But this time it was an exact and precise reversal. He was wasted when he saw her, did not wish to be with her, had lost his spirit and his energy, and she had seen it and known what to do.

She did not expect the release. Nor in herself. Setting free some ghost in him, some dispossessing energy free at last, reminding him of the passion that lay in his bones, she had been born again. Born again. Bearing Abraham. She felt lighter. She didn't quite know how to explain it, but she felt pounds and pounds lighter. And something more. She was not afraid, not afraid of whatever it was that had always made her cautious. Or reckless at bank robberies, reckless about being caught, but more than that a deep fear that made her cling to Bacco like a child and shun the men who loved her. And then she heard the gunfire.

# 11

I do not know when it happened, or how it happened but only that it happened. Perhaps that is all we ever know. But the next few days were the days of Anna's transformation. She went to sea. Something of that night at Hussein's party had remained with her— I do not know if it was Abraham—and what happened with him, something I only suspected—or the gunfire at the palace. Anna, I knew, was very upset. And it was not only because it was a terrorist victory. The next day she announced she was going marlin fishing on Hussein's yacht. Anna was an excellent marlin fisherman, but in addition to that she had taken enormous sums of cash in order to play baccarat. I knew this because I helped her pack, and there were reams of hundred-dollar bills in her yellow suitcase alone.

Things on the yacht got quite out of hand. Anna, on the first day out, caught a 400-pound marlin and won a fortune in baccarat: Then one afternoon quite suddenly she asked to be let off on a small Mediterranean island consisting of not more than a few rocks and trees, and she told Hussein to head the yacht back to shore immediately as they were in danger of being torpedoed by Silverstein. Hussein thought this mere female hysteria and was unfortunately torpedoed the next day. He, happily, and his crew managed to survive, but the lovely boat sank, baccarat tables and all.

Anna returned somber and serious several days later, much to everyone's surprise since it was at least eight miles to the nearest port from her island. She said that swimming with the tide, which was running about four miles an hour, only took her two hours. But the sea was very rough, and Hussein was surprised to see her, to say nothing of Silverstein. In her determination to avoid "death by Silverstein" Anna had not only swum the eight miles to shore in rough sea, but upon getting out of the water had immediately contacted her agents who, in their handy submarine, had chased Silverstein all over the Mediterranean, giving him a considerable fright. I did not know why Anna did not have Silverstein killed at once, but clearly she had some reason for waiting.

Santiago had suddenly gotten worried, which is contagious, since Harcourt had suddenly and mysteriously appeared in a local café. He had information for Anna, he claimed, and the very afternoon she returned he arranged to see her.

Anna did not discuss any of this with me; I only observed it. In fact she said very little to both Santiago and myself until we were on our way to the airport. At that point she seemed to return to her usual contentious manner. Santiago remarked how the Greeks had always understood the nature of things in a way other Mediterranean cultures never could.

"That is because," Santiago said, "they spent a great deal of time discussing the nature of reason and refining it. Although people are skeptical of it," he said, "self-conscious intellectualism is what the Greeks spent most of their time at."

"Really?" Anna said, turning to him in her most skeptical tone. "I thought they spent all of their time fucking each other in the ass and worrying about hubris."

Bacco interrupted and said she ought to be careful about simplistic statements regarding history, but I was glad, for I felt the old Anna had returned with considerable new determination. What was she going to do? I do not know. I only know she was going to do it. She seemed particularly concerned about Victor, so much so that although she became violently upset at the news, she wasn't altogether surprised. For when we landed at the airport in Rome, Farthingdale and Avian met us and told us that Victor had been murdered.

The details of the murder were not very clear yet. Near Victor's body no erotic manuscript was found, just a straight description:

———————————

I asked, "Do you think it means they killed him because he was a writer, because he was a spy, or because the Liberation of Paris was his birthday?"

"I don't know," Avian said thoughtfully.

DOCUMENT #21

And the aging Cocteau, asleep in dreams, as his two beautiful companions played tennis on the lawn, while in Paris, all of Paris writing, the city stilled now as motorbikes and motorcars made a silent trespass past the writers, white papers on white tables, at the Café Deux Magots, at the Café Royale, writing, all pen in hand, pages turning, writing, writing, Sartre and de Beauvoir, Cocteau, Leduc, Hemingway and Adamov, Sarraute, and Genet, all at little tables, every little table in every sidewalk café with pens and paper flashing only the sound of scratching herds escaping to the world beyond.

The day of Victor's funeral, several things occurred. I was standing in a corner of the underground, somewhere near the center of Milan. Their voices were very loud, carried along the tiles, echoing harshly. Farthingdale who was walking slightly behind and to the left of Avian said, in response to something Avian must have said but which I did not see, "There *is* no man in a bowler hat on that platform."

"But I see him," Avian said.

"You must be hallucinating," Farthingdale replied.

At that moment, Anna came down the stairs, smoking a cigarette. "What are you staring at, Avian?" she said smiling. "That man in the bowler hat on the opposite platform?"

Avian looked at Farthingdale, "You said there's no one there."

"There isn't," Farthingdale said.

Anna said, "*I* see him. *You* must be hallucinating, Farthingdale. You know you can hallucinate a void as well as a presence." And drawing on her cigarette she walked out of the station, the beat of her heels echoing in the cool damp silence between trains.

When Avian next looked at Farthingdale he had an expression on his face like none Avian had ever seen. "One of the three of us is lying," Avian said.

"One of three usually is," said Farthingdale and they walked slowly out of the station, saying nothing.

The day of Victor's funeral was one I shall never forget. Anna had been acting very strangely the last few days. She called out in her sleep, Bacco said, she was red-eyed and nervous and yet seemed more angry than sad. Some of us wondered if she had wanted perhaps to kill Victor herself and had been angry that someone else had beat her to it. This, however, made no sense at all, although I privately noted that if sense were our criterion, we would never understand anything.

In any event, Victor's parents had insisted on somewhat conventional funeral services, and so we all agreed to attend. I knew it would be a difficult time for Anna, and yet I could hardly have anticipated her behavior. We arrived at the church late, but the service had not yet begun.

The priests were gathering at the base of the altar. On the raised dais stood the casket, supported on four small pillars, draped in black velvet, strewn with roses and small white petals. We entered a pew and pretended to pray. The hum of the organ was making me nervous. I stood quietly, however, throughout the prelude until suddenly I realized that Anna had slipped from my side. Anna the implacable, Anna contemptuous of sentiment, disgusted by drama, Anna was walking stonily, quietly, strangely toward the altar. Silent, before the stunned crowd, Anna mounted the steps to the altar, her high heels clicking viciously against the metal clasps on each step, the muscles in her legs hard with a new fury, something new in the kind of animal tension Anna radiated now, something that kept the audience from even a whisper, she walked like a sleepwalker with a stare, and then moving to the casket Anna stood, speaking in a harsh whisper, "You stupid son of a bitch," her face twisted in a green rage now, she screamed, "YOU LOUSY LYING SON OF A BITCH, YOU PRICK MONSTER, YOU LOUSY STINKING CUNT," and then Anna, before all of us stunned, too stunned to move, to cry out, Anna pushed against the casket, kicking it screaming, "YOU PRICK YOU LOUSY PRICK," the casket falling to the floor, Anna kicking at it until the top opened and Victor's body fell forth, the scream released now from the watching crowd, Victor's body, wooden, his hands in rigid prayer. I thought I saw Victor's spirit hovering near some corner, mocking Anna, knowing he had her now, cornered in her rage, Anna spinning, grabbing things from behind the pulpit, Anna searching, like a furious wife discovering a husband's hidden closet, throwing forth the holy figures, Jesus soaring by, the crucifix the Madonna, the holy water vessels sailing through the air, the people moaning, the hidden anguish in a hundred throats, one did not scream before God and madness. And Victor, rigid and alone outside the casket now, like a misplaced mannikin. Then Anna spent and fearful, her face tear-stained, staring at us all, The Lady in her hand, Anna before an audience, recognized and recognizing, Anna turned and fixed her hair and began to sweep up the broken figures. No one moved now as Anna picked up the pieces, two priests I saw, anxious, pacing before the altar, then another in prayer, keeping back Santiago, keeping back the men while Anna alone and shaking picked up the broken figures and dumped them into the casket, askew. Then, righting the casket, she closed the top of it and walked over to the rigid figure lying close to the end of the dais. Softly, gently, in full control, seeing the hands raised in prayer, took off her necklace and placed it in the hands and, bending, kissed those cold manacled parts and then straightening, she placed her high-heeled black shoes against the corpse's back and pushed him off the platform into the baptismal basin. The water splashed. No one touched her. She walked then down the aisle stunned and strange, with a slight smile, some small artifice of her grief, with flowers gathered in her hands like a jilted bride, a face in pride and wounded envy, walking slowly to the end of the chapel, and then, leaning against the door, she turned and whispered, "Fuck you," and entered the sounds of the street.

---

"I wasn't crazy," Anna said later, calmly munching on a piece of pizza. "Funerals are too restrained."

None of us knew what to say. We sat there feeling quite odd eating pizza and drinking beer and waiting for her to have some appropriate response, like a nervous breakdown. But Anna only ate lustily, licking the cheese from her fingers, saying, "He was a stupid prick, I hate him for dying."

"I thought you loved him," Santiago said, looking mystified.

"That's just what I said," Anna said. "I am very tired."

The fact was Anna was very frightened. Victor was like a father to her. She never expected Lola would kill him. She would have her revenge, she didn't care about the risks, very soon.

---

Unexpectedly, Avian and Farthingdale found themselves invited to poolside tea at Anna's the very next afternoon.

"Odd," Avian said, "I thought she'd be mourning Victor."

"In her own way she is, I'm sure," Farthingdale said.

He had not told Avian that now he knew who Snow was. What he wondered about, however, was the daughter.

## 14

Anna had a very savage expression in her eyes I noted as I slipped into a lounge chair by the pool. And her usual soft, full mouth was now hard and I thought mean. What surprised me most of all was that Bacco was not around. I figured immediately that something very special was being planned. Nonetheless I was not prepared for the conversation that ensued. We had no sooner gotten our drinks and settled ourselves than Anna lashed out at Lola suddenly. Lola had just announced that she had such severe menstrual cramps that she couldn't possibly go swimming.

"Don't flatter yourself," Anna said. "You have to have blood to menstruate, venom won't do."

Lola turned over slowly, hearing the new sound in Anna's voice as well as the words. "Do I really have such reptilian qualities?" she said.

"Only sometimes," Anna said.

"Like when?"

"Like today, when you returned to the scene where your mate was killed."

"What do you mean?" Lola's voice was hard.

"Victor was not shot," Anna said, "as I'm sure Mr. Braine and Mr. Farthingdale know. He was drowned. In this very spot."

"Who did it?" Santiago asked rather nonchalantly.

"Lola," Anna replied.

"What is your proof?" Lola asked.

"A photograph," Anna said. "You were being watched."

"Have you got the photo?" Avian said quickly.

"I've seen it, I know who has it, but you'll never get me to testify, Mr. Braine, not me nor anyone else here." Avian looked around expectantly. No one moved.

"The stakes are different," Anna said, "but very high for each of us."

Then Lola said, "Anna has a fantastic imagination. I'm getting dressed for dinner." She got up and excused herself.

I turned to Santiago and asked if he'd like to take a swim. I did not like to swim alone these days. He said he would and we walked toward the rocks.

---

"What do you think?" Avian said to Farthingdale.

"She's quite right," Farthingdale said, "he *was* drowned and then shot. The autopsy showed it."

"Why didn't you tell me that?" Avian said harshly.

"Because up until now," Farthingdale said, turning to him, "you were my prime suspect. Now, however," he said, "it's time we visit Miss Apricot and Papa."

# 15

It was several days later, when, it seemed by coincidence, if indeed there is such a thing, Anna was skiing at her favorite mountain in the Italian Alps, that she took a seldom used trail and came upon Plato and Lola. She saw them from a distance at first and then, when certain, came in closer. If she had not taken that particular trail she never would have seen them, for they were in the center of a clearing surrounded by tall pine trees, and only a skier on the steepest trails above would have noticed them.

Anna knew that Lola would be meeting Plato in the woods at four o'clock on a snowy afternoon in a secret meeting for only one reason: a contract. She knew too as she paused at the top of the hill watching the two of them in the cluster of pine trees below her that it was an arrangement they could not have made in front of her, knew that it was something they didn't want her to know, her teeth chattering, tears beginning to fall down her cheek from fear now and the cold, she still cried when she was afraid, really afraid, she stood on the hill trembling, remembering Plato saying a contract is a contract, but when the dagger hits the ground, that means you agree to slay your brother. Or your sister. Or someone close to you, Anna thought. Oh, they were going now, they had only met and now they were going; she saw Lola paused on the rim of the hill about to race through the trees, Plato had half turned from her and then Lola spun about suddenly, Plato must have called her, and Anna's heart leaped at the flash of silver in the snow. The dagger had risen through the air catching the fire of the sun in its brief arc before it hit the ground. She cried and turned swiftly into the wind, swiftly down the other side of the hill, going as fast as she dared, turned expertly through the trees, wanting to die, to hit the tree in her terror: they were going to kill her, her heart was pounding, there was no mistake, taking the dagger; maybe she thought tearing through the trees, they were meeting to buy me a birthday present, yes, perhaps that was it, the tears stung in her eyes, now, her face burning from the speed of the wind against it, but she could not slow her speed now that she knew she was racing for her life, and those forces that had always doubted her value of it now forged ahead with a new strength and savagery that amazed her. At the bottom of the hill she got out of her skis and walked to the road. She got into her car and drove, at never less than one hundred ninety kilometers per hour, straight to Rome. There she telephoned Avian Braine and told him to meet her in an hour.

In a castle high in the Italian Alps lived a history professor, Noland Armbruster, who dabbled in science fiction and inventions. He was enormously fond of the nineteenth century and his castle was full of nineteenth-century diaries and nineteenth-century inventions. In addition to several early models of typewriters, telegraphs, telephones and elevators, he had several balloons and early airplanes. His daughter was a beauty queen, with skin, it is said, "the color of apricots."

A particularly popular pastime in the late nineteenth and early twentieth centuries was an activity known as "the séance." On these occasions, a medium, a person of gifted spiritual powers, would call upon the spirits of those persons now dead and ask them to speak to the living. Occasionally the spirits of the dead complied. At other times they only rapped on tables and moved the furniture about. This, however, which bore testimony to their presence, was sufficient. It was only the more demanding of the live ones who required actual conversation with the dead ones.

Anna did not expect to find herself invited to Armbruster's séance so soon. She thought possibly her conversations with Avian had effected this; yet she did not know. In any event Farthingdale seemed particularly eager to pay a visit to one of the strange ceremonies in the hills.

"I'm warning you," Anna had told him, "he's absolutely dotty. And he sleeps with his daughter. Or rather," Anna hesitated, "she constantly seduces him, and he desperately tries to resist her and she becomes furious."

"Father-raper?" Farthingdale had asked piquantly, and Anna laughed.

"Something like that. She's never succeeded, or so he claims. The girl is positively indecent. She's built like Venus de Milo and she makes him give her a bath."

"Upon my soul," Farthingdale said, "what she needs clearly is a responsible baby-sitter. Perhaps I should volunteer and thus wheedle my way inside the castle."

"Do you really think Armbruster knows something?"

"More than we ever guessed," Farthingdale said, his eyes opening wide in that peculiar way he had. Then he asked Anna about Miss Apricot. Anna had met her only once, and was not impressed. "She talks like Baby Snooks, she sounds about three years old, and the time we had lunch, she ordered apricot ices, and then licked them, in what I assumed she thought was a lascivious manner, off her fingers, occasionally feeding some to daddykins."

"Is her skin . . ." Farthingdale paused.

"Yes," Anna said, "damn it, it's gorgeous. She looks like an apricot, fore and aft, only . . ." Anna hesitated.

"Yes?" Farthingdale asked.

"She giggles."

"Ah," Farthingdale said, "a giggling apricot," taking her arm, or rather, he thought, a pretended giggler. This little lady, he discovered, was a biochemist with a special interest in hallucinogens.

When they were all settled in the car, Bacco put up something of a fuss about the fact that he heard they never served decent food at these affairs and he should have been allowed to pack a picnic basket. I did my best to shut him up, but he grumbled driving up the mountain, which didn't help our spirits at all.

"What sort of things does he invent?" Avian asked.

Anna shrugged. "All kinds of machines, particularly flying machines. He's an interesting sort of quack."

"How did you get to know him?" I asked.

"He came to me for uh, er treatment for this particular difficulty."

"What difficulty?"

"The uh, impulse to fuck his daughter," Anna said.

"Oh. What did you do about it?"

"There wasn't a thing I could do. First of all, courtesans are no treatment for incest, and secondly, he really was a creep. God knows *I* couldn't go to bed with him."

"You're really awfully judgmental about things like that," I said, rather tartly, since she had never been to bed with *me,* preferring always Santiago, and I never did accept this too well.

"Things like that *require* judgment," she said, smiling and stroking my thigh. Oh, she knew just how to wind me about her nine-million-dollar fingers.

"Good God," Avian cried suddenly, "is that a *moat?*"

"It's a moat," Farthingdale said, leaning out the window, "I'm sure there will be ghosts as well."

"Don't act as if you'd never seen a moat before," Bacco admonished them. "You just have to ring for the drawbridge."

"Well, I never have seen a moat before," Avian said, "certainly not an active moat."

"It's terrifyingly active," Bacco said, "he keeps alligators in it. It's heated."

"He sounds very diabolical," I said, thinking I didn't like the way things had turned out at all. Perhaps I shouldn't have come.

I changed my mind, however, when Miss Apricot, looking gorgeous in a low-cut velvet jacket and shorts with high boots greeted us at the door. She did have a bit of a baby-poo voice, but this could reasonably be put aside when considering her other endowments.

As we entered the castle, she giggled and cooed on about her father and her father's collections. Then she turned to us like a tour leader and said, "My daddy has a beautiful flying machine that works. Have you ever seen it?"

"No," Anna said tartly before any of us could shut her up, "I've never seen Daddy's flying machine, but I know *you* have, and I bet it's a beaut."

Bacco nudged Anna fiercely in the ribs and we all heard him whisper to her to please be careful as he was absolutely terrified that we would be thrown to the alligators.

The castle, as far as I was concerned, was smelly and damp and quite huge. The dining room was impressive enough, as was the library. Mr. Armbruster had made no effort to disguise the fact that he was the proud owner of, as far as I could count, at least fifty paintings, all Impressionist.

"An extraordinary collection," Anna said, her face turning quite pale.

"Yes," Avian said, "is it new to you?" He turned to Anna.

"Why yes," she said, surprised at his question.

"How is it," he said, "you've never been to the castle before?"

"I've never been invited," she said directly and moved off down the hall, talking animatedly to Noland Armbruster.

Bacco of course had immediately made a beeline for the kitchen, no doubt throwing his prized oregano rosemary and homegrown chervil and mustard seed into every pot he could find. He also had developed the habit of carrying a coriander grinder in his pocket and backing up to stoves and giving a twist or two into stews and stuffings that needed livening. The last time we'd gotten stuck at some party in Rome, I told him he ought at least to *stir* it as my soup had enough coriander in it to stock the larder for an army, and everyone's eyes at *our* table turned red and watery.

I saw he had taken me seriously this time and had concealed a long-handled soup spoon beneath his friar's cloak and was no doubt stirring absolutely everything in the kitchen.

Armbruster as far as I could tell was something of a dullard, whose redeeming quality seemed to be his passion for history, particularly the late nineteenth century, and harboring a magnificent library.

The ability it took to acquire such a collection, I really didn't understand, although all of us were by now aware that the search for the Nazi storehouse of Impressionists was somehow tied up with the murders. The other question was of course was this in fact the storehouse, or were these copies, part of some intriguing game plan the professor had set up?

I knew of course we would find out at the séance, but I began to suspect things even sooner.

We sat down to dinner rather quickly, all of us except Bacco who came running in late, obviously hiding out in the kitchen until the last gong, and while we were eating Noland Armbruster said suddenly, "You know, these murders I've been reading about, which I'm aware," he smiled stiffly, and condescendingly, I thought, "you are all trying your best to solve, bear in every detail, in method, those used at the end of the last century by a man called Albert Hale. If I didn't know better," and at this Noland Armbruster gave a smile, "I'd think they were being executed by Albert Hale himself. He was a clever man, he stole thirty-six guns from the famous Cartwright collection, and placed one near each body, just as the papers have reported here. Hale was interested in implicating Cartwright, someone he had worked closely with for many years."

"What of the guns?" Farthingdale said, "How can you be sure they're from that collection?"

"Oh, I know for a fact," Armbruster said, "I know the collection well. I have it."

"Are they from the thirty-six that Albert Hale stole," Avian asked quietly, "or are they from your collection?"

"Since I am not the murderer," Noland Armbruster said, "we have to assume they're from the thirty-six that Hale stole."

"And how would the murderer get the guns that Hale stole?" Farthingdale asked.

"Impossible to tell," said Armbruster, "unless they were gotten from Hale himself."

"I see," said Farthingdale quickly, "are you suggesting then that Mr. Hale has been reincarnated?"

"Only that," he said, leaning over the table, "in the realm of the mind, anything is possible."

"But this is not the mind," Farthingdale said firmly, "We are speaking directly of bodies. Dead ones at that."

Noland Armbruster ignored this and continued to tell us about Albert Hale, the amazing gun collector who had been with Chinese Gordon in 1885 in China and brought back some oracle bones, which had since been lost. He had the guns stolen from Cartwright, apparently in a fit of jealousy.

"You don't say," Farthingdale said, almost smirking.

"I see," Avian said. "Perhaps you'll let us see your collection?"

"No," Armbruster said abruptly, "I'm afraid not. No one has ever been allowed in the gun room." He turned to his daughter and patted her hand gently. "Not even Madeleine."

"No one?" Avian said. "Then how is one to know that you have in fact the Cartwright collection, or that the thirty-six that Albert Hale stole are not in fact part of that collection?"

"Well, you know, since I am not the murderer, the Hale guns couldn't possibly be part of the collection. No, Mr. Braine, I'm afraid the room is guarded by a very complicated series of locks. No one but myself can get in. It contains the guns and several priceless nineteenth-century inventions. It's an idiosyncrasy about privacy, that's all."

"Idiosyncrasies must go when we are talking about murder, Professor," Farthingdale said. Avian watched Armbruster closely. Who was he protecting, he wondered? Armbruster had gone to some lengths to implicate him, Avian thought. Armbruster looked at me and then at Avian. He was trying, I could see, to discover which of us was the more likely murderer. Armbruster stared at Avian and thought, "He hasn't changed much after all these years. I'm still smarter by that important degree." The rest of the dinner was a bit stiff, so I was relieved when Armbruster announced that the séance would soon begin and asked if we minded if a certain Maria Buccaletti joined us. We all said no, since it seemed that Maria Buccaletti paid monthly visits to the castle in order to have conversations with her grandmother and none of us wished to interrupt a sacred family tradition.

Armbruster asked me to close the shutters, and I was surprised when I moved to the window to see that, as high as we were, I could nevertheless see the ocean quite clearly. It was a beautiful night, and I stood there quite transfixed as I looked out at the black Mediterranean night, the moon casting orange circles on the water, the waves trancelike beneath the window. I shut the dark shutters and locked them; Anna turned out the lights.

"It is time," Miss Apricot said, in a tone of new authority "for the séance."

I reached quickly for the last of the canapés to pop into my mouth before it began, as I was still a bit hungry, the dinner having been far from suited to my tastes, and as I did so my fingers ran into Bacco's ringed hand clutching mightily at the loaf of bread still on the table. As I wrestled with him, I asked him what he had and I saw he had a roll of salami beneath his habit. Seeing I saw him he said apologetically, "You can't go into a séance on an empty stomach. God wouldn't like it."

Just before it began I overheard Farthingdale remark to Avian that Armbruster was rather effective with optical illusions. It was only then that I noted that Armbruster, when the light fell on his face in a certain way so that the shadow covered his beard, bore a striking resemblance to Avian Braine. Fascinated by this, I made several attempts to get closer, but I noticed that each time on some ruse or other I attempted to get a very close look at his face, Armbruster maneuvered himself away. Nonetheless I thought I had stumbled on something important. I was fairly certain that Armbruster was wearing stage make-up to make him look at least ten years older than he was. I was fairly certain the lines in his face were not his own, but part of an extraordinarily effective make-up job. I could not see, but I also strongly suspected he had, through the use of contact lenses, changed the color of his eyes. I thought it quite possible that Avian had noticed this too, as he seemed extremely uncomfortable.

Bacco giggled throughout the entire affair, which made it difficult for me to be attentive, and I was miffed at this because Maria Buccaletti's grandmother was coming through with a most interesting conversation, in particular a critique of Burkhardt (with whom she claimed she'd had an affair; I didn't know, of course, that these women, once ghosts, are very eager to establish randy pasts) and I missed most of its main points thanks to Bacco sneering, Bacco the belcher in the back row with a roll of stolen salami.

Just before the lights were turned on, as I remarked to Bacco that it hadn't been a very exciting séance after all, a most extraordinary thing occurred. Suddenly, the shutters were thrown open, and the light of the moon flooded the hall. Everyone turned, and there before the shutters was Miss Apricot, stark naked, wearing only a bowler hat. A strange metallic record was playing "Tit for Tat in My Photographic Hat," and then she began to sing the song. Armbruster was up in a minute, screaming, "Madeleine, what are you doing! Madeleine!" he screamed with some vehemence, "take off that hat, where did you get that hat!" and then Miss Apricot pulled from under the hat two guns and, twirling them about her fingers, continued her song and dance, and then, suddenly turning to her audience, she pointed the pistol but just then the lights went out. I heard Avian yell, "You're under arrest for murder," then I heard a fearful scream, and to my terror and incredible surprise heard the sounds of swords slashing in the air, the sounds of chairs overturning. It was pitch black and I didn't know where to go. I just ran, remembering I had to get out of the castle, remembering there were alligators in the moat, and suddenly I felt a hand grab mine. It was Anna I felt certain. "This way," I heard her voice and I followed her as she pulled my hand into someone else's hand, "Follow them, don't unlock hands," she said, and I do not know whom I followed or how I followed, slipping my way in the pitch darkness down a stairway, I thought Anna was leading us, I didn't know. There was a massive sound of gunfire and explosions.

I heard Anna's voice, "We have four minutes to get out of the castle until it explodes. You must all swim, I've taken care of the alligators," and in a minute I was in the water. The moon at least let me see the other side. Part of the castle was on fire. There weren't any alligators, or Anna had perhaps fed them. When I hauled myself up out of the water, I was face to face with Farthingdale, pointing a gun at me as he stood panting and soaking wet.

Anna was screaming on the bank, "Bacco, Bacco,

where is he?" Santiago was on the bank and yelling to a group of men who were throwing what looked to be grenades at the castle.

"He's there!" I heard Anna scream, and looked up and saw Bacco waving frantically from a window far above us. Anna was quite prepared. In a minute she took some sort of power-driven spear gun from around her waist and shooting it into the wall in a cliff opposite the castle, on the rear side of the moat, pulled once or twice on the rope and then shinnied almost halfway up it. I could see her outlined now in the glare from the castle fire against the sheer stone cliffs. I could see Bacco's arms waving in the castle window, and then I saw Anna push against the wall of the cliff out over the moat up toward Bacco's window. Once I saw her push off, twice I heard Santiago's voice behind me, "They'll drop in the moat, that's where the alligators are feasting, she's right over the alligator pool, she can't possibly hold his weight, she'll never make it," and in another second Santiago was up the rope himself, making a huge leap and jumping from the edge of the moat out toward the rope, catching it and gliding upward. Anna looked down screaming at him to leave her alone but he shinnied up with great speed, and then I saw his plan. In another few seconds, Anna and Santiago were both swinging from the rope, their feet pushing against the wall, Santiago holding Anna's feet in his hands as his feet were entwined around the rope. They pushed from the side of the cliff three times leaning out in a great arc toward the burning castle. But they could never swing that far out I thought, they could never get the momentum and I saw the little priest on the edge of the window, the smoke billowing behind him, and then I heard Anna yelling, "Wait wait wait," and saw her and Santiago swing back from the wall one last time, just reaching the outstretched arms of Bacco, I thought the three of them would plunge to their death but by a miracle, by their combined strength Bacco was tossed from Anna's hands and landed safely on the grass on our side of the moat. They swung out again, gaining momentum, and then, as they swung back Anna leaped, just making it on the edge of the land, and then Santiago was left, swinging back and forth, trying to gain enough momentum to land on our side of the pool. He would have to jump very far, and then he leaped, landing in the water, far from where we were. In a second, Anna leaped in after him. The fool, I thought, now they'll both go under and in the clear light of the moon I saw the alligators descending on them, saw the flash of knives in the air, saw the huge tails slamming against the water, saw Bacco throwing a rope from somewhere, saw someone hit one of the creatures with a rock, as I stood paralyzed by fear, paralyzed at what we had uncovered and discovered, and sooner than I thought possible Santiago and Anna were on the shore, safe and bleeding, but safe. Then I heard the explosion and felt the hot ashes in the air as we ran as fast as we could, I ran as fast as I could run with a gun in my back.

# 18

Farthingdale met her at the Rome airport, as they had agreed. "Well?" he said.

"I found out what you need to know," Anna said.

"How was it?" Farthingdale said, taking her arm.

"It was nothing," Anna said. She turned to Farthingdale as she settled down in the plane. Then she pulled out the photograph. "He gave me this. It's a photograph of my mother."

"You look something like her," Farthingdale said, looking at the picture, "but she has more mystery."

Anna smiled, "She was a spy after all." Waiting a few moments she said, "And this is my father. I've had this one for a long time." Farthingdale startled looked up.

"Yes, did you think I didn't know? My mother slept with him for years, they lived together for six, so my assumptions were quite correct. He didn't know until the very end she was Italian after all. I found out what I needed to know. He turned her in."

When they were aloft, Farthingdale said to her, "Plato is dead."

Anna said nothing for some time. Then she said, "And Lola?"

He hesitated for a moment before saying softly, "And Lola too."

Anna knew, knew they would both have to die and was surprised only that she did not feel sadness, only release. Release. "I thought I loved them," she said, "and yet I am glad."

"Perhaps you did," Farthingdale said.

Anna shook her head, "You can't love people who control you. You can't love people who make you detest yourself." She opened her purse and took out a cigarette. It seemed like a very long, satisfying smoke. "Is Plato buried near Rome?" she said after some time.

"Yes, somewhere in Trastevere," Farthingdale said.

"I must have the exact location of his grave," Anna said.

"Are you going to visit it?" Farthingdale asked.

"No, I'm going to dance on it," Anna said.

"It was Silverstein who got Lola," Farthingdale said. "She double-crossed him."

"That was her business."

"Well, he didn't like it, so he fed her to the alligators."

Anna's voice caught, "That night, Lola too?"

Farthingdale nodded.

"Did you catch him?"

"Of course," Farthingdale said. "We've got the entire bunch. The Russians have completely lost their intelligence hold in the Middle East."

"Good," Anna said, and then, "And what about your murderer?"

"You knew all along, didn't you?"

"No," Anna said, "I only became certain at the séance."

"My plans for the murderer are uncertain," Farthingdale said.

"You mean about disclosure."

"Yes, the identity issue is awkward."

"Well," she said, "it's all over now. There's really not much point, other than satisfying curiosity, something I've always found rather vulgar as a motive." Farthingdale nodded.

"We'll be in Buenos Aires in four hours," Farthingdale said. "I think I'll nap until then, although the real strain is on you. Are you sure you don't want someone with you?"

"No," Anna said, "this is the last step. I have to do this myself."

Farthingdale sat back and they were quiet for the rest of the trip. Anna free, at last, and Farthingdale already thinking about the phone call he had received yesterday morning concerning a murder in a bathhouse in the East End.

# 19

In the middle of a small Brazilian city was a modest, well-kept pink-stuccoed home, comfortably furnished and equipped with elaborate communications equipment. It was quite far back from the street and surrounded by trees. Inside was a small dignified man in his seventies. He was an expert at hiding out, had spent most of his life at it in fact and so he was surprised, very surprised indeed when he heard a woman's voice behind him in the door of the house as he had heard no noise from his dogs or the bodyguards.

"You're covered," she said. "Turn around with your hands up or I'll shoot." He had no time to reach for a gun. He waited a second until she said, "I'll count to three." Anna's voice was trembling as she said this, and Martin Bormann nervously turned around in the chair to face a very tall very beautiful woman standing in the doorway.

She stared at him for a long time, her hand quivering on the trigger before she said, "Hello, Daddy."

*THE NEW YORK TIMES, SATURDAY, MAY 5, 1973*

# Auction Brings $13-Million

### By SANKA KNOX

A marathon art auction that began Wednesday night and will end today, has so far brought in $13,279,850 and has become even before its close, the most remunerating public sale of its kind.

Its kind began with Impressionist and post-Impressionist paintings—two of which each brought more than $1-million —and last night canvassed the field of modern and contemporary work, which proved to be the least successful of the areas covered. At Sotheby Parke Bernet, 980 Madison Avenue, where the sale was held, a company expert in the modern field, confirmed findings that contemporary artists, by and large, do not yet enjoy, at auction, the status of their artist-forbearers.

Several pieces did not reach their reserves, or minimums at which they could change ownership.

Nevertheless, about 60 paintings and pieces of sculpture grossed $1,406,000 and posted several records. Three record pieces, purchased by an anonymous New York collector, included Antoine Pevsner's "Le Dernier Elan," the last work of the artist in 1962. A curious construction of brass wire and bronze with gold patina that brought $97,500. Three bronze casts were made of this original work, one of which is on the Russian-French artist's grave.

The same collector also acquired "Photograph" in mixed media by Robert Rauchenberg for $70,000 and Hans Hoffmann's painting, "Joy Spark of the Gods" for $50,000.

Another record went to Rene Magritte's "Le Therapeute," a dark bronze sculpture of somewhat obscure significance, with such elements as the lower part of a trousered figure, a bird cage and bird forming the upper structure and the whole swathed in drapery. A hat rests atop.

**FINIS**

---

May 18, 1973
Coney Island

## ABOUT THE AUTHOR

Carol Hill's first novel was
*Jeremiah 8:20*. She is also co-author,
with photographer Bruce Davidson,
of a nonfiction book,
*Subsistence U.S.A.*